OF MUTTS AND MEN

A CHET & BERNIE MYSTERY

OF MUTTS AND MEN

SPENCER QUINN

THORNDIKE PRESS
A part of Gale, a Cengage Company

Copyright © 2020 by Pas de Deux.
Thorndike Press, a part of Gale, a Cengage Company.

ALL RIGHTS RESERVED
This is a work of fiction. All of the characters, organizations, and events portrayed in this novel are either products of the author's imagination or are used fictitiously.

Thorndike Press® Large Print Mystery.
The text of this Large Print edition is unabridged.
Other aspects of the book may vary from the original edition.
Set in 16 pt. Plantin.

**LIBRARY OF CONGRESS CIP DATA ON FILE.
CATALOGUING IN PUBLICATION FOR THIS BOOK
IS AVAILABLE FROM THE LIBRARY OF CONGRESS.**

ISBN-13: 978-1-4328-8419-2 (hardcover alk. paper)

Published in 2021 by arrangement with Tor/Forge

Printed in Mexico
Print Number: 01   Print Year: 2021

For Bob Edwards

ONE

A rooftop chase? Who's got it better than me?

Chasing down perps is what we do, me and Bernie. We're partners in the Little Detective Agency, Little being Bernie's last name. I'm Chet, pure and simple. When it comes to chasing down perps, rooftop chasing is what you might call a specialty within a specialty, if you see what I mean. And if you don't then . . . then actually I'm right there with you. The point is that rooftop chases don't happen often, so when they do you've got to enjoy them with all your heart. No problem. Enjoying with all my heart is one of my best things, right up there with leaping and grabbing perps by the pant leg.

There are two kinds of perps who get involved in rooftop chases. The first kind — and most perps are the first kind — realize pretty quick that it's game over unless you're up for doing something daring, and they're all dared out by that time: you can see it in their eyes. The second kind of perp believes somewhere deep down that he can fly. What we had on this particular warehouse rooftop in the most run-down section of South Pedroia, which is the most run-down part of the whole Valley, was the second kind of perp.

Our perp was tall and lean and ran very well. For a human, I should add, meaning he was in fact on the slowish side. I loped along behind him as he headed toward the edge of the roof. At the same time, I glanced back to see what was keeping Bernie. And there he was, popping up through the open hatchway from the top floor of the building. My Bernie! The sky was a fiery orange, the way the sky gets around here when the sun goes down, and so Bernie's eyes and teeth were orange, too. There's all kinds of beauty in life.

"Stop!" Bernie yelled. "Where the hell do you think you're going?"

The perp — have I mentioned that he was carrying a painting under one arm, a gold-framed painting of old-time cowboys around a fire, stolen, of course, which was why we were all here — turned to Bernie and said, "None of your damn business."

"You're missing the point." Now Bernie

was running, too. A very graceful runner, in my opinion, but hampered by the old war wound in one of his legs, only coming into play in situations like this. "Which is," Bernie went on, huffing and puffing from all those stairs we'd climbed to get up here on the roof, "that you've got nowhere to —"

Whatever was coming next — sure to be brilliant, since Bernie's always the smartest human in the room — remained unsaid, because at that moment the perp reached the edge of the roof and just kept going. Yes, with his legs churning in the air, high over the alley separating this warehouse from the next one! This was something I'd seen in cartoons — of which Bernie and I had watched many in the period after his divorce from Leda — but never in real life. Nothing beats real life, amigo. I was thinking that very thought as I soared off the edge of the roof myself. Free! Free as a bird, although the tiny eyes of birds always look so angry to me, meaning all that freedom was wasted on them.

Meanwhile the perp was touching down on the next rooftop. More or less. In fact, more less than more, since he ended up a bit short. All that actually touched down were the fingers of one hand, clutching desperately at the tarpaper surface of the roof. And now his other hand was clutching desperately, too, meaning the perp had to let go of the painting. It went spinning high in the air, the golden frame turning sunset orange.

What a lot going on! No time to even think, which happens to be when I'm at my best. In a flash I snagged the painting right out of the air, landed on the roof, nice and smooth — sticking the landing, as Bernie calls it — then let the painting go, wheeled around and trotted over to the perp.

He seemed to be hanging from the roof by his fingertips. That couldn't have been easy. I felt proud of him in a way, as though he belonged to me. Which he sort of did, although he probably didn't realize it yet. I looked down at him. He looked up at me. His eyes were . . . how to put this? Terrified, maybe? Something like that.

"Help. Help me."

He turned out to have a squeaky voice, not at all pleasant, especially to ears like mine, so sensitive to the tinny and the shrill.

"Chet?"

That was Bernie, calling from the first rooftop. He stood at the edge, his lovely face a bit worried, for no reason I could see.

"Be careful, big guy. Don't take any risks."

"Huh?" said the perp, still hanging off the

roof and now kicking his legs a bit, as though . . . as though he might swim his way up. What a strange thought! Meanwhile I was trying to remember what a risk was, but it just wouldn't come.

"Help! Help me!"

Poor guy. The swimming thing wasn't working at all and he seemed to be slip-slip-slipping. I went to the edge with the idea of leaning over, grabbing him by the scruff of the neck, and then digging in with my paws and hoisting him up, but before I could start any of that, he flailed out with one hand and grabbed onto one of my front legs.

"Let him go!" Bernie shouted.

"But — but then I'll fall."

"So what?" Bernie said.

"Really?" said the perp.

Although not particularly strong-looking, he turned out to have an iron grip, at least in this particular situation. I tried to pull my leg free but got nowhere, and began sliding closer and closer to the edge.

Bernie reached into his pocket, drew the .38 Special. "Let him go or I'll shoot," he said.

"I'll take my chances," said the perp.

Whoa! Didn't he know Bernie was a crack shot, could shoot holes through dimes spinning in midair? What other reason could there be for such a strange remark? I decided to forgive him, although Bernie didn't look like he was in a forgiving mood. In fact, I'd never seen him so mad. His face looked almost ugly, maybe the most astonishing sight I'd seen in my whole life. He jammed the .38 Special back in his pocket, lowered his head, started running in a quick little circle, and then charged toward us across the roof.

No, Bernie, no! Not with your bad leg! Stay! Sit! Stay!

Sit stay, as I knew very well, only works some of the time. It didn't work on Bernie, not now. He came soaring — kind of — across the gap between the warehouses, cleared it by plenty — or at least some — and stuck the landing . . . just about!

"Ouch," he said, but not loud. Then he picked himself up and hurried over, reached down, grabbed our perp by the collar, and kind of flipped him right up and onto the roof.

The perp lay panting on his back. Between pants, he said, "Thanks, buddy. My whole life flashed before my eyes."

"Punishment enough," Bernie said.

The perp's eyes widened. "You . . . you mean you're letting me go?"

Bernie gazed down at him. His anger

12

faded away, real fast, and he started laughing. He laughed and laughed, not in the least angry anymore, but happy. That made me happy! I was so happy I came close to prancing around on the rooftop. But that wouldn't have been professional, so instead I grabbed the perp by the pant leg, the most professional move that came to mind. Case closed.

"Oh, thank you, thank you, thank you!" said Mr. Rusk, taking the painting from Bernie. He held it up at arm's length and gazed at those cowboys around the campfire. "Remington at the height of his powers. Did you ever dream we'd see it again, Irene?"

We stood at the front entrance to a huge house way up in the hills above High Chapparal Estates, the richest neighborhood in the whole Valley, although no neighboring houses could be seen from this spot: me, Bernie, and Mr. and Mrs. Rusk, the clients. They looked much younger than they smelled, true about a lot of the folks up here in the hills, but perhaps not something you yourself would have noticed, your sense of smell being what it is. No offense.

"Not at first," Irene said. "But I changed my mind after meeting Bernie." She reached out as though to take Bernie's hand in both

13

of hers, a handshake move I was familiar with, but ended up doing something new, namely grabbing onto his forearm and not letting go. "How can I ever repay you? Ezra would have been grouchy for the rest of his life."

Ezra frowned. "We're repaying by paying his requested fee, Irene. That's how it works."

"You take the fun out of everything," Irene said. She tilted her head, smiled up at Bernie. "Why not throw in a bonus, Ezra? I know you give out bonuses."

"Only at Christmas," said Ezra. "And only to top producers."

"You're saying Bernie's not a top producer?"

"Whoa," Bernie said. "I don't want a bonus."

No bonus? With the state of our finances? Had Bernie forgotten about our self-storage in South Pedroia, stacked from floor to ceiling with Hawaiian pants, not one pair sold? It couldn't have slipped his mind completely, because sometimes after a few drinks he says, "Hawaiian shirts are big, so why not Hawaiian pants? I just don't get it." And then there was the tin futures play. We would have been rich, except for an earthquake in Bolivia, or possibly the earth-

14

quake not happening. *Bernie! Bonus! Yes!*

But no.

"No bonus?" Irene said. "Did you hear that, Ezra?"

"I did." He peered at the painting. "But what are these? They look like two little . . . punctures in the canvas."

"Come and join our little party," Irene said, tugging on Bernie's arm. "It's the least we can do, isn't it, Ezra?"

"But . . . but these punctures. They almost look like teeth marks or something."

"For god's sake, stop fussing. You got your stupid painting back."

"Stupid? It's one of the loveliest evocations of the old West I've ever —"

"Give it a rest. You're not fooled by all that old West crap, are you, Bernie?"

Irene pulled him into the house.

"Well, in fact," Bernie began, "there's lots to be said for —"

"And this beautiful creature's invited, too, of course." Irene glanced my way. "All in all, a very pleasing team to the eye." She squeezed Bernie's arm, her hands by now quite high up, more above his elbow than not. "Chet, wasn't it? Does he like fillet? I'll have Emilia grind some up."

Well, well. What a very considerate woman! For just one moment, something unpleasant, possibly having to do with teeth marks, snagged in my memory, but then it was washed away, like by a mighty river of fun flowing through my mind. A mighty river of fun in my mind? What a life!

We joined the little party, actually a very big party. The backyard was a sort of water park, with a waterfall, a stream, and lots of pools, some with fish swimming in them, and some with human swimmers. I polished off a bowl of ground fillet and another, and possibly one more. Not long after that, we were alone — the usual case at big parties, Bernie being better at small parties — just the two of us at a table by a palm tree, Bernie with a glass of bourbon and me underneath, watching him through the glass tabletop. He was gazing at the waterfall.

"Water, water everywhere," he said.

Not the first time I'd heard that. Water was often on Bernie's mind, the aquifer being one of his biggest worries. Once I'd actually laid eyes on the aquifer, a tiny mud puddle down at the bottom of a deep construction site, which was when I finally understood the problem. We needed lots more aquifer. Was it for sale somewhere? That was as far as I could take it on my own.

Bernie took a sip of bourbon, more of a big swallow than a sip. "Probably the same water cycling round and round," he said, "but didn't anybody consider the evaporation effect?"

A man by himself at the nearest table sat up straight, a trim white-haired man who was also drinking bourbon, the smell impossible to miss. "You don't know the half of it," he said.

Bernie turned to him. "No?"

"You in the business, by any chance?" said the man. He had one of those deeply tanned and lined faces you see here in the desert, his blue eyes washed out and pale.

"What business is that?" Bernie said.

"Hydrology."

"Meaning the study of water?"

"That, plus the practical applications of." He made a sweeping hand gesture at the waterfall, stream, pools. "I designed all this — meaning the guts of it, the parts you don't see. Evaporation effect? I was worried sick about it, told these . . . these plutocrats I had no interest in their project, period."

At that moment Irene went by, a glass of champagne in her hand. "Plutocrats, Wendell? Is that nice? Tell him we're not plutocrats, Bernie."

"Um, I'm not even actually sure about the

exact dictionary —"

"But I'm glad you two have found each other," Irene went on, or maybe just kept going. "This is the private eye I told you about, Wendell. Who brought home the bacon for us. Bernie Little, say hi to Wendell Nero, chairman emeritus of the geology department at Valley College. And he did end up doing our project, which is why it's such a success. Wendell's fierce on the outside but he's really just a big pussycat."

Don't rely on me for the details of what happened next. Because: Bacon! Pussycat! There'd been no bacon whatsoever at any time during our work on the cowboy painting case. You can take that to the bank, although maybe not to our bank, where there'd been some recent issue with Ms. Mendez, the manager. As for pussycat, this white-haired dude did not smell, look, or sound at all like any pussycat on the planet, and I'd had many pussycat experiences in my career, none pleasant. I wrestled in my mind with these problems, bacon and pussycat, getting nowhere. By the time I gave up, Wendell Nero was sitting at our table, and the two glasses of bourbon, his and Bernie's, seemed to have been topped up.

". . . safe bet," Wendell was saying, "because I didn't think they'd get to square one on the permitting. But they waltzed right through."

"Uh-huh," Bernie said.

"You don't look shocked."

Bernie smiled.

"I suppose it's funny in a way," Wendell said.

"A rueful way," said Bernie.

Wendell gave him a long look, then nodded. "So I ended up doing the project after all."

"Because anyone else would have done it worse," Bernie said.

"Exactly. I mitigated at every turn. There's much less volume than it appears, and the flow shuts off automatically from noon to five p.m." He watched the waterfall, took a big drink. "But . . ." His voice trailed away. Then his gaze found me. "This your dog?"

"His name's Chet," Bernie said. "He did the actual recovery of the painting."

Wendell's snowy eyebrows rose. "Yeah?" he said.

"Chet can be very persuasive."

How nice to hear! I tried to remember the exact meaning of persuasive, but before I could come up with it — these things take time — Wendell reached down and scratched my head, right between the ears where it's so hard to reach. Just from how he did it, I knew he was a friend of the nation within the nation, which is what Bernie calls me and my kind.

"I've had a number of dogs myself," Wendell said. "Characters, each and every one, if you know what I mean."

"I do," Bernie said.

"No more dogs now," said Wendell. "All in the past."

"Why is that?"

"The life span discrepancy. Couldn't take it anymore. Like a lot of things." He looked down, almost as though shielding his eyes from view. Bernie turned away, sat still and quiet. It felt like something was going on, but if so it went right by me.

At last Wendell looked up. "Do you handle other kinds of cases, Bernie, besides stolen property?"

"We do," Bernie said. "Did you have something in mind?"

Wendell's pale eyes got an inward look, like . . . like maybe he was trying to see into his own mind. Then he took a deep breath and said, "Can we meet tomorrow morning?"

"Where?" said Bernie.

"I'll be on-site. Do you know Dollhouse Canyon?"

"No."

Wendell drew on a cocktail napkin, handed it to Bernie. "Ten o'clock?"

"See you then," Bernie said.

Next morning we hit the road, Bernie behind the wheel and me riding shotgun, our usual setup. Although once we ended up doing it the other way! A rather exciting outing, but no time for that now. Our ride's an old Porsche, not the one that went off the cliff or the other one that got blown up, but our new one, the oldest of all, and the best, mostly because of the martini glasses pattern on the front fenders.

We crossed the Rio Vista Bridge — the smells rising up from below rich and indescribable, something about a Superfund cleanup — took the West Valley freeway all the way out of town, turned onto a two-lane blacktop, came to a fork with paved road in one direction, dirt track in the other. Bernie checked the cocktail napkin, followed the dirt track, and at last we were in the middle of nowhere, where we liked it best, me and Bernie. I could feel him relax inside.

"Ah," he said.

That was Bernie. He always knows just the right word.

The dirt track led us past a huge red rock with a big black bird perched on top, then down into a long and narrow box canyon.

"Dollhouse Canyon," Bernie said.

At the end of the canyon stood a white trailer with blue writing on the side. Bernie read the writing. "Nero Hydrological Consulting. Water Equals Life."

We parked near the trailer and hopped out, me actually hopping. And almost landing in a thicket of jumping cholla! I've had a lot of experience with jumping cholla, all of it bad. Those yellow spines are capable of doing some hopping of their own, which is the whole point of jumping cholla, but hard to remember for some reason. I moved to Bernie's other side, getting him between me and the thicket. Did that mean I'd rather he got stuck with the yellow spines instead of me? I hoped not and left it like that.

We stood side by side in front of the trailer. The day still smelled fresh and new, and so did we, Bernie because he'd taken a shower before we left, and me because . . . because I just do. He was wearing jeans, flip-flops, and the Hawaiian shirt with the laughing pineapples. I had on my everyday collar, the gator skin one I'd picked up on a case down in bayou country that there's no time to tell you about now. Bernie knocked on the trailer door. No answer. He knocked again. No answer. "Wendell? Dr. Nero?" Zip.

Bernie turned, cupped his hands, called out, "Wendell? Wendell?"

From the sides of the box canyon, the call came back. "Wendell? Wendell?"

Then there was silence. I sniffed at the crack under the door. Uh-oh. I have this certain low, rumbly bark that's only for Bernie. I barked it now. Bernie looked at me and stopped feeling relaxed inside. He turned the doorknob. The door opened. After a moment of confusion, we went inside. Me first.

TWO

The trailer had windows but the shades were drawn, meaning it was pretty dark inside. The shaft of light that slanted in through the open doorway fell just short of a shadowy desk at the far end. A shadowy figure sat behind the shadowy desk, leaning back, like maybe sleeping or in deep thought. Humans tend to close their eyes when deep thoughts are going on. Maybe it helps them. I'm not the one to ask, deep thoughts not something I bring to the table. But there's a lot to be said for shallow thoughts, or even none at all. The Little Detective Agency was successful for a reason, except for the finances part. But we're way off track. I almost left out something important, namely that I knew right away that the shadowy figure wasn't sleeping, wasn't thinking thoughts of any kind. A faint smell, in its very early stages, was coming off that figure. It's not a smell I miss. I also knew he was a man, of course, and exactly which man. Once I meet you, your smell sticks in my mind and stays there forever. Remember that if you're ever tempted to do something perpy when I'm around.

We moved forward. "Wendell?" Bernie said. "Wendell?" Bernie's a hopeful guy, one of the very best things about him.

But there was only silence, except quiet bubbling sounds coming from a bunch of glass tanks stacked along one wall. Beside the other wall stood a workbench with racks of test tubes, all of them filled with dirt.

"Wendell?"

Silence.

Bernie raised one of the shades, the kind that rolls up real quick with a noisy clatter. It came close to scaring me, kind of strange since I'm the type that doesn't scare. It frightens me just to think of being scared, so I avoid it completely, if you see what I mean.

Light fell across Wendell's face. Yes, sitting at his desk, leaning back, eyes closed — just as I'd already known. I'd even known there would be blood, although not from where on his body. It turned out to be from the throat, slashed open from one side to the other. Not something we hadn't seen before, me and Bernie, but we both went still. Some sights just stop you, no matter how tough you are, and we're the toughest. Just ask the Frenzies, a motorcycle gang originally from down in Immler Springs but now up at Northern State Correctional, sporting orange jumpsuits and breaking rocks in the hot sun. All their Harleys ended up in a tar pit, but no time to go into that now.

Bernie took surgical gloves from the back pocket of his jeans, put them on, and raised all the shades. All of sudden, in the bright light, Bernie looked so alive to me! A wonderful sight. I knew then and there that things were going to be okay forever.

He walked around the desk, put a finger to the back of Wendell's wrist, looked at me, shook his head. Not news, but so nice Bernie wanted to include me. You had to love Bernie, and I did.

Next came examining the crime scene. I'm in charge of sniffing around. There's really not much to it. Mostly you just breathe and soon a whole scent world rises up in your mind. Well, maybe not yours. After not much time at all, I knew that two humans had been in the trailer recently, one man and one woman. The man was a gum chewer who liked cherry flavor and also had toe fungus — human toe fungus is impossible not to pick up, like it was spraying from a fire hose. The woman had a smell that reminded me of flowers just before they get thrown out; she also had a hamster in her life. I'd known a hamster once, name of Harry, who'd gotten out of his cage, which had somehow tipped over, and we'd ended up playing a game called nudge Harry all over the floor with your paws. A game that had ended too soon, as I recalled, an unhappy ending that included the loss of the client, who turned out to be Harry's human companion, a fact I learned too late, if at all.

Meanwhile Bernie was looking on top of things, under things, opening desk drawers, examining papers, patting Wendell's pockets.

"No wallet," he said.

Bernie gazed at Wendell, almost like . . . like he was waiting patiently for some explanation about the wallet. Interesting moments like that happened from time to time with Bernie, as though some other world was just around the corner. I was always glad when they ended.

Bernie turned away from Wendell, went over to the workbench, and peered at the test tubes full of dirt. Although all the dirt looked the same, the smells were not. Some of them were even new to me, and I'd thought I'd smelled everything when it came to dirt.

"No phone, no computer of any kind," Bernie said. "I wonder . . ." He didn't finish his thought, at least not out loud. Instead he took out his own phone and called the sheriff.

A squad car pulled up outside the trailer and a pudgy guy in a too-tight uniform climbed out. His cheeks puffed up a bit — possibly one of those burps that doesn't quite get free — and he turned to us.

"Hey," he said. "You the one who called?"

"Correct," said Bernie.

The pudgy guy took a notebook from his chest pocket, wet his thumb, paged through. "Bennie Little?"

Uh-oh. Bennie? We were off to a bad start.

Bernie gave the pudgy guy a look. The pudgy guy blinked and checked his notebook again. "Says here you're a PI?"

"How's Bennie spelled?"

The pudgy guy squinted at the notebook. "B-E-R-N-I-E."

There was a long pause. Then Bernie said, "Where is Sheriff Gooden?"

"Laid up for the time being. Pesky gall-bladder. I'm Deputy Beasley." His cheeks puffed up again. This time he covered his mouth with his fist, but a burp escaped, no doubt about it. Deputy Beasley had been eating Honey Nut Cheerios, and also dill pickles. "What kind of PI are yuh?" he said.

"I don't understand the question," Bernie said.

"There's the kind that's on the side of the law and the other kind."

"What about the kind that's on the side of justice?"

"Huh?" said Deputy Beasley.

"Or," Bernie went on, "the kind that just discovered a homicide in your jurisdiction?"

"Homicide?" Deputy Beasley hitched up his belt, a move you often see from paunchy types, and the deputy was on the big side of paunchy. "I'll be the judge of that."

"Be my guest," said Bernie. We were standing in front of the trailer door. Bernie pushed it open with his heel. Is anyone cooler than Bernie? Also, if Deputy Beasley was our guest, did we now own the trailer? This case felt promising.

We followed the deputy inside. He stopped in front of Wendell and gazed down at him.

"Had one a few years back where some loser slit his own throat," he said.

Bernie folded his arms across his chest. The things he does! I could watch him all day, which I actually do. "You're saying suicide's a possibility?"

"Can't rule it out."

Bernie nodded. "Meaning he did it with his bare hands?"

"You nuts? Had to be a knife or some such."

"Which he hid somewhere before plunking himself back down and expiring?"

"Huh?"

"We'll wait outside," Bernie said.

On the way out I saw a small photo thumbtacked to the wall, a photo of Wendell Nero and a girl — older than Charlie, Bernie's kid, but not grown up — standing side by side, both of them smiling on a sunny day. Wendell's RV was in the background. Also, the girl was holding some rolled-up papers under her arm, and what looked like a baby goat was sitting on her feet. All in all, a very nice picture: happy people are such a nice sight. A nice picture, except for the baby goat. I've had problems with goats, although not, it's true, with baby ones.

We went over to the car, had a nice drink of water, Bernie from a bottle, me from my portable water bowl. It was the hot time of year, when water always tastes best. Bernie held his water bottle in the sun, gave it a close look, as though hoping to see some-thing. All I saw was water, but so clear in the bright light that it was almost like see-ing water for the very first time. The next moment, I understood water completely. The moment after that, I didn't understand it at all. I felt a bit dizzy. Now would come feeling pukey, but before pukiness arrived this strange little — would you call it a spell? — passed and I got back to being normal me, which is all in all my favorite type of me, certainly the most relaxing to be with.

"Why did he want to see us, big guy?" Bernie said.

A tough one. I had no idea, also wasn't sure who Bernie was talking about. Mean-while I was picking up the toe fungus smell. I followed it around the trailer to the base of the steep slope at the end of the box canyon, where it mixed with the cherry gum smell. The cherry gum smell got stronger and stronger and then there it was, an actual glob of cherry gum. It lay on the ground beside a scrubby gray bush, not hardened but not fresh either, just somewhere in between. I'd tried gum all those ways, hard, soft, in between, with never a single good experience. So now I told myself, Chet, don't touch that gum. But what harm could there be in nosing at the crumpled-up gum wrapper? I nosed at that, nosed at another little scrap of paper, and the next thing I knew I was nosing at the gum itself! There's just no end to life's surprises. I nosed at the gum for a bit, then opened my mouth and —

"Chet? What you got there?"

Nothing really, nothing at all. I paused, realized my mouth was open, closed it, and resumed pausing.

Bernie came over, squatted down, put on the surgical gloves, poked around at the gum, the wrapper, the little piece of paper. He picked up the piece of paper. "Receipt from QwikStop in San Dismas, yesterday at one thirty-seven p.m., one pack of Big Chew Cherry Gum, one dollar seventy-nine cents, one fish sandwich, three dollars nineteen cents, total four ninety-eight, amount tendered five dollars, change two cents, clerk Sofia." Bernie took a baggie from his pocket, put in the gum. "Some gum chewer tosses this away." He stuck the crumpled wrapper in the baggie. "Then reaches into a pocket for a fresh piece." And finally he put the receipt in the baggie as well. "Meanwhile dislodging the receipt." He glanced back at the trailer. "A nice little narrative, Chet. Good work."

My tail started up, meaning the pausing

was over. Good thing: pausing gets very bothersome after a while.

"Even if it turns out to be irrelevant," Bernie added.

That part zipped right by me. I was still back at the good work part. My tail, in a very good mood, kept on wagging as we walked around to the front of the trailer. The door opened and Deputy Beasley stepped out.

"You still here?" he said.

"Figured you'd want to talk to us," said Bernie.

"About what?"

Bernie didn't answer. An ambulance and a squad car appeared at the open end of the canyon, lights flashing but sirens off.

"It's a robbery gone bad, by the way," the deputy said.

"Yeah?" said Bernie.

"No wallet on him."

"Ah."

"Exactly. Thief comes in, old dude resists, things go south. Seen it a thousand times. Probably some dope fiend, or one of them traffickers from down on the border."

"Good luck," Bernie said.

We headed for the car. I had already hopped in and Bernie was sliding behind the wheel when Beasley came running up, an odd paunchy run with lots of motion but not much of the forward kind.

"Hey! Shoulda asked — what were you doin' here in the first place?"

"Looking for water," Bernie said.

"Huh?"

Bernie pointed to the sign on the trailer. "He was an expert."

"Hydrology is water?" said Beasley. He did one of those dry spitting things. Spitting is a big subject. Men spit and women don't, for example, and then there's the special kind of man who goes in for dry spitting. There's also the spitting up that babies do after feeding, spit up that tastes quite nice, actually, as I learned when Charlie was still in his high chair. "Ain't no water anywheres near here," Beasley went on, "not for miles."

I wasn't so sure about that. There was our water bottle, of course, under Bernie's seat, but was I picking up something else, very faint yet at the same time very big, from far far down beneath us? I kind of thought so, but then we drove away and it was gone. After a while Bernie gave me an odd look and said, "That discrepancy Wendell mentioned works both ways, doesn't it?"

I had no answer, didn't even understand

the question. My mind was at peace, a very nice feeling.

THREE

We drove away, silent for a long time, the car full of Bernie's thoughts. I loved the feeling of Bernie's thoughts. They were giants! And the West — which was where we lived, a fact I'd learned quite recently — was a giant land, so we matched up perfectly, Bernie and the land, and me, too, of course. Don't forget me. I like being in the mix.

Back on the two-lane blacktop, Bernie took a deep breath and all the giant thoughts went still, as though fallen fast asleep. "Got to beware of simplistic ideas, big guy," he said. Whoa! Those — whatever they were — had never occurred to me. I knew to beware of perps bearing guns, and also bears — ever since that time we'd come between a mama bear and her cubs, mama bears turning out to be amazingly fast on their feet — and now I added simplistic ideas to the list.

"But sometimes," Bernie went on, "simplistic is better than nothing at all. Water equals life, for example. And the reverse — no water equals death. Isn't that, way down deep, why I feel so strongly about . . ."

Whatever Bernie felt so strongly about remained unspoken, so I never found out. But still it was nice to be zooming along in the Porsche, the wind ruffling my fur, lots of wind since the top was down, in fact actually lost, and — and whoa! A road-runner! A roadrunner was also zooming along, practically right beside us. I've chased the odd roadrunner, never successfully. Not yet. And this was not the time. I knew that so well. But then, as we passed him, the little bugger turned his little birdie head and gave me a look with his little birdie eyes. There's only so much anyone can take. I barked my most savage bark, a great feeling, but not quite great enough. All on their own, the muscles in my legs bunched and got ready for a mighty —

"Ch—et?"

Bernie has a way of saying my name — slowly more than loudly — that causes this strange tapping of the brakes inside me, hard to describe. He laughed and gave me a pat. What was funny? Pat pat pat. I didn't know and didn't care.

We passed some big orange mounds, almost

hill-sized, but smelling of copper — meaning they weren't hills but tailings, and this was mining country — and entered a small mining town.

"San Dismas," Bernie said, as we rolled down the main street and stopped at a red light, the only stoplight in sight. We have two kinds of mining towns out here. The kind with stuff still in the mines is where you see lots of brand-new pickups. The kind where the mines are all mined out is where you see boarded-up buildings. San Dismas was this second kind of mining town.

We pulled over in front of a convenience store. Bernie read the sign. "QwikStop. A long shot, big guy, which should come after all other possibilities have washed out, but let's do things backwards today." He paused. "Call it the Beasley method."

Deputy Beasley was still in the picture? A bit of a surprise, but if Bernie said so, then that was that. We hopped out of the Porsche, me actually hopping, and entered the Qwik-Stop.

Here's something about convenience stores — and I've been in many: they always have Slim Jims for sale. How convenient is that! I followed the Slim Jim smell over to the Slim Jim display. A whole rack! What a fine convenience store — even if business seemed a little slow, what with the only customers being me and Bernie — maybe the best I've had the pleasure to visit. The Beasley method — whatever it was, exactly — was working already.

Meanwhile Bernie was at the cooler, picking up a water bottle or two. He carried them up to the counter. The clerk was a very small old lady wearing huge hoop earrings.

"Anything else?" she said, running the little scanner thing over the bottles. Her movements turned out to be surprisingly speedy.

"Got any Big Chew Cherry Gum?" Bernie said.

The woman turned to a shelf behind her. "How many?"

"I'll take a couple."

She laid two packs of gum alongside the water. "That it?"

"Yes, thanks," Bernie said.

Uh-oh. Had I heard right? Not a real question, since I always do — meaning something of the highest importance had slipped Bernie's mind. I forgave him at once, of course, even before I blamed him, meaning I didn't actually blame him, blaming Bernie being something I've never done and will never do. But none of that stopped me from barking a quiet little bark just to get his attention.

When humans are startled by some sudden sound — a car plowing into a plate-glass window, for example — they do this sort of spasm and whip around to see what just happened. Which was what Bernie and the old lady did now, both of them gazing in my direction, mouths open.

"My god," the old lady said, "never heard a bark like that in my life, and I used to run a kennel."

"Sorry," Bernie said, "I —"

"Nothing to be sorry about," said the old lady. "How many Slim Jims should I ring up?"

"Make it one of those eight-packs."

And very soon after that we were all gathered cheerfully at the counter, Bernie paying, the old lady making change, and me sitting quietly, like an obedience school champ. I'd actually been a K-9 school champ, by the way, except for flunking out the very last day on the leaping test. Even though leaping was my very best thing! My memory of the details is a bit sketchy. All I remember is that a cat was involved, and possibly some blood. But that was the same day I met Bernie, so it turned out to be the best day of my life.

"Want your receipt?" the old lady said.

Bernie nodded. She handed him the receipt. He checked it. "Sofia?" he said.

"That's me."

"Any chance you'd remember a certain customer from yesterday?"

Sofia gave Bernie a close look. A little old lady, but her eyes were big and bright and didn't seem old at all. "Depends," she said.

Bernie reached into his pocket and handed her the other receipt, the one I'd found at the base of the slope in Dollhouse Canyon. Don't forget we're a team, me and Bernie. "How about this particular customer?" he said.

Sofia took one quick glance at the receipt and said, "What's he done now?"

"We don't know yet," Bernie said. "What's he done before?"

"Taken too many shortcuts," Sofia said. "Are you a cop? You don't look like one, not exactly." She tilted her chin at me. "And this guy has that K-nine look, but he's not quite right for it either."

Bernie's face lit up, the way it does when he gets real interested in something. "Not right how?" he said.

"Too independent-minded," Sofia said.

Bernie laughed and handed her our card. This was the card Suzie had designed for us, the one with the flowers at the bottom.

Suzie was Bernie's girlfriend, although maybe not anymore, what with her being in London, which I knew was far away. And also Eliza was now in the picture. "Can you love two women, Chet?" Bernie had said the other night. "Or is that the road to madness?" The meaning of that had escaped me completely, but I hadn't liked the sound, so I'd pressed up against him, preventing any movement down any road whatsoever.

But no time for that now. "Never met a private eye before," Sofia was saying.

"We don't bite," said Bernie.

An absolute stunner! True, we didn't bite often, and only when we had to, but we did bite, as more than one perp now sporting an orange jumpsuit could tell you. And when it comes to biting and the Little Detective Agency, it's not just me, amigos. Mostly me, yes, but there was one time — this was during the rather surprising finish of the dental hygienist case, best forgotten — when Bernie had brought his own teeth into play. So, what was he up to, here at the QwikStop counter? I locked my gaze on him and kept it locked.

Sofia pocketed the card. "Florian Machado is who you're looking for," she said. "He really needs to stop."

"Stop what?" Bernie said.

42

"Taking what doesn't belong to him."

"Such as?"

"Cell phones, laptops, the odd car or two — whatever's easy."

"Wallets?" Bernie said.

"Not to my knowledge. But if it was easy . . ." Sofia shrugged. "Is that what he did? Snatch somebody's wallet?"

"Could be," Bernie said. "What if one of these theft opportunities turned out to be not so easy?"

"You're asking if he's violent?"

Bernie nodded.

Sofia shook her head. "Flory's just a big baby. He'd never hurt anyone. Well, there was that one time, but it wasn't deliberate. He doesn't know his own strength, is all."

"What happened?"

"One of those traffic stop things. He ended up with an assaulting a police officer charge, did some time."

"Where do we find him?"

"It's a little tricky." Sofia drew us a map on a scrap of paper. She pointed with her pen. "Look for a blue boat hereabouts."

"And then?"

"You're there. He lives on the boat."

"A stolen boat?" Bernie said.

Sofia nodded.

43

The desert is dry, but some parts are drier than others. No saguaros, mesquite, or paloverde in the real dry desert, which is mostly rocks and sand and maybe a droopy and dusty bush or two. That was the kind of desert we found as we drove out of San Dismas, past the last mound of orange tailings, toward a distant gray stone butte, which turned out to be not that distant and we arrived in no time, just another one of those strange things that can happen out our way. The pavement ended and we followed a dirt track, past a parked ATV, and to a blue boat up on blocks in the shadow of the butte. A strange kind of sight, for sure. Do I love this job or what?

Bernie turned off the engine. It got very quiet. Bernie said, "I can almost hear the sea."

I gave him a close look. Although Bernie's ears aren't small for a human, they're not in my class when it comes to hearing, nowhere near. And what did almost hearing something even mean? So therefore . . . so therefore it had to be a joke! Bernie can be a joker at times. Once he'd done a brief stand-up routine at LaffRiot, something about a bet with a few buddies from Valley PD, very successful from my point of view, although the riot part had pretty much taken over. But . . . but whoa! Had I just done a so-therefore? So-therefores were Bernie's department. I brought other things to the table. So therefore — oh, no, not again! — I dropped this whole thing at once, made my mind a complete blank, and felt much better, more like myself. In fact, exactly like myself, which is when I'm at my best.

We walked up to the blue boat. A cabin cruiser: on our San Diego trip — we'd surfed, me and Bernie! — we'd gone out on a cabin cruiser belonging to an old Army buddy of his, a much nicer cabin cruiser than this one, since it didn't have peeling paint or holes in the hull. "The hardest part of surfing is popping up on the board," Bernie had said. But of course I was popped-up to begin with, so the whole thing had been a snap. Now here we were working on a case involving boats in the desert and possibly making money — too soon, in my experience, to rule out the moneymaking part completely. Who wouldn't be feeling tip-top?

We stepped around some flattened beer cans and stopped at the bottom of a ladder leading up to the deck. The sound of snoring came from inside the boat.

"Ahoy," Bernie said, not loudly and with a flicker of a smile crossing his face, the smile that showed work can be fun. "Permission to come aboard."

Inside the boat, the snoring continued. Did Bernie hear it or not? I didn't find out, because the next thing I knew he'd started up the ladder. This was a problem. Don't think for a moment that I can't climb ladders. I just run right up them, easy-peasy. The problem was I like to be first in this sort of situation, especially if the other guy is Bernie. So I did what I had to do —

"Chet! For god's sake!"

— which was to sort of run right up Bernie's back, one paw — possibly the take-off paw — possibly landing on his head, and spring onto the deck. There! Can't make something or other without breaking eggs: you heard that all the time. Uh-oh. All at once I was starving! Not now, big guy, said a voice in my head, Bernie's voice, which was often there. I waited for more, specifically something about steak tips if I was a good boy, but that didn't happen. Maybe it went without mentioning.

In my most good boy way, I turned to Bernie, now stepping onto the deck, his hair somewhat askew. But that only made him look better! Meanwhile, the sound of snoring was starting to remind me of the thunder we sometimes get in monsoon season.

"Hear that?" Bernie whispered. "He's snoozing." He tiptoed toward the cabin. You had to love Bernie, and I did.

The cabin door hung off its hinges. We went through the doorway, me first. Smells were coming the other way, kind of like a river you might not want to swim in: a river all about toe fungus, stale beer, unwashed human male. Shafts of light shone through holes in the walls, falling on a huge drooling guy in a tank top and tighty whiteys sleeping on a bunk; a pizza box open on the floor, one slice left; and up front, on the control console, a black leather wallet. Bernie, a hard look on his face and no longer on tiptoes, strode to the console, picked up the wallet, checked inside. Then he turned to the sleeping dude, a slow turn that . . . that reminded me of a tank in a movie we'd watched, slowly swinging its big gun around. And then: *KABOOM.*

"Wakee wakee," he said. Not a kaboom, his voice soft, if anything, but somehow that soft wakee wakee had kaboom force. The sleeping dude's eyes snapped open at once.

Very small eyes for such a big potato-shaped head. They shifted Bernie's way, then to me, and back to Bernie.

"What the fuck?" he said.

"On your feet, sailor boy," Bernie said. "Hands where I can see them."

FOUR

Hands up where we can see them is one of our best techniques. Humans can't do much in a fight without their hands. Biting — except in dentist-hygienist cases, as I mentioned — is pretty much a non-factor, which leaves kicking, and most humans are slow and clumsy when it comes to kicking, although we have run into an expert kicker or two. Take Joe Bobb Wu, owner of Wu's Wonderful World of Martial Madness — a spot on the wrong side of the tracks in Rio Vista, where both sides of the tracks are wrong — that turned out to have martial madness in front and a meth lab in back. Joe Bobb had lost his temper a bit when Bernie and I discovered the meth lab part — we'd been so palsy until then — and he'd come flying at Bernie feet first, high off the ground and lashing out with speedy kicks at Bernie's head. At least in his mind. But in real life, the moment that leading-edge foot just twitched, who was up in the air with him, grabbing him — yes, this is pretty amazing — by both pant legs at once? I think you know the answer to that one.

Back on board the blue boat, we had what you might call the beginning of a problem, namely this huge dude on the bunk not getting his hands up where we could see them, but in fact sliding them under his pillow, a stained pillow with no pillowcase. Here's something funny about Bernie: he won't sleep on a caseless pillow. No matter how tired he is, or even if he's had a teensy bit too much in the bourbon department, and he comes home to find no pillowcase, he roots around for one, maybe in the laundry pile, and puts it on.

"Florian!" Bernie said. "Hands!"

Florian frowned. "How do you know my fuckin' name? Who the hell are you, anyways?"

"Hands up. Then we'll talk."

"Okeydoke," Florian said. And slow and easy, like a nice, cooperative perp, he slid one hand out from under the pillow. But after that, things speeded up. First, out came his other hand, real quick, and not empty. A knife? In some ways knives are scarier than guns, but no time to get into the reasons, if any. This was a long knife, the blade golden for a moment as it passed through one of those shafts of sunlight, and then silver as Florian came lunging toward us in the shadowy cabin. Yes, a huge guy, one of those mountain-of-a-man types, surprisingly quick and seeming to fill the whole space. He raised the knife high, his face all twisted from the force he was gathering inside himself, and stabbed down at Bernie. At the same time, I flew right at him. And also at the same time, not looking like he was in any kind of hurry, Bernie launched that sweet, sweet uppercut.

CRACK!

A lovely sound. Bang on the chinny-chin-chin. Florian's eyes fluttered up, his eyelids fluttered down, he toppled backwards, and I soared right over him. The knife clattered down on the floor. Bernie picked it up.

"That's not the way to attack with a knife," he said. "First of all, you hold it like so. And the motion is this, not that." Bernie demonstrated the motions. Who for? Florian was out cold on the cabin floor and I had no need for knives or weapons of any kind. I was . . . a weapon all by myself! What a thought! Did you get smarter as life went along? Something to look forward to.

We got busy, Bernie taking out the plastic cuffs, flipping Florian over and cuffing his enormous wrists nice and tight behind his enormous back, and me . . . well, just sort of tidying up, if taking care of that last slice of pizza counted as tidying up. Meanwhile Bernie found some bungee cord, flipped Florian back over, and then bungee-corded his legs together from ankles to hip.

Bernie sat on the bunk, the wallet and the knife on his knee. "Wendell's wallet, murder weapon, murderer," he said. "The whole package in" — he checked his watch, not the one that had belonged to his grandfather, our most valuable possession, currently with our buddy Mr. Singh at Singh's Pawnbroker and Financing for All Your Needs shop, but the everyday watch, that had come in a cereal box — "less than three hours. This could be some kind of record, big guy."

I sat beside Bernie, got patted a bit. We really were pretty good. For a moment I thought: Who is paying? A bothersome thought and it quickly vanished. We waited peacefully, nice and comfy in this blue boat in the middle of the wide wide desert.

After a while, Bernie gave Florian a little kick, not hard, on the sole of one of his huge, bare, and toe fungusy feet. Florian groaned. Bernie gave him another kick. Florian groaned again and his eyes fluttered back open. He . . . how would you put this? Took in the situation? Something like that. That went on for what seemed like a long time. At last he spoke.

"Whaddya want from me?" he said.

Bernie's eyebrows have a language of their own. Now they rose in a very interesting way that made Bernie look like the huge one and the huge guy look small.

"Nothing," Bernie said. "We don't want anything from you." He glanced down at the wallet and the knife, still resting on his knee. Very slowly, Florian's little eyes shifted in the same direction, gazed at the sight in a confused sort of way, like he didn't quite understand what he was seeing.

"Uh," Florian said. "What are you, like, saying?"

Bernie shrugged, didn't say a thing.

"You a cop?" Florian said.

"Nope."

"Then . . . then what are you? You're on my property. I got rights."

"What about Wendell Nero?" Bernie said. "What about his rights?"

"Who the fuck is he?"

Bernie didn't like that, not one little bit. He didn't show it on the outside. Was Florian sensing what I was sensing? Probably not, and maybe if he'd been back on his feet and unbound, he'd have been in big trouble. But right now he was safe from harm. Bernie would never hurt someone tied up, not even the worst of the worst. Was Florian the worst of the worst? We'd only come up against one single man who was the worst of the worst for sure. That was at the end of the broom closet case, the only one where we'd failed completely. We'd found the missing kid — Gail was her name — but not soon enough. Later that night, we'd taken care of justice ourselves, me and Bernie, also a onetime thing in our career. After it was over Bernie had said we had to forget what we'd done and never think of it again. Yet here it was back on my mind, and not for the first time.

Bernie rose, opened the wallet, took out the driver's license, and held it for Florian to see. "This is who he was," Bernie said.

Florian's face scrunched up in thought, not a pleasant sight. Then his eyes opened wide. "Wait a goddamn minute. You think I killed that old man?"

Bernie didn't answer, simply pointed at the long knife, resting on his knee.

"But . . . but that's crazy!" Florian said. "That knife never leaves the boat. It's under my pillow at all times."

"Why would that be?"

"I got enemies is why."

"Any of them on the inside?" Bernie said. "Because that's where you'll be spending the rest of your life. Unless you get the death penalty, still a real possibility in this state."

"You . . . you bastard!" Florian starting wriggling around on the floor. "You're framing me."

"Oh?" said Bernie. "This" — he gave the wallet a little shake — "was lying right there when we came in." He pointed to the console.

"So what?" said Florian. "Maybe I stole the wallet. But that don't make me a murderer. The old man was dead when I got there."

Bernie sat back. "Go on."

"Like I said — he was dead when I went in the trailer, sitting back in his chair, throat cut from ear to ear. I almost had a heart attack, for Christ's sake. But then I happened to see the wallet, lying right out there on the desk. So I made myself go up and take it. Not easy, I can tell you. The sight was like . . . like a fuckin' horror movie. The slasher kind. I hate those."

He studied Bernie's face. Good luck with that, amigo. When Bernie wants his face to show nothing it doesn't. Florian was getting

55

nowhere. Where was he even hoping to get?

"And, uh," Florian went on. "Um — what's your name?"

"Bernie Little."

"Well, Mr. Little, one more thing, going back to the . . . the situation in that trailer. I'm not a lawyer, but is taking something that belongs to no one theft? See what I mean?"

"Belongs to no one?" Bernie said.

"Sure," said Florian. "When you're dead you're no one. That's . . . that's the whole point of, like, everything."

Bernie looked down at Florian, gazed at him for what seemed like a long time. A bright sort of hopefulness rose in Florian's eyes, one of those perp things you saw from time to time.

"What about his phone?" Bernie said. "His computer?"

"Don't know nothin' about that," said Florian.

"You had no problem taking the wallet, but the phone and the computer were a bridge too far?"

"Bridge?"

Bernie gave him another look. This one made Florian turn away.

"Did you know Wendell Nero?" Bernie said.

56

"Not from Adam, Mr. Little. I swear on . . . on my mother's grave, except she was cremated so she don't have one."

Bernie gave Florian a look. "Ever had any concussions?" he said.

"Hell, yeah. You just gave me one, for Christ's sake. With that sucker punch."

"Sucker punch?" said Bernie.

"Um," Florian said. "No offense." From somewhere overhead came the sound of the beating wings of a big bird, probably heard only by me.

"What were you doing at the trailer in the first place?" Bernie said.

"I was just ATVin' around, happened to come across it. Had no idea anyone was inside, else none of this would ever have happened."

"I believe that part," Bernie said.

"Yeah?" said Florian.

"One hundred percent. But then when you did go inside, there was this rather well-known scientist working at his desk. An old man, but feisty. He didn't like you coming in uninvited, didn't cooperate when you demanded his wallet. So" — Bernie took out two baggies, big and small, tucked the knife in one and the wallet in the other — "some sort of scuffle broke out and your temper got the best of you, just like it did

57

when Chet and I came in here, and you went for the knife, also just like in here."

"No!" Florian shouted. His face went red, bright bright red, although Bernie says I can't be trusted when it comes to red. "I'm tellin' you the truth! This is a frame-up. You cut his throat and — and —"

By that time Bernie and I were back outside, and Florian sounded much farther away than he really was. Bernie walked around the boat to the back. Stern, was that the name? There's all sorts of boat lingo, which I'd learned on our San Diego trip but mostly forgotten. Bernie scraped some dirt off the peeling paint and read: *Sea of Love.* Then came a long silence. After that he took out his cell phone.

"Deputy Beasley, please."

Beasley came on. "Yeah?"

"Bernie Little here," Bernie said. "There are tides in the affairs of men, Deputy Beasley."

"Huh?"

I was with Beasley on that, but would never admit it, especially not to myself.

Deputy Beasley and some other officers plus some crime scene dudes showed up pretty soon. The officers hauled Florian out of the boat and got him into the caged back seat of one of the squad cars. The crime scene dudes climbed into the boat. Bernie started in on the explanations. Maybe Beasley hadn't been a huge fan of ours the first time around, but now he was warming up.

"Well, well," he said. "The wallet, huh? And the knife. Well, well. Hot damn. Glad I encouraged you from the get-go. I'm a good judge of talent, ain't I, boys?"

The officers all gazed at the ground, or kicked at a pebble or two, except for the one non-boy officer. She folded her arms across her chest and gazed into the distance. For a moment I thought she was going to spit, a very interesting prospect: I'd seen lots of spitting in my time, but never by a woman. The moment passed with no spitting. Still, you could always hope and I always did.

"Got an idea," Beasley went on. "Officer Zurburan?"

The woman officer turned to him.

"See that Bernie here gets one of those honorary sheriff's badges. And maybe throw in a couple of them commemorative T-shirts."

Officer Zurburan nodded the tiniest nod.

At the same time Bernie said, "Not necessary. And one thing you should be aware of, Deputy: the suspect admits to the theft of

59

the wallet but claims the victim was already dead when he entered the trailer."

"That's a good one," said Beasley.

Not long after that, the crime scene dudes and all the officers had driven away, with Florian in his caged back seat, head hanging down. Only Beasley remained.

"How's Sheriff Gooden doing?" Bernie said.

"Pesky gallbladder," said Beasley.

"You mentioned that. When's he expected back?"

Beasley shrugged. "They're runnin' some tests. Might not be the gallbladder, I heard. What's the pancreas? Part of the gallbladder, maybe?"

Bernie didn't answer. He walked over to the stern of the boat. I went with him. "How come he's been living in this?"

"The boat?" said Beasley. "Dunno. Probably stole the goddamn thing. No right to keep it here, of course. This is county land. I'll have DPW haul it away."

"Away where?"

"The dump."

"Don't do that," Bernie said. "We'll take it."

"Why? It's a wreck."

"I'll have someone come today," Bernie said.

"Suit yourself." Beasley hitched up his belt, got in his car, drove away.

Much later, the big wrecker from Nixon's Championship Autobody — owned by our buddy Nixon Panero, who was also a part-time screenplay reader for a big Hollywood studio — drove up, Nixon's sister Mindy Jo at the wheel.

"Hey," she said, tossing me a biscuit, which I caught in midair. Then she got to work.

"I'll help you with that," Bernie said.

"Bernie. Please."

We watched Mindy Jo with hooks and chains, winching the boat onto the wrecker. Mindy Jo has powerful arms, covered with tattoos of all the boyfriends she's had.

"Is there a man alive who could . . ." Bernie said as Mindy Jo drove away with . . . with our boat, if I was following this right. I waited for Bernie to finish the thought, but he did not. Thoughts can be hard to finish, as you might have learned sometime in your life.

Then it was just me and Bernie. Whoa! Maybe not exactly. Because from a ridge far far away came a glare, in fact a sort of double glare that I'd seen before, and it meant one thing to me and one thing only: binoculars. The glare passed over me and my eyes cleared and I made out a small figure standing on that ridge. A very small figure — a stick figure really — about which I could tell nothing, except that it was a woman. A woman stands differently from a man, that's basic in this business. Was the woman on the distant ridge something Bernie should know about? I thought so, and barked my low, rumbly bark.

"Something up, big guy?"

Bernie shielded his eyes from the sun, looked this way and that. When his gaze finally found the distant ridge, the small figure was gone. At that point I suddenly remembered the Slim Jims eight-pack, a powerful memory that caused the forgetting of everything else.

FIVE

"Damn it," said Bernie, as we pulled up in front of our place on Mesquite Road, not entering the driveway on account of Mindy Jo already being there, busy unloading *Sea of Love,* if I'd caught the name of the blue boat. Our place on Mesquite Road is the best place in the whole Valley, in my opinion, and probably yours, too, after you come to visit. We've got the canyon out back, and on one side are the Parsonses, this old couple — maybe not doing so well these days — and my pal Iggy. On the other side lives old man Heydrich. Not long ago we found out — actually from our buddy Mr. Singh of Singh's Pawnbroker and Financing for All Your Needs, who I think I may have mentioned already, although I may not have gotten to Mrs. Singh's curried goat, a reason to visit even if you have no needs — that old man Heydrich collects Nazi memorabilia. Whatever those might be, Bernie's not a fan, but that's not the worst thing about old man Heydrich. What's worse is the way he waters his lawn — not a desert-style lawn like ours and the Parsonses', mostly about rocks and cactuses and dirt, really the nicest kind of lawn, Bernie says, but the green-grass golf-course kind, which is the worst. Even if it feels the best under your paws, but that last part's just between you and me.

Now, switching off the engine, Bernie said, "There's only one aquifer — what's so hard to understand?" Possibly he raised his voice a bit, but I would never have called it shouting. It didn't matter. Old man Heydrich wasn't out there to hear, so the only answer was the hiss of his sprinklers spraying water high in the air, making a rainbow, yes, which had to be good, but also a puddle out on the street, and that was bad.

Bernie glared at that rainbow for a moment, then gave his head a quick little shake. I do the very same thing sometimes. We're a lot alike in some ways, me and Bernie. Then, not looking angry anymore, he walked up the driveway to where Mindy Jo was at the controls of the winch, slowly lowering *Sea of Love* beside the house. I gave my head a quick little shake and followed.

"Anything I can do to help?" Bernie said.

"Pour me a cold one," said Mindy Jo.

Bernie went into the house. I stayed outside. The boat touched down without making a sound. Mindy Jo started unhooking the hooks, paused when she saw me watching.

"One fine hombre, arn'cha?" She glanced toward the house. "Make that two f—"

Whatever was coming next didn't come, because the side door of the Parsons's house opened and out stepped Mr. Parsons, not actually stepping, but stumping on his walker, one of those hospital bands on his wrist.

"Hi, there," he said. "I see Bernie got himself a —"

Boat.

That was my guess on where Mr. Parsons was headed with this. But I might have been wrong. The point was that Mr. Parsons didn't get the word out because at that moment who squeezed between his leg and the door frame, a very small space? Why, that would be Iggy!

One thing about Iggy: he can squeeze through spaces even when there are no spaces. Once — this was before the electric fence guy got the Parsonses to put one in, an electric fence they could never get to work right, meaning nowadays Iggy was pretty much inside — when we were roaming in some distant neighborhood where the mailman left a biscuit in the box outside every house that included a member of the nation within — Iggy had actually jumped up — an amazing jump for such a little guy — and squeezed himself into a mailbox, the opening of which was way smaller than he was! And then he'd hopped out with that biscuit in his mouth and a crazy look in his eyes that got crazier when a sort of howling rose up from the nearest house. Around then was when I snatched the biscuit from Iggy — it seemed like the right thing to do — and he chased after me going yip-yip-yip, his tongue, astonishingly long, flopping out the side of his mouth. Of course there was no way Iggy could catch me unless I let him, which I did, although by that time there was no biscuit to be had. What a great game, and we'd made it up all on our own! We played that game over and over — the game of Iggy snatching biscuits out of mailboxes and me snatching them away from him — going from one neighborhood to another until the mailman checked his rearview mirror and hit the brakes. After that came a period of confusion, involving animal control, thornbushes, and several members of Valley PD, including one I happened to know, namely Leo "Kittycat" Leone, so everything turned out all right. Did I poop or what the next day! Poop and poop and —

But maybe too much information. And not really the point, which was all about Iggy squeezing through narrow spaces, just like he was doing now, and the next moment he'd be on the loose and headed for the hills, and me right with him. Iggy! My best buddy! I got ready to ramble and rumble and who knows what? But at the very instant when Iggy was popping free, Mindy Jo glanced his way, stuck a thumb and one finger in the corners of her mouth and whistled.

This was a whistle like none I'd ever heard, except maybe one time when Bernie and I were mixing it up with a couple of perps on a railroad track in the middle of nowhere and a train suddenly came zooming round the mountain. That train whistle, somewhere between a scream and a roar: the scariest sound I'd ever heard. The perps gave up and raised their hands immediately — when the right move actually was to leap off the tracks and get clear of that train, which was what Bernie and I had done. So then we had to go back and get them, with the train now practically on top of us! And they didn't even thank us later that day when we went to check on them in their cells.

But forget all that. The only reason I brought it up is on account of that train whistle and Mindy Jo's whistle being pretty similar. Cleared my head, I can tell you, and it was clear to begin with. Mr. Parsons's mouth opened wide and he leaned back a bit, as though facing a storm. As for Iggy, he forgot about being on the loose, wheeled right around and darted back into his house.

To look at someone in awe — is that an expression? If so, that was how Mr. Parsons was looking at Mindy Jo. She looked at him in alarm.

"You okay, pal?"

"Perfectly okay."

"Whew," Mindy Jo said. "Thought for a second there you were having a stroke."

"That was last week," said Mr. Parsons. He went back inside and closed the door.

Not long after that we were out on the patio back of our place and having drinks — beer for Bernie and Mindy Jo, water for me. The swan fountain — the only thing Leda left behind after the divorce — made soft splashes, just the sound cooling off the day a bit. The sound of water! I came close to having a thought about that.

A lot of humans have trouble with the heat, but not Bernie and not Mindy Jo. They sat at the little round table, both relaxed in that easy way strong bodies have when they're relaxing. Mindy Jo took a big sip of beer.

"What're you going to do with the boat?" she said.

"Fix it up."

"Yeah?"

"Am I hearing something in your tone?" Bernie said.

"Don't know what you're hearing," said Mindy Jo, "but what's in my mind is no frickin' way."

Uh-oh. Had Mindy Jo just said something not nice about Bernie's fixing things up skills? Was it possible he and Mindy Jo would soon be throwing down out here on the patio? No way — Bernie could never hurt a woman, not even a big strong one like Mindy Jo.

And in fact he started laughing. He laughed and laughed, all of a sudden so happy. Mindy Jo laughed, too. They polished off their beers. Bernie went inside and brought out two more. They clinked glasses.

"Nixon always says you're a special guy,

Bernie," Mindy Jo said. "And I agree. Older, true, but special."

"Well," said Bernie, "um, I wouldn't say they're mutually exclusive. No reason you can't —"

"I had an older boyfriend once." Mindy Jo leaned across the table, held one of her muscular arms so Bernie could see. She pointed at one of the tattooed faces, halfway down her forearm. "This guy," she said.

Bernie peered at the tattoo. "Hard to really tell a whole lot from —" he began.

"Never again," Mindy Jo said. "That's what I told myself about older men."

"Kind of sweeping, but —"

"You know why?"

Bernie shook his head.

"Take a guess."

Bernie looked up at the sky. A plane was flying by high above, trailing one of those long white tails. Tails of any kind were always interesting, of course, but Bernie seemed to gaze at it for a very long time. Finally he said, "They start doubting themselves."

"Exactly!" Mindy Jo punched Bernie's shoulder, not particularly gently. "And then they stop being fun. How did you know that?"

Bernie smiled this quick little smile he has.

You hardly ever see it. I think it happens when he's pleased with himself, but don't go by me. "I just tried to imagine myself in the shoes of an older guy," he said.

"Ha!" said Mindy Jo. "Ha!" She started to make a fist, as though to give Bernie's shoulder another pop, and then stopped. What was going on? I checked Bernie's footwear, saw he was wearing flip-flops, got no further ahead. Meanwhile Mindy Jo was looking at Bernie in a new way. But he'd gone back to watching that plane, so he missed it.

"Bernie?" Mindy Jo said.

His gaze came back down. "Yeah?"

"Got any tattoos yourself?"

He shook his head.

"Look down your nose at people with tats?"

Look down your nose? I'd never heard that before, and it sounded like something I should have known about. I sat up straight, tried looking down my nose and . . . and found I could do it easily! And what a nose, by the way! Absolutely fascinating, especially from this angle. It went on and on and on, a total champ of a nose. Who's got it better than me?

"No," Bernie said. He glanced at me,

blinked, turned back to Mindy Jo. "Not at all."

"Sorry," said Mindy Jo. "My bad — didn't mean to stereotype you."

"No problem."

Mindy Jo swallowed some more beer. "My first serious boyfriend played in a Beatles tribute band up in Vegas."

"Yeah?" said Bernie. "Which mop top was he?"

"Ringo, of course," said Mindy Jo. "Want to see?"

Here is where I should maybe describe our patio a little more. It's fenced in on both sides with a high wooden fence and at the back a high adobe wall with a high gate, all this highness is really high so someone — say Bernie — would never have to worry about someone else — say me — taking off on what you might call an unplanned outing. A very smart idea and it had worked for the longest time, with that second someone not even dreaming of even taking a crack at leaping up and over. But then one night had come a sound unlike any other from across the canyon, namely the sound of she-barking. Bottom line: you don't know what you're capable of unless you try. For now let's leave out the complications of the later appearance of a puppy supposedly resembling — if that's the meaning of "spit and image" — me, a puppy now going by "Shooter" and living with Charlie — that's Bernie's kid — Leda and Daddy Malcolm, which was what Charlie was supposed to call Leda's new husband, a rich dude with very long toes, Bernie being simply Daddy.

But forget all that, or at least part of it. The only point was the high fence on both sides, the Parsons side and the old man Heydrich side. On the Parsons side the fence has a door — the very door we'd come through after the boat was all nicely in place — now closed but not locked.

Okeydoke? Back to this Ringo person. A perp-type name, in my opinion, so if you're out there right now, Señor Ringo, I hope you look good in orange.

"Uh, sure," Bernie was saying. He glanced at Mindy Jo's arms. "Which one's Ringo?"

"His name wasn't actually Ringo, of course," Mindy Jo said. "It was Jerry."

"Got it," said Bernie, although that was where I myself stopped getting it.

"And he's not with the others," Mindy Jo went on. "Being my first, and all."

"Ah."

"Still want to see?"

"Um, well, maybe better to just let the

imagination kind of —"

Right about then was the moment the side door of the fence opened and someone looked in. This someone was Eliza, sort of Bernie's girlfriend now that Suzie didn't seem to be speaking to Bernie these days. All so complicated, not at all how we handle these things in the nation within. When we first met Eliza, Bernie was still in Valley Hospital after the saguaro case — no way I'm getting into all that now — and she was Dr. Bethea to us, in charge of getting Bernie better. Which happened, just one of the reasons I'm a big fan. Also she turned out to be a cousin of Cleon Maxwell of Max's Memphis Ribs, my favorite joint in the whole Valley! I was a big fan of Suzie, too, although I didn't recall any of her cousins being in the same league as Cleon.

Bernie did not notice Eliza at the door. He was too busy watching Mindy Jo, who was trying to lower one shoulder of her T-shirt, and when that didn't quite work out the way she wanted, moving on to just plain taking the whole thing off.

"Here we go," she said, pointing to the now-visible tattoo of a long-haired dude with a big, crooked smile on his face. "You like?"

"Uh, remarkable," Bernie said. "Remark-

74

able, like, likeness."

"You knew Jerry?"

"I meant of Ringo."

"Jerry wasn't really Ringo, Bernie. It was an act."

"Right, right, of course. Line between art and life and all, and —" He tore his eyes off the sight, and that was when his gaze swept over the door in the fence, now closed again, with no sign of Eliza.

Mindy Jo's phone buzzed. She checked the screen. "Wreck on the airport cut-off," she said, jumping up. "Sanitation hauler and two eighteen-wheelers." Ringo, or Jerry, or whoever it was, disappeared from view, and Mindy Jo was gone right after that.

Bernie and I sat quietly, Bernie gazing at the fountain and me gazing at him. All at once, he slapped his hand on the table. "Evaporation! What's wrong with me?"

That was an easy one. Zilch, zip, nada. For some reason, Bernie went behind the fountain, shut off the water. The flow from the swan's mouth dwindled to a trickle, then a few drops. He watched those last few drops.

"Why did Wendell ask us to go out there in the first place? That got lost in the shuffle." Bernie turned my way. "What did he want to talk about?"

Our fountain? Hey! A pretty good guess by me! I felt tip-top.

Six

"Wow. See what that dog just did?"

"Chet? Can you give the Frisbee back, please?"

"Is that your dog?"

"We're more of a team."

"I can't believe he jumped that high. Does he have a YouTube channel?"

"Don't give him ideas. Chet? The Frisbee, please?"

Why, certainly! It wasn't my Frisbee. I knew that very well. I'd just been sharing it with these college kids. College kids were the greatest. Bernie said it was exam week now, so they'd probably be studying in their rooms, but this time — maybe for the very first time in his life! — Bernie was wrong. The college kids were all doing their studying out on the quad, learning about catching rays, smoking weed, chugging beers, and lots of other stuff they had to — what was the expression? Get their heads around? —

before exam time. Plus, on top of all that, mastering the Frisbee, too! So much work for the poor kids. Thinking it over, I realized that I'd only been trying to help. Not to criticize, but that last throw, the one I'd snagged, had really been pretty wild, totally uncatchable. Although not by me. So picking that Frisbee right out of the air just as it fluttered away over a food truck was going to help the hollow-chested pipe-armed kid who'd thrown it with his confidence. And maybe now would be a good time to build up his stamina by having him chase me around a bit. Suppose I went up to him and almost gave him the Frisbee, but not quite, instead smoothly backing away just as he reached for it and —

"Chet!"

Prof was our expert when it came to money — everything about money except making it, which took me some time to realize. His office overlooked the quad, an office with stacks of books all over the place and a couch. Prof was lying on the couch when we came in, his hands folded over his big round stomach.

"Well, well, been a while," he said as we came in. "Perfect timing — I just now figured out what's happening on our college campuses — although not yet this one, thank god."

"Yeah?" Bernie said. "What is it?"

"You expect me to simply tell you?"

"Why not?"

"That would be spoon-feeding, Bernie, the sign of the teacher who has thrown in the towel."

Spoon-feeding? Totally unexpected. I smelled no food whatsoever in Prof's office, but I was ready to be surprised. I've licked spoons from time to time, also forks, plates, and bowls. But none of that happened now. Instead Bernie said, "I'm not your student."

"Good point. None of my students are remotely like you." Prof sighed and sat up, not easily. "My breakthrough came when I stumbled on the following quotation. Can you identify the writer? Quote." He raised a pudgy finger toward the ceiling. "To right a wrong it is necessary to exceed the proper limits, and the wrong cannot be righted unless the proper limits are exceeded. Unquote."

"Someone very dangerous," Bernie said.

"Precisely!" said Prof. "Would you consider coming to one of my classes and giving a little talk?"

"About what?"

"The life of action."

"No."

"No to the theme or no to the talk?"

"Yes."

That right there was the most confusing human conversation I'd ever heard. Anyone called Prof had to be brilliant, of course, and Bernie was always the smartest human in the room, so the fault had to be mine. I lay down and licked my paw for a while.

"Feel free to change your mind at any time," Prof said. "The quotation comes from Chairman Mao. The self-righteous violating proper limits — that's what we have today. But you probably didn't come to hear me pontificate."

"I could listen to you pontificate all day," Bernie said.

Prof smiled. "You could?" His face changed and for a second or two I saw him as a cheerful, chubby boy instead of a sick old man. Yes, poor Prof was sick. The smell of something wrong inside him was in the air, faint but unmissable, at least to me.

"But," Bernie went on, "we're working a case, involving someone you might have known."

"And who would that be?"

"Wendell Nero."

"Terrible news," said Prof. He rubbed his beard. Did a tiny crumb or two fall out?

"But what case? I understood there'd been an arrest."

Bernie nodded. "I'm just poking around. How well did you know him?"

Interesting, because at that moment I was poking around myself, hunting for those crumbs, soon found beside some balled-up papers on the floor. Bacon crumbs? I couldn't believe my luck.

"Not well," Prof was saying. "We've been on a committee or two over the years. And his office is just down the hall."

"Let's take a look," Bernie said.

"See! Right there! The life of action!"

"We're just walking down the hall."

"But because of a murder, Bernie. Intent changes everything."

We walked down the hall, one of those chilly halls where the AC's turned up to the max. Bernie's not a fan of AC turned up to the max, or of AC at all. Is it because of the aquifer? That was as far as I could take it.

"Here's his office," Prof said. "Wendell wasn't around much these last few years, busy with his consulting work. Did you know he actually lived in that RV?"

"I did not."

"Saved time, according to him, time for his research. There isn't a geologist west of the Mississ—"

At that point Prof opened the door. Wendell's office was about the same size as Prof's but it had a desk instead of a couch and was much tidier. A man was standing by the desk, peering into one of the drawers. This was a bit of a surprise. For one thing, I hadn't smelled him through the door. Must have been on account of the AC, which can sometimes be like a river, washing smells away on a current of cold air. I smelled him now, of course, an everyday Valley male aroma of aftershave and weed, but mixed in very very faintly was a female scent, a scent of flowers a day or two before they get thrown out. Not his smell, if you see what I mean, but the smell of a woman he'd recently been near, riding in a car, for example. Just throwing that in, since I also picked up a hint of gasoline, the kind humans always have on them after they do their own pumping.

Whew! A lot of information, and maybe none of it as interesting as how the man looked, which was like surfers I'd seen in San Diego, especially one who hadn't been enthusiastic on sharing a wave with us — a whole big wave, belonging to everyone! Same sun-bleached hair, same tan skin, the big difference being the scar on this dude's cheek, the sort of little round puckered scar a bullet leaves, something I'd seen many times in my line of work, way more than two, the biggest number my mind is comfortable with.

"Hey, guys," he said. As for what Bernie calls the element of surprise — a big thing in our line of work — he seemed a little surprised, but in a friendly, smiling way. Prof looked very surprised, his wild and bushy eyebrows raised high. No surprise at all on Bernie's face. That was Bernie, a cool customer, especially in moments of danger, which this was not, so maybe he was just practicing.

"Hi," he said. And then nothing. Nothing is part of Bernie's technique. He's that good.

"You folks with the college?" the man said right away, filling the silence, which showed that nothing was working its magic again, as it almost always did. "I'm Uncle Wendell's nephew. What a terrible thing! But somewhere there's a photo of him and my dad when they were kids. I was hoping to salvage it before everything got . . . disposed of."

"The brother who died a long time ago?" Prof said.

The man nodded. "And they weren't

particularly close. But there's a photo of the two of them on a horse when they were little boys that my dad often mentioned — like toward the end." He closed the drawer, gave Prof a big smile. "But it doesn't seem to be here, so I'll get going. Hope I haven't caused any trouble."

"No, no," said Prof, "no trouble at all."

The man gave us one of those little salutes and was almost out the door when Bernie said, "When was the last time you saw your uncle?"

He turned and gave Bernie the same sort of smile he'd given Prof, but now it wavered slightly. "Been years." He got a faraway look in his eyes. "But it's still kinda . . . emotional."

"Condolences," said Prof.

"Thank you, sir," said the man. He moved out of the room and down the hall. I heard an odd papery crinkle as he walked away.

Bernie went over to the desk. "Any reason I can't take a look around?"

"I don't see why not," Prof said. "Looking for anything particular?"

"Wendell wanted to see us," Bernie said. "I'd like to know why."

"Because?"

Bernie shrugged. "It's a gap."

"A point of commonality between us — I

84

can't bear gaps either." Prof gestured toward the room. "Fill in the gaps, Bernie."

He left us by ourselves. Bernie's an expert at searching a room, a pleasure to watch, which was what I did, curled up in a corner. Bernie went through everything, sometimes muttering things like "You'd think he'd . . ." or "so tidy he's almost not even . . ." which I didn't understand at all, but finally, "Aha!"

I sat up.

Bernie raised a small leather-bound note-book. Leather has always been an interest of mine. I rose and moved closer.

"His appointment book, Chet. Was he the type who jots down the subject matter of his meetings? That would be nice."

Bernie leafed through the notebook. He paused, looked more closely, went through the notebook again, this time page by page. He turned to me, the notebook open so I could see. "Someone cut out yesterday, big guy, the day we were scheduled."

He gazed at the door. Then all at once he was on the move, out the door and running down the hall. I ran after him, very soon taking the lead, running because Bernie was running. He ran for reasons of his own, more than good enough for me. We ran down a few flights of stairs — me mostly airborne the whole way — then burst through a doorway and out to the quad, running this way and that, along a street to a parking garage, up, up, up through all the levels, Bernie's eyes so alert, looking here and there for something, no doubt about that, and finally we reached the roof and came to a stop. Bernie, huffing and puffing, went to the low wall at the edge, peered down. I got my paws on the top of the wall and helped with the peering. Very nice to see things from up here: the college, the quad, the surrounding streets, all the little people moving around. So busy and yet . . . so helpless. You had to love them. Whoa! What a strange thought! I pushed it aside and watched a Frisbee gliding through the sunshine, tiny suns glinting on its surface, a lovely sight.

But maybe not to Bernie. "Damn," he said, in that quiet tone he used for talking to himself. Was something wrong? I tried to think what it could be. My mind went on a little trip, sort of . . . how would you put it? Peering into dark corners? Something along those lines. Except there were no dark corners. So that was that.

SEVEN

Deputy Sheriff Beasley was having lunch at a table out back of the Noshery, a strip mall place that was new to me. I'm the type who gets excited by somewhere new, especially somewhere new that smelled like this, so even though Deputy Beasley didn't seem at all excited to see us there was plenty of excitement to go around.

"Mind if we join you?" Bernie said.

"Uh," said Beasley, talking around a sandwichy mouthful, a sandwich filled with thin strips of meat that gave off wave after wave of powerful, complex aromas, some of them previously unknown to me. I faced the fact that Deputy Beasley had made a poor first impression on me and decided to give him a second chance. Who in this life doesn't deserve a second chance, and maybe even one after that? "The thing is," he said, "I'm kind of in a — what the hell?"

"Ch-et?"

Uh-oh. Somehow my paws — only my front ones, so it could have been worse — seemed to have placed themselves on the table, not far from the deputy's paper plate. I got that situation cleared up and pronto.

"He just gets enthusiastic about things," Bernie was saying. "It's probably because he's never been to a deli before."

"Never been to a deli?" said Beasley.

"Not an authentic Jewish-style deli like this one."

"Huh?" said Beasley. "You got something against Jew—" All at once, his face turned purple and he began coughing, choking, and gasping. Bernie went around the table and pounded him on the back. A small — but by no means tiny — piece of that fascinating meat popped out of his mouth, across the table, and almost directly into my own mouth. I hardly had to move a muscle!

After that the next thing I really remember is the waitress coming to the table to take Bernie's order, Bernie by then sitting down and me right beside him, highly alert.

"I'll have what he's having," Bernie said. There: a perfect demonstration of his brilliance.

"One pastrami and corned beef triple decker on pumpernickel coming up," said the waitress.

Beasley, back to eating again, his face its normal color — grayish, with pink splotches here and there — raised a finger. "Side of fries."

"You got it."

Jewish-style deli? Had I gotten that right? My whole life up to now had been . . . not false, oh no, what a frightening idea — but for sure I'd been missing something and hadn't even known! But why be hard on yourself? I stay away from that as a rule.

Beasley took a nice big bite. He chewed for a bit, then gestured at Bernie with a handful of sandwich. That handful of sandwich came oh, so close to me. I could easily have . . . but I did not! Instead I proved that . . . that . . . whoa! What had I proved? Can a dude change his mind? This dude can and did! But too late.

Meanwhile Beasley was saying, "I'm not Jewish."

"No?" said Bernie.

"But my stomach is, if you get what I mean."

"I actually don't."

"Put it this way," Beasley said, biting the end off a dill pickle with a sharp, crunching sound. The dill pickle he could have — I've tried dill pickles on more than one occasion, never with good results. "You can eat Jewish without being Jewish. It's a free country."

Good news! Not the free country part — I already knew that, on account of it being something Bernie often said, but the Jewish part. Was I Jewish, whatever that happened to be, exactly? I doubted it, had never even heard of Jewish until now, but it didn't matter because if Beasley was right I could still eat Jewish no matter what, and eating Jewish was all I wanted to do at that moment. Did Beasley look like the kind of human who tended to be right about things? He did not. That was worrisome.

"Yes, a free country — with liberty and justice for all," Bernie said. "I want to discuss the justice part."

"Huh?"

"Specifically as it relates to the Wendell Nero case," Bernie said.

"What case?" said Beasley. "I closed it already, with some help from you. Got no problem sharing credit. What's the matter? Didn't get the honorary badge and T-shirt yet?" He crunched off another bite of pickle. "I could maybe get you a couple hunnert outa the tipster fund."

A sort of iciness appeared in Bernie's eyes, there and gone in a flash. You don't see that every day — in fact, I didn't remember seeing it ever. "It's not about the money," he said.

"Whoa? You really a PI?" A joke of some sort. Beasley laughed and laughed, spewing a few pickle shreds, useless to me although I snapped them up anyway. What was the joke? Bernie was the best PI in the Valley. He'd even given the keynote address at the Great Western Private Eye convention, and plenty of people had still been in the room when it ended, or at least some.

"I'm the kind of PI who doesn't like loose ends," Bernie said.

Beasley shrugged. "So what? You got a client?"

Good question. Clients were part of our business plan at the Little Detective Agency, possibly an important part.

"Client or not," Bernie said, "there are loose ends in the Nero case."

Client or not? Uh-oh.

"I told you," Beasley said. "There ain't a case. And the DA's office says it's a slam dunk."

"Who's handling it?"

"Some gal? Deena? Dinah?"

"Deirdre Dubois?"

"Yeah. A ballbuster if there ever was one."

That didn't sound good, but Bernie didn't

seem alarmed so neither was I. "Where's the RV?" he said. "I'd like another look at it."

"Why?"

"Unless you've already recovered any phones or computers Wendell owned."

"Nope."

"He was a scientist with a consulting business," Bernie said. "He must have had a phone, a laptop. Where are they?"

"Search me."

Wow! We were going to pat down a deputy sheriff? Had that ever happened before? Actually, yes. And had I enjoyed it or what! Maybe it would become part of our routine! I moved around the table, took up a spot right behind Beasley's chair, standard procedure. Bernie shot me a quick glance, possibly a little puzzled. Was I being too obvious? I went as still as I could, hoping to look less obvious. Did that mean smaller? I tried to look smaller. But how? Think small thoughts? I tried to think small thoughts but came up with none at all.

Around then was when the waitress arrived with Bernie's sandwich and Beasley's fries. On her way back to the kitchen, without even looking — like a behind-the-back pass in basketball! — she slipped me a thick rolled-up slice of that lovely meat.

Pastrami? Corned beef? Both? What a talented waitress, sort of the Steph Curry of the restaurant business! After that my memory of events isn't reliable, although I did get the impression that those fries — maybe the biggest plate of fries I'd ever seen — put Beasley in a better mood. The fry or two or possibly more that I somehow ended up with certainly made me more cheerful, and I'd been feeling pretty cheerful to begin with.

". . . don't really care what you do on your time," he was saying, dipping his napkin in his water glass and wiping his chin, which had become pretty greasy. "The RV's still at the shed, last I knew. The exes are fighting over it."

"Exes?" Bernie said.

"Turns out your pal the scientist had some ex-wives. Three? Four? Something like that. It's a wonder he lived as long as he did."

Deputy Beasley thought that was pretty funny. He was still laughing when we left.

The shed's in the part of South Pedroia where the last boarded-up buildings end and the desert begins. It's a huge fenced-in dirt yard, really, full of all the cars, trucks, SUVs, RVs, tractors, motorcycles, bicycles, and a few strange homemade wheeled things with no name, that end up in possession of the law. The shed itself is at the gate, where we were waved through no problem. We're known in places like this, me and Bernie.

Wendell's RV, with the beautiful waterfall on the side, was in a middle row between a smashed-up truck cab and a pile of motorcycle parts, some of them red-stained. A group of women had a big shaved-head dude backed up against the RV. The women were all new to me, but the dude was Itsy Bitsy Litzenberger, a perp at one time and now the junior assistant attendant of the whole shed experience, which just shows you. He saw us coming and called out over the heads of the women.

"Bernie! Help!"

"Hey, Itsy," Bernie said. "What's going on?"

The women all wheeled around. We had an old one, a not-quite-so-old one, and a younger one than that, although you couldn't call her young. They all wore yoga pants and gold watches. I sensed trouble.

"Flat out goddamn theft!" said the youngest one.

"Look who's talking!" said the not-quite-so-old one.

"Pot calling the kettle!" said the oldest one.

Bernie held up his hand. "Ladies, please."

They all spoke at once. "Don't call us ladies!"

I got ready to run.

"Uh, women," Bernie said. "Please, women. Maybe Itsy here can fill me in."

"Well, Bernie," Itsy said, shifting from foot to foot, "these three . . . visitors are all former wives of the guy who owned this RV and —"

The middle one jabbed her finger, the nail painted bright red, at the youngest one. "He never married *her*. They were just shacked up."

"I'll take that as a compliment," the youngest one said. "We didn't need a ring to keep us together. We had heat in the bedroom, foreign territory to you as I know from the horse's mouth."

"I was never a professional like you, that's true," said the middle one.

"More like a semi-pro," the oldest said.

Then came a lot of shouting, including a few words I hadn't heard since an all-you-can-drink night at a biker bar we went to once by mistake, all of it impossible to follow. But if horses — prima donnas each and every one — were involved then we had problems.

"Excuse me," Bernie said several times to no effect. Finally he added, "We were the ones who found him, Chet and I."

The women went silent and turned their gazes on us. "Who's Chet?" said the oldest.

Bernie pointed my way.

"What a handsome boy," she said. The others nodded. Had we turned a corner? Simply based on my looks? I couldn't think why not.

Bernie rubbed his hands together like we were getting somewhere at last.

"I'm guessing you're all united in feeling, um, or having felt, a certain . . . fondness for Wendell."

He paused. None of them said no.

"Wendell had asked us to call on him yesterday morning," Bernie said. "He didn't say why." He took out our business cards, handed one to each of the women.

"Can I have one, too?" Itsy said.

Bernie reached over the women, gave Itsy a card. Itsy glanced at it. "Hey. Cool flowers."

I missed Suzie, but those flowers? Nothing we could do about it, since it was Suzie, although now that things weren't so good with her anymore, maybe . . . I didn't want to go there. I'd already gone further than I wanted.

"You're a private eye?" said the youngest one.

"At least you can read," the middle one told her.

"Why did Wendell want a private eye?" said the oldest.

"That's the question," Bernie said. "Have any of you been inside the RV yet?"

They all turned on Itsy. "He won't let us!"

Itsy raised his hands. "Just doin' my job, Bernie. Gotta establish ownership."

"The owner passed," said the youngest one.

"Deceased," said the middle one.

"Dead," said the old one.

"In which case," Bernie said, "maybe there's something in his will."

"There is no will!" the women said.

"How do you know?" said Bernie.

"We called the lawyer," they all said.

"Um, one at a time or all at once?" Bernie said.

"Is that meant to be funny?" said the youngest one.

"Separately, of course," the middle one said. "We haven't talked together all three in years."

"Thank Christ," said the oldest.

The women exchanged glares.

"Who made the last call to the lawyer?" Bernie said.

"Me," the oldest one said.

"What's your name?"

"Felicia."

"Let's talk, Felicia, just the two of us, for simplicity's sake."

"Simplicity's sake?" said the other women. I was with them on that.

Bernie led Felicia away, toward the smashed-up cab. I followed — and soon led — feeling the gazes of the other two women all the way.

"I need to search the RV, Felicia," Bernie said.

"Why?"

"There are unanswered questions in this case."

"But haven't they caught the murderer?"

"Nevertheless."

"Are you saying they got the wrong guy?"

Bernie gazed down at her. "I'm saying two things. One: I want no objection from you or the others when I ask Itsy to let me search the RV. Two: I'm going to need a client."

Felicia gazed back up at Bernie, eyes narrowed and suspicious at first, and then just narrowed. She gave him a nod, very slight, hardly any movement at all.

Not long after that, we were inside the RV, me, Bernie, and Itsy — Itsy along not because he didn't trust us, but because he wanted to see pros in action. We have fans, me and Bernie. With fans you need to throw them a bone from time to time. Whoa! An actual bone? Never. I mean an unactual bone, whatever that might be. Meanwhile our search, for a phone or a laptop, if I'd been following things right, was turning up nada. Bernie stood very still, gazing at something far beyond the walls of the RV. That seemed to go on for a long time, and then he snapped out of it, an inner snap I could feel, and now his gaze was on the actual wall, focused, in fact, on that thumb-tacked photo of Wendell and the girl. Bernie took the photo off the wall, checked the back, and slid it into his shirt pocket.

We went outside. The women were waiting. Bernie shook his head.

"Does that mean you're giving up?" Felicia said.

I was hoping Bernie would say, *What a question!* Instead he went with, "No."

"Good," said Felicia. "Because we want to hire you."

Bernie swallowed. "Meaning . . . the whole lot of, um . . . ?"

"Exactly," said Felicia. "The whole lot of um."

EIGHT

There's a nice little park across from the courthouse. We waited there in the late afternoon, Bernie on a bench, me underneath, the heat of the day still strong but tiny breezes starting to stir. Were we going inside? I'd done some work in the courthouse during my career, once as Exhibit A. The judge had slipped me a Rover and Company biscuit, my very favorite, from under his black robe. I'd even gotten to know a few members of the jury. The walls of that little box they sit in is not high at all. They could have easily jumped out of it at any time. Why didn't they? I'd been thinking along those lines when I . . . did whatever I did, and soon after that I'd been back out here in this very park! Wow! Sometimes you just have to sit back and say, What's this all about? Although I never do.

From inside the courthouse came — at least to me — the sound of humans on the move — the heavy-footed, the light-footed, the sneaker-wearing, high-heelers, wing-tippers, and flip-floppers, all of them in a hurry. The front doors opened and out they came in a big mob, which was when Bernie became aware of what was going on.

"Five o'clock whistle," he said. Whistle? There'd been no whistle, but if Bernie said . . . I listened my hardest and . . . and from far beyond the Valley, came the faintest, tiniest woo-woo of a train, one of those long, long trains you sometimes see out there, like a black line inking itself across the desert. "They just blow that whistle because they're feeling lonely," Bernie likes to say. But that's not the point, which is about his hearing. True, Bernie's ears aren't small for a human, but was it really possible he'd heard that train whistle? If he had, then . . . then I really didn't know my Bernie. But I did! I did know my Bernie! That had to mean he wasn't himself for some reason. I gave him a close look, just to see what was going on. Did he seem a little tired? That had to be it.

"Chet? Something up? You're kind of in my face, big guy."

Hey! He was right! Our noses were practically touching. How had that happened? I had no clue, but why stop at practically? I pressed my nose right against Bernie's.

He laughed. "What am I going to do with you?"

What a question! Same as always — chase down perps pedal to the metal! And weren't we on a roll? First that rooftop dude, who I could hardly remember, and then Florian almost the next day. Or maybe exactly the next day, days having a way of sometimes merging into one another. But nothing beats chasing down perps. Who's next? Who's next? Who's next? Perhaps I was getting a little too excited, almost to the point of pawing at the top of Bernie's head, or . . . or, yes, I seemed to be at that point, not much question about it, but Bernie didn't mind. He laughed again, patted my side, and then paused, his gaze on the courthouse door.

"I think that's her," he said, using his business voice. I climbed down at once, turned, and sat at his feet, facing forward, facing the world. When Bernie means business, I mean business.

A not-very-tall but strong-looking woman had appeared on the courthouse stairs. She was towing a wheeled suitcase behind her, with another suitcase on top of it; smallish suitcases or maybe biggish briefcases. Instead of bump-bump-bumping them down the steps, she just lifted them clear with one hand and carried the whole load down to the sidewalk, easy-peasy, all of this in high-heeled shoes. She came into the park, sat on the bench next to ours, took sneakers out of one of those briefcases — yes, a briefcase for sure, full of papers in different slots — and started changing her shoes.

Bernie rose. "Deirdre Dubois?" he said.

The woman turned to us. She had deep dark eyes that reminded me of Suzie's except they didn't shine. Suzie's shone in a way that made me think of moonlight; this woman's eyes were hotter.

"Yes?" she said, in the kind of tone most humans use for *no*.

"I'm Bernie Little and this —"

"I know who you are," said the woman, Deirdre Dubois, if I'd been following this right.

"Have we met?" Bernie said.

"That seems to be happening now," said Deirdre. "But you're a PI. I have files complete with photos on every PI in the Valley, the licensed ones and the ones whose licenses I've stripped."

That sounded not very friendly, but Bernie just smiled. "Then you know that Chet here's my partner."

"Correct," Deirdre said. "His K-nine school summary report is part of your file."

104

When Bernie gets surprised he looks much younger — you can suddenly find Charlie in his face. It's an expression you hardly ever see because Bernie's not easy to surprise, but it was there now.

"I'm thorough, Bernie," Deirdre said. "I even know he flunked out on the very last day."

Oh, no! Why did that have to come up? I hoped her file included the part about a cat being involved. *Please, Bernie, ask her about the cat part! Please.*

But he did not. Instead he stopped looking surprised, instead looked just himself, his very best self. "That was a very lucky day for me."

"Because you ended up together?"

"Correct."

Deirdre's gaze went to me. I gazed back, showing zip, a total pro. Had one of my ears turned inside out for some reason? Unfortunate timing perhaps. Sometimes you just have to carry on. I doubled down on my total pro look.

Deirdre turned to her bag, dropped the high heels inside. "Is this simply a chance meeting, Bernie? Or do you want something?"

"The second."

"Let me guess. You're feeling put-out that

you made the collar on the Wendell Nero murder and ended up with nothing to show for it. I'll have my office forward you a check for $500." She zipped her bag closed. "Anything else?"

"I get it that you're tough as they come, inside and out," Bernie said. "So you can ease up a little." Whoa! He sounded angry? Not by raising his voice — that wasn't part of his angry sound, more like just the opposite. But why? Five hundred dollars was nothing to sneeze at, as humans like to say. Once I'd seen this coke dealer name of Snorter sneeze on an enormous pile of cash, way more than $500. This happened to take place on a high-rise balcony downtown, but no time for a description of what came next.

Meanwhile Deirdre had gone still. Her color didn't change, no vein throbbed in her forehead, none of that stuff. But her eyes, hot to begin with, were blazing.

"I don't want money," Bernie said.

But . . . but surely money was part of our business plan. I didn't understand. Maybe we would be paid in gold or diamonds from now on? I felt better right away.

"What I want," Bernie went on, "is a meeting with Florian Machado, just the three of us."

Deirdre's head shifted slightly back. "Me,

you, and him?"

Bernie shook his head. "Chet, me, him."

"Has Beasley already turned you down?"

"I didn't ask him."

"Why not?"

"I'm guessing you have a file on him, too," said Bernie. "Meaning you already know why not."

Did I catch a tiny twitch at one corner of Deirdre's mouth, like a smile was on the way? I wasn't sure, but probably not, since no smile came.

"Too bad about Sheriff Gooden," she said. "Maybe he'd have given you the okay. Weren't you in the military together?"

Bernie nodded. "When's he coming back to work?"

"You haven't heard?"

"Beasley said he's got a pesky gallbladder."

"Pesky gallbladder?" Deirdre said. "It's stage four pancreatic cancer. He has a few more weeks, if that."

Bernie went quiet. Sometimes, not often, I get the feeling he's far away even though he's right here. I moved a little closer.

"But back to business," Deirdre said. "Why do you want to meet with Florian Machado?"

Bernie was slow to answer, like he was

waking up. He took a step or two, sat on the end of Deirdre's bench. "We met Wendell Nero the night before the murder. He asked us to visit him the next morning but didn't say why."

"So?"

"So I'd like to know why."

"And what does Florian Machado have to do with that?"

"Nothing," Bernie said. "Unless his alibi is true."

"He was innocently riding around on his ATV, went into the RV on a sudden larcenous impulse, saw the victim with his throat slit from ear to ear but kept from puking long enough to steal the wallet, which he'd never have even considered if he hadn't been so upset by the gory sight," Deirdre said. "That alibi?"

"Yeah," Bernie said.

"Tell you what," said Deirdre. "I was thinking of offering him a deal — no death penalty in exchange for a guilty plea. But for you I'll take him to trial. Then if the jury buys his alibi, you'll be able to question him at leisure." She smiled at Bernie — just the teeth part, her eyes not joining in.

Bernie has a temper, way way down. I've seen it only once or twice, but now felt it waking inside him. Then I felt a sort of internal effort and he put it back to sleep. "What if there's a small chance — ten percent, five, even one — that Florian's telling the truth, at least on the most important part?" he said.

"I can live with uncertainty," said Deirdre. "And I'll bet you can, too. I'm not reopening the case." She took a file from one of her bags. "Anything else?"

Their eyes met. Bernie's were as hard as I've ever seen them, but hers were harder. I got a bad feeling about what was coming next, but I never learned what it might have been, because at that moment a woman came running up, a happy-looking woman with a tiny member of the nation within in her arms. In its tiny mouth was a tiny toy.

The happy-looking woman leaned forward and gave Deirdre a nice big kiss. "Hi, babe," said Deirdre, smiling again, this time her eyes joining in and in a big way. But none of that was important. What mattered was the toy, suddenly slipping from the mouth of the tiny dude — or dudette, in this case — and rolling away on the grass. The dudette scrambled free of the happy-looking woman's arms and chased after the toy. How cute! Would you look at those teensy-weensy legs, just churning away, although her forward progress was just about nothing. Because I'm the kind who believes in fair play, I waited till she was almost there, one or two teensy steps from that toy — a very interesting toy, it turned out, part lopsided ball and part chewy — before soaring right over her, snatching up the toy, barreling around a tree, leaping over a bench, charging onto a basketball court I hadn't even noticed before, jumping right up to one of those hoops just as a basketball was on its way in, batting it away with a twist of my head — uh-oh, possibly a no-no called goaltending, but not to worry because by then I'd put a lot of distance between me and the court, in fact was zigzagging across the park, paws digging in, clods of earth flying, toy still securely in my grip, and — Bernie suddenly in sight! There he was, my Bernie, now on his feet in front of the bench, Deirdre and the other woman also standing, all of them with their eyes and mouths wide open. The tiny dudette was right where I'd last seen her, sort of bouncing up and down, mostly on her hind legs, barking the tiniest barks I'd ever heard. I dialed right down to a slow trot and for absolutely no reason at all dropped the toy — a very nice toy, by the way, with unusually pleasant mouth feel — right at the dudette's feet.

What furious little eyes she had! Just adorable. She snapped up the toy and hurried back to the bench, where Deirdre's friend — if I'd gotten things right — scooped her up. Then they were all watching me.

I sat down, calm and professional, and watched them back. It got very quiet. I actually heard that deep desert train whistle again, now from even farther away.

Deirdre turned to Bernie. "I've changed my mind," she said.

"First, Chet, a little detour."

We were back on the road, Bernie behind the wheel, me in the shotgun seat, the sun low, the sky starting to get that fiery glow. In short, everything was great, except for one thing, namely that there was no sign of a detour, like a roadblock, guys in vests waving stop signs, cops lounging around and chewing gum. But if Bernie said we were taking a detour, then that was that. Actually, now that I looked around, a very nice detour, into a quiet hilly neighborhood that was new to me, the houses not big and fancy, and also kind of old, but nice at the same time. Were there other neighborhoods like this in the Valley? Not that I remembered, but don't take that to the bank, especially not our bank where things were a bit awkward, as I may have already mentioned.

We turned into a circular drive, parked in front of a low but longish adobe building, and went inside. Right away I smelled some hospital-type smells, as well as the smells of old humans, but also lots of nice flower smells as well — which I almost always find quite relaxing. Was this a hospital? Someone's home? There was a front desk, which made me think hospital, but it was quiet and peaceful, which made me think home.

"Oh my goodness," said the woman behind the front desk, putting her hand to her chest, "that's the biggest therapy dog I've ever seen."

Bernie glanced at her name tag. "Well, Lois," he said, "I wouldn't exactly call Chet here a —"

"And I didn't even expect you." Lois took off her glasses and checked a screen. Some humans take their glasses off for screen checking and some put their glasses on. I still have a lot to learn about humans, but luckily enough I had plenty of time, unless I was missing something. "Weren't you booked for tomorrow?"

"This is a private visit," Bernie said. "We're here to see Bo Gooden."

"That's nice." Lois rose. "He hasn't had a

visitor in some time."

"No?" Bernie said. "What about Cynthia?"

"Cynthia?" Lois opened a door and led us down a wide hall.

"His wife," Bernie said.

Lois shook her head, then paused in front of a door and in a low voice said, "When did you last see him?"

"Been a year or two," Bernie said.

"Be prepared." She knocked on the door.

"Come on in," said a man, his voice starting out pretty strong but trailing off into a whisper.

Lois opened the door. Inside was a nice little room, clean and tidy. A man in pajamas lay on top of the bed, head propped up on pillows. His bare feet were big and so were his hands, plus he had thick wrists. Bo Gooden, if that's who we had here, must have been a big man at one time, although not now.

"Sheriff Gooden?" said Lois. "You've got visitors."

He turned his head our way. His eyes were dull and lightless, and I smelled something strong and not good coming from inside him — not pee or poop or puke or any of that normal stuff — which actually doesn't smell bad to me, interesting being the way to put it, always worth a sniff. This particular bad smell was something I'd smelled in a human or two before. It was the smell of a living thing inside them, a living thing that wasn't them — a scary thought. Had I smelled something similar in a few members of the nation within? Uh-oh. My mind stopped right there. I have the kind of mind that looks out for me, at least most of the time.

"Bernie?" he said, his voice a soft sort of croak. He cleared his throat, making a horrible metallic sound that seemed to pain him, and tried again. "Bernie?"

"Hey," said Bernie, moving toward the bed, me right beside him.

Behind us Lois said, "Can I get you anything, Sheriff?"

"Two," said the sheriff. He took a breath and raised his voice a little. "Two bourbons. Doubles."

"Ha ha," said Lois. "Coming right up." She went out and closed the door.

We stood beside the bed. "This is Chet," Bernie said.

Those dull eyes shifted my way. "Heard about him," the sheriff said. Then he looked at Bernie. Bernie sat on the edge of the bed and took the sheriff's hand. Nothing else happened. They just stayed like that.

After what seemed like a long time, the sheriff said, "I dream of ocean waves, big ones."

"Yeah?" said Bernie.

"Not just at night. Always."

Bernie nodded. "I got a boat."

"You did?" A tiny glimmer of light flickered in the sheriff's eyes. "What kind?"

"A wreck."

"Of course."

Bernie laughed. Bo's lips, cracked and dry, turned up at the edges.

"It's kind of a long story."

"Go on," Bo said. "I've got all day. Maybe."

"Well," Bernie said, "it actually started up in your jurisdiction."

"Don't tell me you've been dealing with —" Bo broke off and began to cough, coughs that went on and on, forced him into a sitting position, Bernie supporting his back. There was a bit of blood, not much. Bernie dabbed it up with a corner of the sheet, filled a water glass from a bedside carafe, held it for Bo to drink. He took a few sips and sank back on the pillow.

"Just the thought of Beasley," Bo said. "That's all it took."

Bernie laughed again. Then he told a big long story all about Beasley, Wendell, Florian, Deirdre Dubois, and lots of other stuff that sounded familiar, but I got caught up in the lovely sound of his voice all by itself with no . . . what would you call it? Meaning? Yes, no meaning attached. That suited me fine. Without a lot of thought — or even any — I circled the bed, climbed up on the other side and lay down. Bernie glanced at me but kept on with the nice, even flow of his story, whatever it was. Bo's other hand, the one not holding Bernie, touched my shoulder.

". . . and that's where we are," Bernie said.

"The usual," Bo said. "Nowhere and everywhere. 'Course, I know Florian."

"Yeah?"

"Comes from a whole long line, just like him. Pussycats at heart, each and every one."

"Meaning?" Bernie said.

I was totally with him on that. Hadn't pussycats come up already in this case? I got the feeling we were in trouble.

"Meaning it's real hard for me to imagine Florian cutting anybody's throat," Bo said. "Big soft lazy dumb — you know the type, Bernie."

Bernie nodded. Bo's eyes closed. Then they opened.

"One more thing," he said. "Fixing up the boat?"

"Yeah."

Bo's eyes closed again. His chest rose and fell, just tiny movements.

"Book me on the maiden voyage," he said.

Bernie gazed down at him. Bo's eyes stayed closed. "Sounds like a plan," Bernie said.

Then came a longish period of doing nothing. Finally there was a knock on the door.

"Come in," Bernie said quietly.

Lois entered, carrying a tray with two glasses of bourbon on it, bourbon one of the smells I know best of all. Bernie rose, slipped his hand out from Bo's.

"Thanks," he said. "Maybe later."

Lois shook her head. "He'll sleep right through till morning now. You don't have to leave, but there's no real point."

Bernie nodded. He took one last look at Bo and then said, "C'mon, Chet. Let's go, big guy."

I stayed where I was, Bo's hand on my shoulder.

"Chet?"

I really didn't want to go. I was okay like this for now.

Bernie looked surprised. "I think he wants

117

to stay."

"Not unheard of," Lois said. "I'm on overnight — I'll keep an eye out. Why don't you come back and get him at breakfast time?"

Breakfast time. Perfect. Something to look forward to. Bernie and the woman went out, closing the door behind them. Bo's chest kept on rising and falling the tiniest bit.

NINE

You can look at the moon but you can't look at the sun. What's up with that? Has Bernie ever talked about it? Not that I remember. Maybe he'll get to it one day. Until then I'll forget the whole issue completely.

Right now, lying beside Bo in his tidy room in this big house or small hospital or whatever it was, I was watching the moon through the window. It was one of those sliver moons, shaped sort of like a sideways human smile. And what was up with that, by the way, the moon changing shape all the time? Whoa! That was something Bernie actually had talked about. He'd explained the whole thing to Charlie on one of those every-second weekends when we had him all to ourselves. We'd been playing miniature golf, never an easy outing for me but I'd been on my best behavior, unfortunately not quite good enough, which eventually resulted in . . . well, no point in dwelling on that whole — what would you call it? Uproar? Good enough. But before any of that, Bernie had suddenly said, "Ever wonder why the moon changes shape?" And Charlie had said, "I'm lining up a putt, Dad." Charlie drew back his putter, eyes locked on the ball — "and not just the ball," as Bernie always said, "but the exact spot on the ball you want to hit" — swung even and firm like he was supposed to and knocked that green-and-yellow-striped ball right under the little windmill, through the whale's mouth and out its tail, over London Bridge and down Main Street, straight into the hole.

"Dad! Mark that on the scorecard! Charlie: One!"

Bernie marked the scorecard and then launched into the whole thing about the moon, good timing on account of the backup at the next hole, Dracula's Dinner Party. "Know what an orbit is, Charlie?" Bernie had said. "A kind of gum," said Charlie. And then we were off on the whole thing about the moon changing shape, which I'll just briefly sum up for you as . . . as . . . .

Before I could get my moon thoughts in exactly the right order, I felt Bo's hand move on my shoulder. I turned slightly and

120

looked at him. He looked at me and smiled. Bo was lying on his side now, so his smile was just like that sideways sliver of moon up in the sky.

"Chet," he said. "A fine name."

How nice of him! Bo was a fine name, too, in my opinion. It was good to be lying here quietly, both of us with our fine names. His chest rose and fell, rose, stopped, fell, stopped, rose.

"Come to carry me across, haven't you?" Bo said. "Lucky all my life, and it's holding right to the end."

Carrying Bo? Was that in the cards? I've carried Charlie lots of times, and some of his pals, but never a full-grown man. I studied Bo. A full-grown man, yes, although kind of shrunken, here in the moonlight. If I had to carry him I could. We were good to go.

"We good to go, Chet?" Bo said.

Wow! We were thinking the same thoughts. I was liking Bo a whole lot. Too bad we hadn't met earlier, but we could still — what was the expression? Make up for lost time? Yes, that was it. Bo and I were going to make up for lost time. I leaned forward a bit and gave his face a gentle lick.

"I'm all set." His eyes shone with moonlight. Then they didn't. His chest fell. Inside

Bo got very relaxed, as relaxed as he could be. Poor Bo. He needed his rest. I could feel his weight through the mattress, but Bo himself didn't seem to be around anymore. Hard to explain. I rose, climbed onto the floor, and crawled under the bed.

The sideways sliding moon moved across the sky. I watched it through the window, a lazy moon in no rush. After a while a shadow fell across the window and the moon disappeared. Then the window made a few clicking sounds. This was turning into a bit of a strange night. Where was Bernie, again? The window slid open. A man climbed into the room.

Whoa! A man was climbing into the room? That made this a B and E! Someone was trying to pull a B and E on me, Chet, a law enforcement professional. That was outrageous. And rage is a big part of outrageous, don't kid yourself. I was starting to get pretty angry as I squirmed out from under the bed and got my back paws under me.

This man — his hair silvery in the moonlight, his face in shadow — came forward. He had some sort of gun in his hand. A dart gun? Yes. A dart gun against me? Think again. I sprang at this B and E dude. At the same moment the gun made a soft thwap and the dart shot out, spinning through the moonlight and hitting me in the neck. Good luck with that, buddy boy. I didn't feel a thing.

A woman said: "Repeat your instructions."

A man said: "Aw, come on. Again?"

The woman said: "Something wrong with your hearing?"

They seemed to be arguing about something. Also they both had unpleasant voices. Although I've liked just about every human I've ever met, even most of the perps and gangbangers, I got the feeling I wouldn't like these two. So therefore I hoped I'd never meet them. Hey! Had I just handled another so-therefore? That was Bernie's department.

Bernie?

Bernie!

I opened my eyes. They seemed to have been closed. I had vague memories of this and that. Now I seemed to be on the move. Had my eyes closed again? I got them back open and pronto. How sleepy I was! But not too sleepy to notice that I was in the back seat of a car. A silvery-haired man was driving and a dark-haired woman was in the passenger seat. Also this was one of those cars where the front and back were separated by a chain-link screen or cage, like in a squad car. But this didn't smell like a squad car and those two humans weren't cops. When you've been in the business as long as I have, you just know these things. My eyes closed.

We had a beautiful blue boat, me and Bernie, called *Sea of Love*. We'd sailed *Sea of Love* all the way to San Diego — which we'd had to do to get to the ocean — and now we were just roaming around on bright shining waters. Forever and a day — was that an expression? It was perfect. These bright shining waters smelled of flowers, specifically flowers a day or two before they get thrown out. Bernie and I were going to sail forever and a day, across the wide Missouri, whatever that happened to be, on and on and —

And suddenly we came to a stop. *Sea of Love* made a tiny squeak, like the brake pads were shot. I knew all about brake pad issues from the Porsche, but boats also had brake pads? Cool. Cool, but everything was much too dark. I tried opening my eyes. That worked.

Uh-oh. I seemed to have forgotten some things, but now they started coming back to me, the most important of them probably being that I was caged in the back seat of a car. Behind the wheel sat a dude with light blond hair and in the passenger seat was a dark-haired woman. Outside were lots of palm trees and flower beds and the glowing entrance to some big fancy place. Hey! Rancho Grande, oldest hotel in the Valley. They had beautiful gardens out back, where'd I'd been a few times, the last one for the bat mitzvah of the older sister of Charlie's buddy Eli. My very first bat mitzvah, so naturally I'd been on the lookout for bats, even though it was daytime and bats only came out at night, in my experience. But you can't be too careful, as a certain type of human often says, and bats — part bird and part rat, couldn't be any clearer, just from the name alone — are no favorite of mine. Did mitzvah mean hunt? That was my take, and I started in on hunting the moment we arrived. And wouldn't you know it? Almost right away I noticed a dark grayish bat all folded up in the lap of a woman too busy downing champagne to even notice. Some humans need more protection than others. I pounced on that bat and gave it what for but good, discovering — maybe a little on the late side, you make the call — that my bat was actually more or less a type of scarf, something to do with Hermès, I found out at a later date, when Bernie was cutting the check.

Bernie!

But no Bernie now. Instead we had the dark-haired woman, opening her door, then pausing to turn to the driver. A green-eyed woman with very nice teeth for a human, on the small side but shining white and even. Did I know her? No, but her smell was oddly familiar: flowers, specifically flowers a day or two before they get thrown out. And what was this? A whiff of hamster?

"One more time," she said.

The man turned to her. Hey! I knew this man! Wasn't he Wendell Nero's nephew, the surfer type dude? From when Prof had taken us into Wendell's office? Hadn't he been looking for a photo of a horse? I should have gotten a bad feeling right then. Instead I was getting it now.

"Seriously?" he said.

The woman said nothing, just gazed at him. He looked away. "All right, all right. I go somewhere out in the middle of nowhere and take this goddamn dog off the board."

"Go on."

He sighed. "Disappear him without a trace."

"And —"

He sighed. "Without being seen. But like,

isn't that just part of without a trace?"

She gazed at him again.

"Just thinking out loud," he said.

"Dewey?" she said.

"Yeah?"

"Am I paying you to think?"

Dewey shook his head.

"I'm paying you to follow instructions to the letter," the woman said. "Any questions?"

"Well, uh, what about Bernie Little?"

"We're not doing a thing about Bernie Little, not going near him, not getting on his radar. We're simply taking him off the board as well."

"Without going near him?"

"We're distracting him, Dewey. We don't need forever, now that . . . things are rolling our way. I've done my research. He has an Achilles' heel."

"I had one of those myself but the doc sewed it up, good as . . ." Dewey's voice trailed away, maybe because he saw the look in the woman's eyes.

"What I'm telling you," she said, slowly and quietly and yet somehow nastily, too, "is that he will do nothing but search for this dog until he finds him."

"Which ain't gonna happen."

"Not if you do your job, Dewey."

The woman got out, closing the door firmly without quite slamming, and walked toward the big glass doors of Rancho Grande. Dewey put the car in gear, then twisted around to look at me. I looked right back at him. His eyes shifted like he was having a thought — probably not a good one, if I knew his type, and I did.

We drove out of the Valley, first on a big highway, then on a pretty busy two-laner. I recognized things going past — a truck stop where we'd once busted a guy with an empty truck who turned out to be smuggling trucks, and a tequila bar with a shooting range out back, now closed. This road led to Mexico. Had the green-eyed woman mentioned Mexico? I didn't think so but wasn't sure. Dewey flipped open the glove box, glanced inside, flipped it closed — but not before I glimpsed the revolver inside. He glanced at me in the rearview mirror. I watched him.

Traffic thinned out. Dewey put on an earpiece, made a call.

"Mig?" he said. "Me, Dewey."

"Whaddya want?" said Mig.

"You in?"

"Why?"

"Got a proposition."

128

"What?"

"More of a show-and-tell thing. I'll swing by."

"Huh?"

Dewey didn't answer. Instead he clicked off and sped up a little. I checked the rearview. He was smiling.

Not long after that, we entered a little desert town, the kind with one main street and a few back streets. At the end of the backmost back street, unpaved and rutted, we pulled into the driveway of a small house with no neighbors and parked beside a shiny new pickup. A light over the side door of the house flashed on, the door opened and a man came out. Dewey climbed out of the car to meet him. He had that slightly rolling gait that comes from wearing cowboy boots.

"Hey, Mig," he said.

"What's up, Dewey?" said Mig, who turned out to be one of those short, wide guys you run into from time to time. They come in types, Bernie says, one type being very strong, so you have to watch out, and the other type being soft through and through. "I'm kinda busy." One thing he'd been busy with for sure was smoking weed. The smell rose off him like he was a little round weed furnace.

"Too busy to make money?" Dewey said.

129

"Check out the back seat."

Mig came closer to the car, peered in at me. "A dog?"

"Know a PI name of Bernie Little?"

"The one with the dog? Heard of him."

"This here's the dog," Dewey said.

"How'd you get him?"

"That's not the point. A dog like this is valuable."

"For what?"

"Guarding, that's what. He's big and strong and real smart. The kind of dog one of your pals on the other side of the border would be itchin' to own."

"Oh?" said Mig. "What do you know about my pals on the other side of the border?"

"Nothing," Dewey said quickly. "Nothing at all. Zip. Business acquaintances of yours, is what I meant. And I didn't even mean that. But I was thinking, since we're buddies, I'd give you a real good price and you could do a resale down there for way more."

"Why me?"

"I already said. We're buddies."

Mig gave Dewey an unbuddy look. "You want the dog to end up in Mexico — that it?"

Dewey looked surprised. "How'd you know?" he said.

130

"Magic," said Mig. He took another look at me. "I'll give you five hundred bucks."

"Five hundred? He's worth ten grand, maybe more."

"Six hundred," Mig said.

"C'mon, Miggy. Make it a grand."

"Six fifty."

"How about seven?" Dewey said.

Mig took a step toward the house.

"Okay, okay, six fifty."

Mig nodded. He took out an enormous roll, peeled off some bills, handed them to Dewey. Then he came to my door. "You got a leash on him?"

"No," Dewey said.

Mig went into the house and returned with a length of rope. He made a loop at one end.

"How are you gonna get that on him?" Dewey said.

"No worries," said Mig, and from his pocket drew . . . a Slim Jim? Yes, a Slim Jim. I love Slim Jims, goes without mentioning, and of course wanted this Slim Jim more than anything. I jumped up and —

But no. I did not jump up. I did not want this Slim Jim more than anything. What I wanted more than anything was to be with Bernie. And all at once — is there anyone luckier than me? — there he was in my head. *Lie down, big guy, like a good, little doggie.* I lay flat down on the seat.

Mig opened the car door, real slow and careful. "He better have more fight in him than this," he said.

"Oh, for sure," said Dewey. "Probably still woozy from the knockout drug."

Mig held out the Slim Jim. "Treat."

Real slow, nice and easy, I rose and moved toward the Slim Jim. But my eyes weren't on it. Instead I was watching Mig's other hand, the one holding that loop of rope.

"There's a good dog," he said.

Very gently, I took one end of the Slim Jim — one of the tastiest Slim Jims I've ever encountered, by the way — in my mouth. At that moment, Mig's other hand twitched. And the next moment —

VA-VOOM!

From zero to sixty in no time flat, whatever that might mean. Did Mig get knocked aside, possibly right to the ground, turning out to be the soft through and through type of short wide guy after all? Was there yelling back and forth? Did I hear the glove box flip open? Who knows? The only sure thing was that Chet the Jet was on the loose! And he still had that Slim Jim! Can you beat that?

I tore around Mig's house, away from light, toward the darkness and the desert. A car engine howled and headlights flashed on, lighting up a bush, a rock, a rusted-out fridge, but not me. Not me at first, and then suddenly I got lit up. *Crack! Crack! Crack!* Gunshots, one of them smacking into the ground close by, one whistling past my ears, one maybe parting the fur on my back.

Zigzag, big guy! Zigzag!

How could I have forgotten the zigzag, one of my primo moves? I zigzagged — *Crack! Crack! Crack!* — up a steep hill, down the other side, across an arroyo, up the bank, down another slope, then straight across some rough ground. I glanced back as I ran, caught the glow of distant headlights, not moving now, their beams petering out way behind me. I ran up another hill, and another after that, and from the top of that hill I could see the glow of the Valley. I took a short break and polished off the Slim Jim.

Not long after dawn — by then I'd settled into what Bernie calls my go-to trot — I spotted a giant donut in the sky. What luck! Donut Heaven. We've got Donut Heavens out the yingyang in the Valley, just one of the things that make it great. I headed straight for the giant donut, got there in no time.

Business seemed a little slow this morning. There was only one car in the lot, a Valley PD black-and-white. I went over to it. Sitting behind the wheel and munching on a cruller was Captain Stine. He was an old buddy, owed his being a captain to me and Bernie. What had we done? I couldn't remember. In fact, I couldn't think at all, beyond one single thought: Cruller! Cruller!

Captain Stine's head snapped around in my direction, like he'd been startled. The air seemed strange, as though some very loud sound, possibly bark-like, had recently passed through it.

"Chet?"

TEN

"What have we here?" said Amy. Amy's my vet — a big woman of what Bernie calls the no-nonsense kind. Was that because she hardly ever laughed at his jokes? I didn't know. Right now we were in her waiting room — I'm not a fan of the whole setup Amy had behind the door that led to the rest of her office — and she was running her hands along my back, the strongest female hands I'd ever come across, although they were always gentle with me.

"That's what I was wondering about," Bernie said.

They were kneeling on either side of me, Amy parting my fur, both of them giving my back a close look. Was there some problem? Not that I knew of. I felt a little bit thirsty, but otherwise tip-top.

"Appears that something grazed him," Amy said, "but superficially. No sutures required. I'll clean him up and put him on an antibiotic. That should take care of it."

"What kind of something did the grazing?" Bernie said. "Thorns, maybe?"

They looked at each other over the top of me. "Could be thorns," Amy said. "Could be from crawling under a wire fence. Could be a lot of things, depending on the scenario. Any idea how long he was gone?"

"Less than ten hours. That's all I can say for sure." Amy went on looking at Bernie. "My fault completely," he added, which made no sense to me. First, nothing was wrong. Second, even if something was wrong, how could it ever be his fault? We're talking about Bernie here, folks.

"Wouldn't want anything to happen to Chet, would we?" Amy said.

"No, ma'am," Bernie said.

"On the other hand, given his occupation, interests, and abilities, it wouldn't be fair to get all overcautious."

"No."

Amy rose. "The wound was made by a bullet, Bernie. Ten to one. He should take it easy for a day or two. And he's dehydrated — make sure he gets plenty of water."

Plenty of water — that sounded good. I went right to the water bowl in the corner of the waiting room. A few members of the nation within had been sipping from it, and

136

not long ago. I'm sure I don't have to point out how annoying that was. I slurped up every drop.

"I let you down, big guy," Bernie said as we drove away, me in the shotgun seat, him behind the wheel, our usual arrangement, and life living out just like it's supposed to. Except for that last remark, whatever it was. "Now," he went on, "we go home and take it easy, doctor's orders."

Sure thing. We went home. I love being at home. We hung around the kitchen and had a snack or two. I noticed that Bernie had taped the smiling photo of Wendell and the girl with the rolled-up papers under her arm to the fridge door. I almost left out the baby goat, who seemed to be smiling, too.

We sat down on the couch and watched some TV. Bernie flicked through all the channels. So many glimpses of so much stuff! There's nothing like watching TV. Bernie switched it off. That was even better.

I wandered into the kitchen, drank some water. Bernie refilled the bowl. I drank again. He cracked open a can of beer — a lovely sound, lets you know that good times are on the way. He sipped beer. I lapped up some more water. We went out to the patio, sat in the shade.

"Feeling all right, big guy?"

For sure, except for being bored out of my freakin' mind. I noticed a tennis ball behind the swan fountain, picked it up, dropped it at Bernie's feet.

"Fetch?" Bernie said. "Maybe tomorrow. Today we're taking it easy."

But I'd had enough of taking it easy! I snapped up the tennis ball, flipped it in the air, caught it, pranced around.

"I'm not paying attention to you."

How infuriating! I was considering ways to possibly get Iggy involved when Bernie took out his phone and said, "Wonder what Eliza's up to today." He pressed a key or two.

"Eliza?

"Hello, Bernie."

"How're things?"

"Fine, thank you."

"Off today?"

"Yes."

"How about coming over? I can show you our new boat."

"Was there a cancellation?"

"Cancellation?"

"In your social calendar."

Bernie shot me a puzzled glance. "Eliza? I don't understand."

"That's one way of putting it," Eliza said.

And then: click.

"Whoa," Bernie said. "What's going on?" He pressed a button. "Eliza? Pick up."

But she did not. "I'll text," he said, and did some quick touching of the buttons. Then he laid the phone on the table. It just sat there.

"Chet? What happened?"

I had no idea. My only thought was that if we'd gone off for a round or two of fetch in the canyon this whole Eliza thing wouldn't have happened. But perhaps not a nice thought. I tried to forget it and was successful at once.

Bernie snapped his fingers. "I know! We can work on the boat. That won't be too taxing."

What a brilliant idea! But that's Bernie. Just when you think he's done amazing you, he amazes you again. In no time at all, we were beside the house and climbing up on *Sea of Love,* Bernie carrying the tool kit and me the tennis ball, just in case.

We walked around, checking things out. Bernie poked his hand into a hole here and there, some in the deck, hardly any in the hull, and none of them big. Only small fish had a chance of getting through, so what was the problem? As for fishiness, I smelled something fishy behind a hatch cover under the rusty, coiled-up anchor chain. Whew. A little of that goes a long way, and this was more than a little. I joined Bernie, standing at the console.

He turned the wheel. "A tad on the loose side, Chet," he said. "Should be a snap to tighten. And I like the idea of starting with the wheel."

So did I! I loved it! Starting with the wheel! Wow!

Bernie opened the toolbox, chose a tool, cast it aside for a bigger one, ended up using a tool even bigger than that.

"The whatchamacallit should be right behind this panel. How about we pry it off like so? Voilà!" Good news! I hadn't heard a voilà in ages. When Bernie said voilà we were starting to cook. "See those wires? The yellow one means caution so we stay away but the green one means go. Stands to reason, right?"

Of course it did! Bernie reached for the green wire.

We have lots of buddies in the fire department. We were happy to see them and they were happy to see us. They smothered the odd little flame or two no problem, and that whole idea of fire spreading to the Parsons's house turned out to be a complete nonstarter, all the shouting and hosing totally unnecessary. The only bad part was that Iggy got to ride on the hook and ladder truck and I did not. In the lap of the driver — no reason to leave that out. The lap of the driver! They went around the block way more than once or twice, Iggy eyeing me out the window on each pass. All sorts of bad thoughts about things that could happen to Iggy went through my head. It hit me for the very first time: life can be cruel. But oh, no, that couldn't be true!

I was still going back and forth on that a little later, when things had settled down, just me and Bernie. He was opening a bottle of bourbon when he paused and looked at me, perhaps actually pacing back and forth in the kitchen, as a way of accompanying my mind, if that makes any sense.

"Right you are," he said. "That's enough of taking it easy." He put the bottle back on the shelf and we were out of there.

"Phew," Bernie said, as we backed out of the driveway and hit the road. Which was exactly what I would've said if I could've. Then he said it again, yes, for me. How great is that! Say adios to taking it easy, all you perps and gangbangers! Here comes the Little Detective Agency! And we even had a client! A number of them, in fact. I went over the clients in my mind, Felicia and those other two — all women, all sporting gold watches and yoga pants, all former wives or girlfriends of Wendell, all quick-tempered — and got a bit confused.

"Oh, I'm so glad you found him," said Lois, rising from her desk and taking off her glasses. She came over and gave me a pat, a very nice pat but slightly higher up the neck would have been better. I twisted around a bit as a sort of hint, but she didn't get it. "Where was he?"

"Actually not that far from here — when he turned up," Bernie said. "But how long he was gone and where he went are mysteries."

Lois shook her head. "I just don't understand. Can he open doors?"

"Some," Bernie said. "Which is why we're here — I'd like to take another look at the room."

This visit was about rooms and doors? Good to know. I prefer to be in the picture, although it's fair to say I can handle being out of the picture if necessary. The Little Detective Agency isn't successful by accident, amigos. Except for the finances part. I don't mean the finances part is by accident. What I mean is . . . Or maybe that is why . . .

By then we were down the hall and entering Bo's room, now just an empty room, bed stripped, no sign of anybody's belongings anywhere. It was no longer Bo's room. I was a little surprised at first. Then certain events of the night — maybe not events but more like feelings — came back to me, and I stopped being surprised.

"All I can think," Lois said, "was when Bo died — sometime in the night — Chet got upset and . . . and let himself out."

"Who found the body?" Bernie said.

"Me."

"Was the door open or closed when you came to the room?"

"Closed. But maybe a breeze . . ."

They both turned to the window.

"It was closed, too," Lois said. She squeezed her hands together. "I feel awful about this. Dogs have stayed overnight, as I mentioned, but we've never had a situation where a resident passed during one of those periods. We're going to have to change the policy."

"I hope you don't, Lois." Bernie closed the door. "I have a feeling this was a onetime event."

"You do? Why?"

"Just a feeling, like I said." Bernie tapped

143

his finger on the doorknob. "Chet? Open."

I trotted over to the door. Open it? Was that the idea? We'd been working on this for some time, me and Bernie, me in charge of the opening part, Bernie in charge of the treats. The lever types were easy-peasy. Knob types were harder. I had to get both my front paws on the knob and then push one up and pull one down, a lot to remember. But I'd been getting pretty good. This was the knob type, not too big and not too small, and also not shiny, the shiny ones being harder to grip. I liked my chances.

I rose up and got my front paws on the knob. It practically started turning on its own. But then came an important thought. What about my treat? There was not the slightest treat smell in the air, meaning Bernie had no treat on his person — on his person being law enforcement lingo.

"Chet? You okay?"

Well, yes and no. Yes, I could open this door. No, I wouldn't, not without a treat. Whoa! I was saying no to Bernie? How shameful! All at once I felt very bad about myself. I was going to do my job — meaning turn this doorknob — and pronto. And not only that, I was also going to put everything I had into it, do my job with all my heart. I pressed down on that doorknob, good and hard, so that doorknob would know what's what. Nothing happened. I pressed even harder, and got more nothing out of the doorknob, a doorknob I was starting to hate, by the way, and then remembered: push and pull! So I pushed and pulled, pushed and pulled, then tried pulling and pushing, pulling and pushing and got all mixed up and went back to —

But nothing worked, even though I knew how to do it. I just couldn't turn that doorknob.

"That's all right, big guy," Bernie said softly. "Not a problem."

Oh, but it was. A huge problem. My tail drooped right down to the floor. I tried to raise it back up. At first it didn't want to. I made it.

"So how did he get out?" Lois said.

Good question! How the hell had I gotten out of this room? You'd think I'd be able to remember something like that. After all, it's not every day that — and then it all came back to me! Whoa! Bad guys were in our lives right now, even if Bernie didn't know it. At that point I had the strangest thought, a thought that made no sense: maybe it was a good thing that I'd failed to turn that doorknob. Made no sense, but my tail sure liked it. It stiffened and stood straight up all on its own, tall and proud.

"Can he have a treat?" Lois said.

A Rover and Company treat! There was a lot to like about Lois. But eventually we had to move on. We're good at moving on, me and Bernie. He says we're going to roam the whole great West before we're done. Hey! Was that our business plan? I understood it at last, all except for the part about being done.

We said goodbye to Lois and went outside, but then came a surprise. Did we hop in the Porsche and blast off into the whole great West? We did not. Instead we walked around the building — small hospital or big house? I still wasn't sure — and had a look at the back. This building had all its fanciness out front, the back being pretty plain. A sort of flower bed ran along the base of the wall, but hardly any flowers grew, even though the ground was kind of damp.

Bernie shook his head. "Irrigation system irrigating nothing," he said. "Over irrigating nothing. You know that expression, vast carelessness?"

I did not.

"Fitzgerald, big guy."

Fitzgerald? A new one on me. A perp? I had no reason to think otherwise. I hoped he looked good in orange.

Bernie stopped at one of the windows. "This should be it." He peered through the glass. I rose up on my back legs, got my front paws on the window, took a peek myself. Hey! Bo's old room, seen from the outside, bare and empty, just how we'd left it. An interesting sight? Not really. But if it was interesting in Bernie's eyes then that was that. I was trying to make the room look interesting — not easy even knowing where to start — when Bernie stepped back, meaning I did, too. Then he put his hands on the frame and pushed up. The window slid open.

He turned to me. "Ring a bell, Chet?"

I listened and yes, heard a distant bell, one of those bicycle-type bells. Was this the first breakthrough in the case? I had a real good feeling.

Bernie crouched down, gazed at the flower bed, damp but flowerless. "Is it true that nothing is completely bad?" he said.

Yes! I'd never been so sure of anything in my life.

"Take the waste of all this water, for example," he went on. "Without it, we wouldn't have that." And he pointed to a footprint in the dirt. "Cowboy boot. Size eleven, maybe?"

Sounded good to me.

Bernie got out his phone, took a picture of the footprint, showed me the screen. Then he rose and gave me a grin. "Whoever it was, you outfoxed 'em, didn't you, big guy?"

Excuse me?

ELEVEN

"How's it going?" Bernie said.

"How the fuck do you think?" said Florian Machado.

Maybe we weren't off to the best possible start. We sat at a table in one corner of the chow hall at Central State Correctional, a metal table with metal benches, all bolted to the floor. Because it wasn't mealtime, we had just the three of us in the big echoey space — Florian sitting on one side and Bernie on the other, me beside Bernie until that moment. Now I got up and moved around the table, sat nice and close to Florian. He gave me one of those double takes. Sometimes they lead to a change in tone, sometimes not. Perp tone is a huge subject that maybe we can get to later.

"Within the obvious limits, is what I meant," Bernie said.

"Limits?"

"Sure," said Bernie. "Just look around.

149

Doing time is about limits."

Florian leaned forward, pointed his big, thick finger at Bernie. "But that's the whole thing. I'm not doing time."

"No?"

"Ain't been convicted yet. Any justice in the world, I'd be out on bail." His hands balled into fists. "Know what I'd like to do to that judge?"

"Tell me."

"Pound his goddamn head to a pulp."

"Had much experience in that line?"

"What line?"

"Pounding someone's head to a pulp."

Florian's brow wrinkled up. "You lookin' to try me or somethin'?"

"We already did that, Florian. It's time to face a fact or two. Yes, you're a big dude —"

"Six three two sixty!"

"But not particularly strong for your size."

Florian glared at Bernie in a way that made me think he didn't like him at all! Imagine that — not liking Bernie at all. Bernie didn't seem upset, just gazed back at Florian in a calm way, not in the least threatening. Once you've taken a guy down, there's no need ever to threaten again. That's something I learned in our work, although I knew it going in, from how we

150

roll in the nation within.

"The toughest guy I know is LeSean Stiller, over at Stiller's Gym," Bernie went on. "Weighs one fifty, tops."

LeSean Stiller — a fan of me and my kind, and a very good patter, in his way. His hands were gentle, no doubt about that, but there was also something in their touch that scared me. Well, not scared me, me being who I am. Forget I mentioned that.

"If this works out," Bernie was saying, "you could take some lessons from him."

"If what works out?" said Florian.

"We'll get to that," Bernie said. "The problem right now is that there are plenty of men in here who have pounded heads to a pulp, practically live for it."

Florian glanced around. Way down at the other end of the chow hall, a dude in an orange jumpsuit was mopping the floor. A guard leaned on the wall, watching him. The mopping dude looked our way, then shaded his eyes — like he was outside in the sun. Humans can be very entertaining.

"Hey!" he called. "Chet? Zat you?"

He was too far away for me to make out his face, but I remember every voice I've ever heard. This one was easy — it belonged to Zdeno "Big Z" Zdeniev, who'd gotten hold of some submarines and was selling them to — well, I don't recall the details, and we brought him in more or less by accident, our actual case at the time being about a Russian hockey player who'd been smuggling something or other inside pucks, a case I'd solved pretty much by myself — if you don't mind me throwing that in here — and all because of my longtime hobby of chewing on pucks whenever possible. No time now to describe the wonderful feeling my teeth get from puck chewing. Just try it, if you haven't already.

Down at the other end of the chow hall, Big Z had a huge smile on his face. "Will you look at zat tail off his!" he said to the guard. "Can I quick go over, say big hello to my puddy, Chet?"

"No," said the guard.

Florian was watching all that go down, a thoughtful look on his face. Bernie was watching Florian. He looked thoughtful, too, but thoughtful Bernie and thoughtful Florian were different kettles of fish. Don't get me started on fish: those tiny bones, stuck in my throat, each and every time! Why were they even called bones? I know bones. Fish bones are something else.

Florian turned to Bernie. "All's they got is the wallet," he said.

"And the receipt from behind the RV,"

Bernie said. "Which puts you at the scene of the crime."

Florian nodded. "Yeah," he said. "She keeps bringin' that up."

"Who are you talking about?" Bernie said.

"What's her name, my attorney."

"From the public defender's office?"

"Kinda."

"What does that mean?"

"She works with them once in a while, or something like that. On loan, type of thing."

"A law student?"

"Maybe too old for that. Point is we're makin' a deal."

Bernie has very nice posture. Have I mentioned that? Even when sitting, like here in the chow hall at Central State Correctional, he always sits up good and straight, but not at all stiff, if you see what I mean. The only stiffening that ever happens is when something really gets his attention, like now.

"What kind of deal?" he said.

"Guilty to lesser charges," Florian said. "Like manslaughter or even maybe aggravated something or other. Instead of murder one, which is what the DA'll go for if I say no." He glanced around the chow hall, bit his lip. "Could be out in three years, even less, what with the overcrowding situation."

Bernie gave Florian a very direct look. "But Florian," he said, "did you do it?"

"Did I do what?"

"Slit Wendell's throat from ear to ear."

Florian looked down and sighed. "I just don't know."

"How can you not know something like that?"

"It happens," Florian said. "Some kind of syndrome."

"Your lawyer told you that?"

Florian nodded. "Like the mind makes new memories — to give you a break, you know? But then you can't sort them out from the real ones. Or maybe the real ones are gone forever — can't remember exactly what she said."

"Leaving Wendell aside for the moment," Bernie said. "Ever slit anybody's throat before?"

"No. Well, not that I remember."

Bernie smacked his hand on the table. "Yes or no?"

Down at the far end of the chow hall, Big Z and his guard turned to watch us.

"No," Florian said. "If it has to be one or the other."

"It does," Bernie said. "Have you ever

154

killed anybody?"

"Not that I —" Florian caught the look in Bernie's eyes. "No."

"Ever seriously hurt anyone?"

Florian thought. "Only in football."

"You played football?"

"Just Pop Warner. I got tackled on the sideline and fell on some old lady's leg. Busted it in three places — she screamed something awful."

Bernie rubbed his hands together, always a sign we were getting somewhere. Were we about to close the case right here and now? If so, would that mean I'd have to grab Florian by the pant leg? He was already locked up in Central State Correctional and wearing an orange jumpsuit. I got a bit confused.

"So," Bernie said, "on one hand we've got the wallet and the receipt."

Florian nodded.

"Not to mention," Bernie went on, "the phone and the laptop, lurking out there somewhere."

"Phone and the laptop? Why the hell does —" Florian jammed on the brakes, but too late — I could tell from the look on his face. Have I mentioned Bernie's not-to-mention technique? One of his very best — he ends up mentioning whatever it is anyway! Who else could have come up with something so

155

brilliant? There's only one Bernie.

"You sold them to a fence?" Bernie said.

"I got a right to remain silent," said Florian.

"That ship has sailed. I'll need the name."

Even I knew that! The name of the ship was *Sea of Love,* once Florian's and now ours. I was a little surprised Bernie had asked the question. And also that Florian couldn't come up with the answer. He just sat there silent, with an expression that reminded me of Rummy, a mule I dealt with in an earlier case.

"What is wrong with you?" Bernie said. "Are you on your own side or against? We're talking about bargaining chips here — to sweeten your deal with the DA."

Florian did that frowning thing again, even more than before. And the lip-biting thing. Not a pretty picture. "How come you want to do that? You're who busted me."

"I'm not Inspector Javert," Bernie said.

"Who's he?" said Florian.

I was totally with him on that. Bernie had never spoken that name before. Inspector Javert — a perp, perhaps? But at the same time an inspector? Heads up, Chet. I took a careful look around. Big Z and his guard were gone. We were alone, safe for the moment.

"He's the type I'm trying to protect you from," Bernie said.

I felt Florian thinking, and again was reminded of Rummy. Finally he took a deep breath and said, "Butchie Dykstra. He operates outta —"

"I know where he is," Bernie said. "Now try to remember your lawyer's name."

Florian squeezed his eyes shut tight, a sight that lasted way too long. "No go," he said. "But I got her card."

Bernie's eyes lit up in a lovely way. How nice to see him having fun!

Florian took a card from inside his orange jumpsuit — a jumpsuit with no pockets, hardly worth pointing that out — and handed it to Bernie.

"She works for Lobb and Edmonds?" Bernie said.

"Like I told you, kind of on loan. Pro bono, if you're familiar with the expression."

Bernie gazed at Florian and said nothing.

We rode up in an elevator in one of the tallest downtown towers, one of those bronze-colored towers that can look like they're melting in the hot sun. Elevators are not my thing, and real fast ones are worse. This was the fastest I'd ever been on, so fast my stomach couldn't keep up. That was a problem because when my stomach falls behind like that, the next thing that happens, which was going to be a big no-no, would be a whole lot of —

Bernie put his hand on the top of my head, nice and gentle. The next thing I knew, the elevator came to a stop, the door sliding open and fresh air flowing in. Maybe not fresh, more like AC, but good enough. I walked out of there head high, unpuking, a total pro.

"A white-shoe law firm if ever there was one," Bernie said in that voice he uses just for talking to himself.

We headed to the reception desk. This whole floor seemed to be one big fancy office, a setup I'd seen before when we'd gotten involved in a cryptocurrency case, incomprehensible from start to finish, the end coming somewhat unexpectedly on our last visit to their HQ, which we found empty, all equipment, furnishings, and people gone, nothing remaining but a miniature lemon tree plant that we took home as payment, the tree dying soon after, although Bernie did make lemonade from some of the lemons, and Charlie sold a few cups out front of the house, unfortunately making the customers sick. But this was a brand-new day!

"Looking for Gudrun Burr," Bernie said to the receptionist. She sent us down a wide and brightly lit hall — lined on both sides with framed blow-up photos of cats and also sculpted cats on pedestals, which was around when I lost my concentration — to another receptionist, this one a dude, a rather large dude with a neatly trimmed beard and wearing a very nice suit, of the kind called cashmere. Cashmere suits have an interesting smell all their own, and also an unusual mouth feel, which I knew from an experience I'd had with a suit belonging to Malcolm, Leda's husband, an experience that will never be repeated, not if I can help it.

He gave us a friendly look. "What can I do for you?" He was a handsome guy, reminding me slightly of a Hollywood actor we'd once worked with, an actor who had a cat named Brando, the case off the rails from the get-go. A difference with this receptionist guy was one of his ears, slightly cauliflowered like he'd done some wrestling in college. Was that a common route to being a receptionist? I didn't know.

"We'd like to see Gudrun Burr," Bernie said.

"Do you have an appointment?"

"No."

"Then I'm afraid —"

"We can wait."

"Ms. Burr's schedule won't accommodate any more meetings today. Her earliest availability is next Tuesday, two forty-five p.m."

"This is about one of her clients," Bernie said. "I'm guessing she'd want to meet sooner than that."

"Which client?"

The receptionist had one of those name plates on his desk. Bernie glanced at it and said, "Well, Mr. Venatti, that —"

"Mason, please."

"Well, Mason, that's for Ms. Burr to hear."

Mason had had a small smile on his face the whole time, and it didn't go away now. "Are you in law enforcement?" he said.

"No," said Bernie. "Why do you ask?"

"Because of your companion here," Mason said. "If he's not in the K-nine corps he should be."

Oh, Mason! You don't know the half of it, whatever that might mean. I flunked out on the very last day! The leaping test, Mason! And leaping's my very best thing! Was this a good time for a demonstration? Perhaps a quick leap right over Mason's head and then scurrying back to where I was, no time wasted?

I was going back and forth on that when

160

Bernie took out our card and handed it to Mason. "Maybe you could show her this."

Mason gave the card a good look. His little smile stayed on his face. "Happy to." He rose — yes, a very big dude — walked over to a door, knocked, and went inside.

Bernie turned to me. "K-nine. That would be like Sherlock Holmes walking a beat."

A complete puzzler. I couldn't make anything out of it. Bernie laughed and gave me a quick scratch between the ears. "Which makes me Dr. Watson." Also a complete puzzler. Holmes? Watson? I'd never heard of them. Perps? For no reason at all, I doubted that. Funny how the mind works. From somewhere far away came a sharp sound, possibly a hand smacking a desktop. Bernie didn't seem to hear it. We waited.

Mason opened the door, still looking friendly although no longer smiling.

"Ms. Burr will see you now."

A familiar scent was suddenly in the air.

TWELVE

A woman sat behind a desk. Her eyes went to me right away. They showed nothing, but her smell sure did. It was all about being surprised in a real bad way. She rose — a dark-haired, green-eyed woman, a woman smelling of dying flowers: Dewey's boss.

"Mr. Little?" She smiled at Bernie, her teeth small, white, even, and very sharp for a human. I was just guessing on that last part, maybe a bit unfair, but I was no fan of this woman. "Gudrun Burr," she said, coming around the desk and shaking Bernie's hand. Some humans have a lot of force inside them, but most less or none. Of the forceful types, some show it all the time, some a lot of the time, a few, who keep it deep inside, hardly ever. Handshaking is when you might see these kinds of things. For example, Gudrun Burr was the forceful type who showed it all the time, and Bernie was the forceful type who kept it deep inside.

"How can I help you?" she said.

"Uh," Bernie said, "excuse me for a moment, please." He turned to me and said, "Chet? What's the problem?"

Problem? I knew of none. We were in a nice big office, way up high; we had views of the Valley that went on and on past the last suburbs and into the shimmering desert; soft music played in the background. So no complaints. Perhaps there was a sound somewhat like growling coming from here or there, not worth a mention.

"Chet? Buddy? What's with the growling?"

Growling? Not worth a mention. Hadn't I just covered that?

"Chet!"

"I don't think your dog likes me," Gudrun said, putting her hand to her chest.

"I'm sure that's not the case," said Bernie. "He's not comfortable in elevators, probably just letting me know."

Elevators? It had nothing to do with elevators. What a weird situation! Bernie was wrong and this woman was right. I didn't like her, not one little bit. And I had every reason! What I would actually have liked to — or more accurately what my teeth were itching to do, especially those long ones,

163

was to —

"Chet? Do you want to wait outside?"

Wait outside? Meaning while Bernie stayed inside? I couldn't believe my ears, except they've always been totally believable. Okay, maybe not quite in the league of my nose, but the next best thing. Wait outside? While we were working a case? I happen to have a way of standing that makes me just about immovable. I stood like that now.

"Then you've got to amp it down."

Bernie gave me a look. I gave him a look back. And then I noticed that Gudrun was also giving me a look, a very thoughtful one. It made me consider possibly going over to her and —

"Chet? I mean it."

Uh-oh. Bernie meant it. That changed everything. The growling — wherever it happened to be coming from — stopped at once.

Bernie turned to Gudrun. Gudrun's thoughtful look vanished just before his gaze fell on her. "Sorry," he said. "Don't know what that was about."

"Probably the elevator, as you said," Gudrun told him. "Dogs usually like me."

I didn't believe that for one second, but now was not the time for any of the violent

— well, not violent, more like . . . active. Yes, that was it! Now was not the time for any of the active things I wanted to do. Instead I yawned a great big yawn. Gudrun laughed.

"What a character!" she said, and motioned Bernie to a chair.

Bernie sat down. I sat on the floor beside him. Gudrun went back around the desk and sat in her chair.

"We're the ones who brought in your client, Florian Machado," Bernie said.

"I'm aware of that," said Gudrun. "So I'll ask again — how can I help you?"

"First I want to make sure I've got the facts straight," Bernie said. "Is it true you've advised Florian to cop a plea?"

"Cop a plea," Gudrun said. "I hate that expression."

"Oh?"

"It's just another way of saying this entire enterprise is jaded."

Bernie's eyes got an inward look. That didn't happen often in company, just when it was him and me. Something must have really caught his attention. As to what that might be, I had no clue.

"You're about to tell me that's the inevitable result of the subject matter," Gudrun said. "Which is criminality."

165

Bernie nodded. "Something like that. But not as eloquently. How about I revise it to taking a plea deal?"

Gudrun smiled, just a quick show of those small, even white teeth, and then gone. "Who told you I'd done that?"

"Florian."

"When?"

"A couple of hours ago."

Gudrun went still, very slightly, more just on the inside — in fact, reminding me of Bernie. Strange, what with their smells being so different, Bernie's having not a trace of dying flowers. "You saw him in prison?" she said.

"Correct."

"I don't understand. Did he ask for you?"

"No. It was my idea."

"Is that your usual practice? Jail follow-ups with men you've — how did you put it — brought in?"

"No," Bernie said. "But it has happened."

"In situations where the case has not been completely resolved, I assume?" Gudrun said.

Bernie nodded.

"Or not resolved to your satisfaction?"

"I won't argue about that," Bernie said.

Good to hear! An argument now might not have been a good thing, almost sure to remind me of my feelings toward Gudrun, which could lead to a certain sort of . . . activity that would end with me no longer in this room and part of the conversation. As to what they'd been close to arguing about, I leave that to you. Some human conversations are harder to follow than others. This was one of those, plus I also had the feeling that another conversation was going on at the same time, but unspoken. That wasn't new, these unspoken conversations giving off certain smells, a snap to pick up if you're someone like me. Otherwise . . . otherwise I guess you're on your own.

One particular kind of unspoken conversation can happen between a man and woman, especially when they're meeting for the first time. We have something not that different in the nation within! It's all about a certain kind of exciting possibility. Do you know what I'm getting at? Maybe you've experienced it. I hope so.

There's also a scent that gets loose when two men — especially the tough kind — meet for the very first time. We've got that one in the nation within, too, and plenty! More than enough, you might say, but it always gets the blood flowing, a feeling I love. The only reason I bring this up is that some of that scent was also now in the air, mixing with the man and woman excitement scent in a very unusual way that actually didn't work for me. In fact, it got me a bit confused.

Meanwhile, since arguing was not in the cards, Gudrun had moved onto something else. "If Florian didn't ask for you, how did you get in to see him?"

Which sounded a bit like arguing, but I must have been wrong about that.

"It wasn't that hard," Bernie said.

"I believe you," said Gudrun. "But you'd still need permission from either the warden, the sheriff — in the current interregnum Deputy Beasley — or the DA. Which one was it?"

There was a slight pause, like maybe Bernie didn't want to answer. I'd seen pauses like this before, but always when Bernie was asking the questions and someone else was doing the pausing. I got a little more confused.

"The DA, then," Gudrun said.

Bernie nodded.

"No reason to hesitate on either of the others," Gudrun went on. "Deirdre Dubois is no pushover and you have no standing and you're for sure not her type. So what's your secret?"

"Chet here did most of the persuading,"

Bernie said.

Gudrun was the good-looking kind of woman, unless I was missing something. She had very smooth skin, plus those green eyes and those shining teeth, but it wasn't just that. The good-looking women also knew who they were and always acted in a good-looking way, hard to explain. And Gudrun certainly acted in a good-looking way, although right now an expression that was almost ugly crossed her face, real quick. Then, back to normal, she said, "You're quite the joker," she said.

Exactly right, although if Bernie had just made a joke, I'd missed it. Was this the moment for some sort of explanation? If so, Bernie was letting it pass by. He just sat there, eyes on Gudrun and saying nothing. I'd seen lots of people bothered by that quiet look of Bernie's, but Gudrun wasn't one of them. She pointed a finger at him — a well-shaped finger with a bright red nail — and said, "Here's the answer to your question. I didn't tell Florian to take a plea deal. I described all the available starting points and the likely outcomes of each. He asked me to make the best arrangement I could. I'm in the process of doing that right now. Is there anything else you want to know?" She folded her hands on the desk.

"Yeah," Bernie said. "Why aren't you going to trial?"

"Isn't it obvious?" Gudrun said. "Because of you." She turned to a screen, hit a key or two, read what popped up. "This is from Beasley's arrest report. 'According to Bernie Little, the private investigator, when confronted the suspect charged him and brandished a knife.' " She turned back to Bernie. "Would that be your testimony?"

"Part of it."

"That's all it would take in the mind of any juror who ever lived. Guilty, murder one." She gave Bernie a close look. "You disagree?"

"Not with your analysis."

"With what, then? What are you doing here? You want to go to trial? You want the maximum punishment? Making the collar isn't enough for you?"

Bernie shook his head. "I want you to slow things down a little bit. Ask for a postponement. Delay, somehow. You'll find a reason. I just need time."

"For what?"

"I want to dig a little deeper."

What great news! Where and when? Clearly not here in this office high over the Valley. I moved across the room and waited by the door.

170

"Into what?" said Gudrun.

I was with her on that, waited to hear. Flower beds are always a good choice, but there's a lot to be said for putting greens.

"The death of Wendell Nero," Bernie said.

"Death? You're not calling it a murder? Now you have my interest."

"Oh, it was murder, all right."

"Then what? Someone else was involved? Maybe did the actual throat-cutting? And my client's covering up for him?"

"It's possible."

"Have you got some evidence for that statement?"

"No."

"So what are you doing?" Gudrun said. "Don't say you want me to hire you."

"I don't."

"Therefore you'll work for free? Or do you already have a client?"

"I do."

"And who would that be?"

"I protect my clients' identities."

"How convenient."

"Usually not," Bernie said.

Gudrun laughed. She gave Bernie a look that some women sometimes give to some men, although not often to Bernie, in my experience. As for what it meant I wasn't sure. If humans had tails they'd be easier to

— Well, I'm sure it's a fine thing to be human, all in all. Let's leave it at that. The important thing was digging, when and where. I was hoping that Gudrun would bring that up, and stat. She sat back in her chair like she was getting comfortable and said, "I'm going to take a wild guess. Your client is — or was, in this case — Wendell Nero."

"No," Bernie said. He has many ways of saying no. They all end up meaning no, but was there something odd about this particular no, like it had a little bit of yes mixed in? What a thought! Way too much for me.

Meanwhile Bernie was sitting up straight like he wasn't relaxed, but I could feel that inside he was. And Gudrun was sitting back like she was relaxed, but I could feel that inside she wasn't. Was this interview going well? I didn't think so. Of course I'd seen Gudrun in action and Bernie had not. *Bite her, Bernie, bite her!* Whoa! What was with my mind all of a sudden? Thinking too-big thoughts, and now this? I tried to shut it down completely.

"Can't you sell that a little better?" Gudrun said.

Uh-oh. Bernie's selling ability. That had come up once before, actually last Christmas, when Bernie's mom paid us a visit, accompanied by her boyfriend, fiancé, or husband, something we never quite got clear, named Tommy Trauble, owner of Tommy Trauble's Auto Mile Dealerships in Flamingo Beach, Florida, which was where Bernie's mom lived. Tommy Trauble had the deepest tan I'd ever seen on a human face, tiny bleached-out eyes, and shoulder-length white hair that gleamed. But, according to Bernie's mom, he was also the greatest salesman in the whole state, and — well, it went something like this: "Bernie? I'll have another one of those lovely old-fashioneds you mix. He really does have all sorts of talents, Tommy, but his problem is he just doesn't sell himself. Can you explain to him, honey, how important that is?"

And things went downhill from there. Was there a point when Tommy Trauble challenged Bernie to an arm-wrestling contest? Something Bernie would never consider, not with an older gentleman. But one thing led to another, until finally the ER doc said the break was nice and clean and Tommy would have that cast off his arm in no time.

Meanwhile Bernie was saying, "Don't see why I have to sell anything to you." One good thing about that: his mom couldn't hear it. "You're Florian's lawyer. You should be welcoming any new evidence in his favor."

"Evidence?" said Gudrun. "I haven't heard any yet. And you're just about the last person who'd want to find any. Unless you're a saint, in which case you'd be in some other line of work." She tilted her head slightly to one side and her eyes opened a little wider. "Are you a saint, Bernie?"

"Only in an upside-down world," he said.

Whoa! Saints were very good, if I was understanding things right, maybe the best. Which is Bernie! So therefore — yes, again! — the world was upside down. This had to be very important, but for some reason I wasn't surprised.

Meanwhile, in the smelling part of life — a huge part, as I hope you realize by now — we had some changes. The female excitement aroma had gotten stronger, and the male excitement aroma had gotten weaker. What was that all about? I had no idea. But the female excitement aroma was coming in waves, all the way to me at the door, and flowing around Bernie en route. Was he aware of these things? I had no idea about that either, but I did notice that the male excitement aroma was back on the scene, and getting stronger.

Gudrun reached for a mug on her desk, took a sip. Tea with lemon, if you're interested. "I'm going to do my job, Bernie, which is to act in my client's best interest."

"Meaning you're taking the deal?" Bernie said.

"He's taking the deal. I'm acting on his wishes." Gudrun rose. "Will there be anything else?"

THIRTEEN

We drove up to our place on Mesquite Road. What was this? Someone at the door? My muscles all bunched up, getting me ready to do who knows what — and then I saw who this someone was, namely Eliza. She had an envelope in her hand and was stooping down, maybe to slide it under the door, but she heard us coming and turned.

"Well," Bernie said to me as we got out of the car, "on a day with some not-so-good surprises, this is a nice one."

We walked up to the house. Not-so-good surprises? I tried to think of one and got the feeling I actually came close. I love that feeling!

Eliza stood on the doorstep, putting her at eye level with Bernie. Was she the forceful type? She had force in her, for sure, but not like Gudrun. Some humans are more complicated than others. Are the really forceful types less complicated? I was in over my head.

Bernie smiled. Had he ever looked more handsome? Not to my way of thinking. And Eliza looked good, too, her hair so glossy and always smelling of fresh rain, even though we hadn't had rain in the longest time. So we were off to a promising start, and soon we'd be inside, whipping up snacks and chillin' — exactly what I was in the mood for, although I hadn't realized it. The only slight possible hitch was that Eliza wasn't smiling back, and in fact might not have been in the mood for snacks and chillin'. I suddenly remembered the last time I'd seen her — looking in from outside the patio, where Mindy Jo had been showing Bernie some of her tattoos — and I began losing the urge to chill. Although not for snacks — that takes some major upset.

"I apologize for barging in," Eliza said.

"We're not even inside yet," Bernie said. Possibly a joke but Eliza didn't get it, and the truth is neither did I. "But, uh, you don't need an invitation."

"That's arguable," Eliza said.

"It is?" said Bernie, rocking back slightly.

"But I'm not here to argue," Eliza went on. "More to explain. And when I saw you weren't in I just wrote what I wanted to say." She handed him the envelope. "I'm actually better at clarifying my thoughts if I put them in writing."

Bernie held the envelope in both hands even though it weighed almost nothing. I myself am a hundred-plus pounder, in case I haven't gotten that in yet.

"Whatever it is, just tell me," he said.

Now Eliza did smile, a very brief smile, possibly happy in a small, here-and-gone way. "Come on, Bernie. I went to a lot of trouble."

Bernie opened the envelope, unfolded the single sheet of paper that was inside and began reading, his eyes going back and forth, back and forth, at first quickly, then slower, and finally stopping. He looked up. Their eyes met.

"I'm not afraid of living life alone," she said.

That was a stunner. Right then I realized that Eliza was the bravest person I'd ever met. Outside of Bernie, of course.

"I know," Bernie said. "But this is so . . . so quick. And based on a misinterpretation of —"

"I've allowed for that," Eliza said. "Maybe I'm making a mistake. But I don't think so. You came along too late — let's leave it at that."

178

"But —"

She leaned forward, gave Bernie a quick kiss on the cheek. "Bye, Bernie. I'll see you around."

Eliza walked away. Watching how she moved, how she held her head, I saw that, yes, she had force. She crossed the street, got in her car, drove off. Should I mention that she seemed to have some trouble fastening the seat belt?

Inside the house Bernie did some pacing. He had Eliza's letter in his hand and he read bits of it from time to time. Like "maybe what I saw on the patio was perfectly innocent, but even if it wasn't you have every right — we had no formal arrangement of any . . ." Or ". . . too set in my ways? But the truth is my work is all about managing uncertainty, and in life-and-death situations to put it too dramatically, so I'm not big on uncertainty in my personal life, not anymore . . ." And ". . . yes, a cliché, but was the starting point me the rescuer and you the invalid? And now the invalid is gone, thank god, and yet . . ."

By then I'd drunk every drop of water from my bowl and licked it dry. Bernie read that last part — the part about an invalid, whatever that was, once more. He looked at me and said, "So the healthy me is worse than . . . ?"

Was this about the saguaro case? I didn't want to think about the saguaro case ever again. I went over to the counter. There's a bread board on the counter where Bernie sometimes slices bread. Right now the only bread on it was the end piece of what I believe is called rye. I'm not a fan of rye — or of any kind of bread, really — but I rose up, snatched that stub of rye off the bread board, and gulped it down. Actually not bad! Maybe I'd rethink my whole position on bread, but right now Bernie was going to say I'd done a no-no and then I'd feel bad for a while, probably not very long.

Instead he surprised me. "Right you are, Chet. Let's get to work."

Bernie has lots of pals from his Army days. He'd pitched for Army, in case you didn't know, until his arm blew out, but even with that blown-out arm he can still throw a tennis ball a country mile, much farther than a city mile, as you're aware if you've ever spent time in both places. But most of the pals aren't from the baseball part of his Army career. They're from the war part, which was where Bernie got his leg wound. You wouldn't even know he had a leg wound unless you saw him wearing shorts, which he doesn't, or maybe at the end of a real long day, tracking perps on foot way out in the desert, for example, when he might limp just the tiniest bit. The wound happened out in the desert — not our desert, if I'd understood things right — on a day when Bernie must have done something good, because whenever we run into guys who were there, they come over and pound Bernie on the back and say "Hey!" and things like that.

Thurgood was one of those guys. Thurgood's name wasn't really Thurgood, just what all the rest of them called him, on account of something to do with his job in the Army, but that was as far as I could take it, except that maybe his old job was why he was our go-to person for everything legal. But why? Legal meant about the law, unless I was missing something, and since me and Bernie were the law, why would we need a go-to person? But I don't ask myself questions like that. Now Thurgood owned a bar called All Rise on a corner in the Mission section of town, where the oldest houses stood. He was shaking a cocktail shaker behind the bar when we walked in.

"Hey!" he said, putting down the shaker and coming around the bar.

"Um," said a man sitting with an empty glass, possibly waiting for what was in the shaker.

Thurgood didn't seem to hear. He sort of hugged Bernie and pounded him on the back. Sort of hugged him on account of Thurgood having just the one arm, and he was using it to do the pounding.

"Looking good, Bernie. Had some of us worried."

"That's all over," Bernie said. "Not looking too bad yourself."

"Lost ten pounds," Thurgood said. "Got to fit into my tux by March."

"Oh?"

"Trina's wedding."

"She's old enough to get married?"

"That's what I said. She told me to stay in my lane."

"Um," said the man with the empty glass.

Thurgood turned to him. "Haven't forgotten you," he said. Thurgood had a deep, rumbly voice and a face that went with it, if that makes any sense.

"No rush," the man with the empty glass said quickly.

"I'll just say hi to my buddy Chet." Thurgood leaned down and gave me a nice scratch between the ears, hitting the sweet spot perfectly. "Is he still growing?"

"Not possible."

"What a specimen!" Thurgood said. "Who would be the human equivalent?"

"No idea," Bernie said.

"Hercules," said the man with the empty glass.

Not long after that, his glass was full — on the house, if I'd been following things right — and he'd moved down the bar to check out a ball game on TV.

"What'll it be, Bernie?" Thurgood said.

"Whatever you want for yourself," said Bernie. "I'll have the same." He laid a bill on the bar.

"Your money's no good here," Thurgood said.

"It's not mine," said Bernie. "It's the bank's."

Possibly a joke, since Thurgood laughed, a deep, booming laugh I felt through the floorboards. A joke, but if so, I didn't get it. Also, who was Hercules? A perp? How could that be, if he was like me? I, Chet, was the chaser of perps! So I could never be a perp. I'd be chasing my own tail, for god's sake. Uh-oh. Had that happened? And more than once? Why would I ever do that? It makes no sense. Yet even at that very moment of knowing it made no sense, I was seized by a powerful urge to —

"Ch—et?"

Me? Something about me? Why on earth? Here I was, peacefully sitting up nice and tall, or I would be, any second. There! Done! A total pro, ready, alert, still. You wouldn't have noticed me.

"How about we try this new drink I'm inventing?" Thurgood said. He poured a deep-golden liquid into two small glasses. I smelled bourbon, plus other liquids I didn't know the names of.

They clinked glasses and sipped. The expressions on their faces changed, becoming pretty much identical, although Bernie and Thurgood didn't look much alike. But whoa! Their smells weren't that far apart. How interesting!

"What do you think?" Thurgood said. "A keeper?"

"Wow," said Bernie. "What's in it?"

"Basically an old-fashioned but with a secret ingredient of my own." Thurgood glanced at me over the bar. "Let's call it the Chetster."

Something about me had just gone by? Perhaps I'd latch on to it some other time. They clinked glasses and sipped again.

"So what's on your mind?" Thurgood said.

"Ever hear of a lawyer named Gudrun Burr?" Bernie said.

"Affirmative."

"Know her?"

"Met her once or twice, wouldn't say I know her."

"Give me the basics."

"Partner at Lobb and Edmunds, most prestigious firm in the Valley — in the state, for that matter. Rhodes scholar, summa at Veritan — their admission rate was four point three percent this year — first in her class at Veritan Law, Ivy League all the way."

"All the right credentials," Bernie said.

Thurgood nodded. "But very good, despite that," he said.

Bernie smiled.

"Divorced, no kids, lives for work," Thurgood went on. "This personal or professional?"

"Professional. She's defending a murder suspect we brought in."

"Yeah?"

"Why the surprise?"

"She doesn't do criminal work, far as I know," Thurgood said. "Her specialty is on some cutting-edge of private capital M and A structuring."

"The cutting part applies, but that's all," Bernie said. "She's acting for the PDS."

"Maybe she's got political ambitions," said

Thurgood. "Wouldn't be the first of her type."

The guy watching the ball game smacked the bar and said, "Chin music!"

Bernie turned toward him and got all thoughtful. Thurgood refilled their glasses.

FOURTEEN

"Do you ever get the feeling," Bernie said, as we drove away from All Rise, across the Rio Vista Bridge and out of the Mission, "that we're chasing our own tails?"

I sat in the shotgun seat, very still, eyes straight ahead and therefore helping with the driving, as usual, but inside I was shocked. Chasing my own tail? Yes, I'd had that feeling — and so recently — and not just the feeling but I'd been doing it for real. We're a lot alike in some ways, me and Bernie, but one way we're not alike involves tails, namely me having one and Bernie not. Was it possible he actually thought he did have a tail? But how could he? He puts on pants every day. Surely he'd notice that not once had he ever had to check whether a tail of some kind was properly tucked in. So how could he have that feeling? It would be like me . . . like me having the . . . having the . . .

I was still trying to find the end of that thought when Bernie said, "And when that happens, there's just one thing to do. We'll have to start from scratch."

Now I shifted position, turning so I could keep a close eye on him. What was the right way to handle this? Wait for Bernie to take the lead on the scratching front or start first to show him I was on board, a team player? I went back and forth, back and forth, back —

"What's up, big guy? Not fleas again?"

Fleas? What was he talking about? No way I had fleas. You can't miss them taking those teeny-tiny bites out of you and it was not happening. And hadn't I just recently finished up on a round of the drops?

"Have we got any of those drops left?"

Bernie flipped open the glove box, rooted around inside, came up with the little bottle of drops.

"Here we —"

The little bottle of drops somehow came into contact with one of my back paws, which seemed to be busily having a go at the fur on my neck. And for the first time I could recall in my whole life, one of my front paws was in action at the same time, taking on a sudden and terrible itch on the side of my nose. Chet the Jet! Wow! But the important part of all this was the back paw knocking the bottle of drops from Bernie's hand — totally by accident — and out the open window. A woman on the street shook her fist and yelled, "No littering!"

We stopped at a red light. Bernie looked at me. I ramped down the scratching to just about zilch and looked at him, a look that said, *If we're starting from scratch, then start, Bernie. What's the holdup?*

But he did not start scratching. Instead he said, "Sometimes I don't understand you."

Well, right back at ya. Which didn't change how I felt about him, not the slightest bit. And just to show him, I put my paw on his leg and pressed down firmly, so he'd know how much I cared. We shot through the intersection, the light luckily turning green at that moment, or just about to.

Not long after that, we were zooming along the West Valley freeway, two best buddies headed out of the Valley and onto a two-laner that seemed familiar. Soon we came to a fork in the road, also familiar, with a paved road leading one way and a dirt track the other. We took the dirt track, like we pretty much always do, soon passing a huge red rock and looping down into Dollhouse Canyon. I knew Dollhouse Canyon very well, of course, the box canyon with Wendell Nero's white RV at the end. But when we got there, I saw it was gone. For a second or two I was puzzled. And then I remembered: the RV was at the shed! With Itsy Bitsy Litzenberger! And all those wives of Wendell's! Chet the Jet, in the picture but good.

Bernie parked near some tread marks in the dirt. I was about to hop out when I remembered the jumping cholla from before and hopped out on Bernie's side instead. Was I ahead of the game or what? I got a real good feeling about this case. Then it hit me that we'd already solved it, bringing in the perp, Florian Machado, now sporting an orange jumpsuit, which I'd seen with my own eyes. So why wouldn't I feel good about the case? But here was a crazy thing: I was starting to feel less good.

For a little while we walked over the ground where the RV had been. There was nothing to see. Bernie sniffed the air a few times. I'd seen that before. Soon he might say, "Smell anything, big guy?"

And I did. I smelled all kinds of things, of course, including water, a distant sort of water. Was there a dry riverbed somewhere near, one of those dry riverbeds with a tiny pool of water or two, usually in the shade of a creosote bush, or sometimes a cottonwood tree? I didn't think so, hard to explain why. It felt . . . bigger than that.

Meanwhile Bernie didn't ask me anything. Instead he'd started climbing the slope at the end of the canyon. The big heat of summer was coming very soon, and the back of Bernie's shirt — one of his nicest, with the flamingos drinking at a bar pattern — was getting sweaty, and he was huffing and puffing a bit. I followed him up the slope, first from behind and then from in front, where I do my best following.

In pretty much no time I reached the top. Had I run the whole way? Probably, and I'm sure you're just like me when you get to the wide-open spaces. Don't you want to just run and run forever?

But I stopped and waited for Bernie, goes without mentioning. After not too long he came up beside me, paused with his hands on his hips. "Sometimes . . ." huff puff . . . "I wish I had four legs like you."

No surprise there — one of those wishes that made perfect sense. But where would his arms go? That was a problem, way too big for me to solve. I prefer small problems, or even better, none at all.

We stood on top of the hill, gazed at what was on the other side, namely a small and narrow valley with some sort of yellowish dwelling in the distance. But I left out the most important part: this little valley was green. Not totally green, like the kind of lawn we didn't like, me and Bernie — although there really isn't any place better for doing one's business, a thought I'll keep to myself — more like rows of green with rows of desert in between.

"A vineyard, Chet," Bernie said. "Couldn't be more than a dozen acres. Heard there were one or two starting up along this way, but I didn't expect . . ."

Whatever Bernie didn't expect remained unspoken. Also I didn't know what a vineyard was. And then from out of nowhere it came to me: a farm of some sort! A farm, and I'd thought of it all by myself. Wow! I was on fire.

"Careful," Bernie said. "Your tail's about to fly off on its own."

Oh no. Please not that. I sat down at once. My tail swished back and forth in the dirt a few times and then went still. I, not my tail, was the boss. My tail was going to have to learn who was the boss, once and for all. I, Chet, am the boss. You, tail, are the . . . what would you call it? Sidekick? Yes! You, tail, are the sidekick, even though you're mostly straight up, not sideways. And straight up was where you should be! The sidekick's job was to make the boss look good. Take me and Bernie, for example. Or . . . or maybe not. I seemed to have stumbled on a tough question. Who was the boss and who was the sidekick? And then came the answer, so right: we were both of us sidekick and boss! At the same time, if you see what I mean. Wow! I'd never felt more tip-top in my life.

Meanwhile Bernie had worked his way down the slope, not so steep on this side, and was walking along one of the green rows. I caught up at once and walked beside him. The air changed around us, became slightly cooler and a little less dry. What we had here looked to me like gnarly little green-leafed trees, the size of bushes, with clusters of what smelled and looked like purple grapes hanging from the branches. Grapes grew on trees? Life was full of surprises.

"Not really unusual, I suppose," Bernie said. "There's Algerian wine, Moroccan wine, Mexican wine, so some grapes thrive in this kind of . . ." He went silent, but I could almost hear the thought continuing in his mind ". . . and of course the padres planted vines going all the way back to . . ." He plucked a grape from a branch. "Still, you have to wonder if it's a smart or even sustainable use of . . ." Bernie popped the grape in his mouth. "Hmm," he said, and plucked another one. "What do you think?" He held out the grape and I snapped it up. Not the best grape I'd ever tasted, but I hadn't tasted many, grapes not being part of what you might call my regular diet. I also have a very wide-ranging irregular diet that includes things like pizza, apple cores, and scraps from around or sometimes in trash bins behind restaurants and bars, but grapes weren't really part of that — call it my regular irregular diet — either. Then they had to be part of a diet I hadn't even known I had — my irregular irregular diet. So many diets! Some of us have all the luck! Or at least lots of it.

"Here's an interesting fact, Chet." Bernie plucked another grape. "There's red wine and white wine, but the juice of all grapes is white."

Was that interesting? I couldn't think why, but if Bernie said it was then that was that. He squeezed the grape between his finger and thumb and sure enough —

"Freeze, you son of a bitch!"

We froze. That's what we do, me and Bernie, when someone behind us says *freeze*. Also Bernie raises his hands, which he did

194

now. Also he let go of the squashed grape. It fell to the ground, making a tiny, damp-ish sound. Then, without any signal at all — we'd practiced this so many times I'd almost gotten tired of Slim Jims — we turned very slowly, so as not to scare somebody into making a wrong move. And if I can just fit this in, I didn't mean it about getting tired of Slim Jims. That could never happen.

We faced this particular somebody. He was a fierce-looking old man, dressed in faded denim, dusty cowboy boots, and a sweat-stained cowboy hat. His skin was leathery from the sun and his legs were bowed. Probably none of that was impor-tant. I should have started with his shotgun, pointed at Bernie's chest, and left it at that.

"What the hell is wrong with you?" the old man shouted. "Didn't I say freeze?"

"We mean no harm," Bernie said, his voice calm, quiet, unafraid. I felt the exact same way. But I was all set to do what had to be done to this old dude in no time flat, just as soon as Bernie said *when.* Actually *when* is not the signal. It's *now!* I could hardly wait. Waiting for now is one of the most difficult parts of life. But I waited anyway. You can learn a lot from Slim Jims.

"No harm?" The old man's voice rose even more, up into a sort of harshness that hurts my ears. "You're trespassing on my goddamn land! It's not for sale, period. And where do you get off stealing my goddamn grapes?"

"My apologies," Bernie said. "I don't want to buy your land. And I'll pay for whatever the grapes are worth. In their final form, I mean."

"What the hell are you talking about?"

"As wine. They're worth more as wine than as grapes, right? Isn't that the whole point?"

"What whole point?"

"Of what you do," Bernie said.

This last part of the conversation was way beyond me, but it seemed to be having some sort of effect on the old man, like a fire raging inside him was dying down. And maybe he would have lowered the shotgun on his own, but at that moment a younger man came running up.

"Dad! What are you doing? Put down that gun!"

The old man turned to the younger man, the fire inside him raging back up so much his face went red. The younger man, wearing khakis and a button-down shirt, was bigger than the old man but looked something like him, except that all the hard facial features had been smoothed out.

"When I need your advice I'll ask for it," the old man shouted.

"I'm not giving you advice, Dad." The younger man — son of the old man, unless I was completely out to lunch . . . uh-oh, Chet, said a voice in my head, don't go there — put his hand on the shotgun barrel and gently pushed it down. "But I know you wouldn't want anyone to get hurt."

The old man's gaze went to Bernie, and then to me. His son, again gently, took the shotgun away from him, broke it open, pocketed the shells.

"Have you had your meds today, Dad?" the son said.

The old man raised his voice again, but now it was all thinned out, kind of loud and weak at the same time. "None of your business. I'm sick of my meds — why can't you get that through your thick skull?"

"At least go on up to the house, have Juana fix you some lunch," the son said.

"I'm not hungry," the old man said. But he started moving away. Then he stopped and pointed in our direction, meaning mine and Bernie's. "I want these trespassers arrested."

"I'll take care of it, Dad."

The old man moved off again. After a few more steps he said, "But not the dog." He walked down the row of vines, turned into a cross row, disappeared.

The son took a deep breath, let it out slow.

"Sorry to cause you problems," Bernie said. "We were nearby, saw the vineyard and got curious. My name's Bernie Little and this is Chet."

The son gave his head a little shake, like he was clearing up the insides. "We had a dog like him once. Maybe not as big." He gave me a close look. "Or so smart." He leaned the shotgun up against one of the vine stocks. "I'm Diego Torrez, Junior." He held out his hand. They shook. "Everyone calls me Jim. My dad is Diego. We, meaning the family, own Gila Wines." He gestured at the green rows.

"I didn't realize there were any on this side of the reservation," Bernie said.

"Wine has been made here since 1632," Jim said. "Although not very good wine and not by us. We bought the land in 1806. But the big jump in quality came twenty-five years ago, when my dad ripped out all the old vines and planted Mourvèdre."

"What's that?" Bernie said.

"A Mediterranean varietal that does well in hot, dry climates. I gather you've sampled it already."

Bernie smiled. "Won't do that again. How

much rainfall do you get?"

"We had an inch last year, nothing the year before, two inches the year before that."

Bernie ran his gaze over the vineyard. "So you must be sitting on top of the aquifer."

Jim's eyes shifted. "You know something about aquifers?"

"Not really," Bernie said. "Does the name Wendell Nero mean anything to you?"

Jim took a step back. "Only from the news," he said. "A scientist, apparently, killed in a robbery just over the hill in Doll-house Canyon. Why do you ask?"

"We knew him slightly," Bernie said. "What do you think he was doing in the canyon?"

"Couldn't tell you," Jim said. "I had no idea he was even there." He glanced at his watch. "Afraid I've got to run. We have tastings the first Saturday of every month." He picked up the shotgun. "Feel free to stop by."

FIFTEEN

"Your hands already know how to catch," Bernie said. "You just have to let them."

"Yeah?" said Charlie.

In summer, Charlie went to day camp on the grounds of Chaparral Country Club, where Leda and Malcolm were members. And I suppose Charlie, too, was a member, since he was Leda's kid and lived with them most of the time. But he was also Bernie's kid and lived with us a little bit of the time, and we weren't members and never would be, on account of Bernie has a sort of attitude about places like Chaparral Country Club. You can see it on his face, a heavy look you might call sulking, if it was on the face of someone else. And it had been on his face as we sat parked in the Chaparral Country Club lot — where we sometimes came to pick Charlie up and drive him home, not to our place but to Leda and Malcolm's, just for the fun of being with him — until the moment he came running up, and Bernie's face changed completely into a face of happiness and beauty.

"How was camp?" Bernie said, reaching out with one hand and hoisting Charlie up and into . . . the shotgun seat, squeezed in beside me. The shotgun seat — can it possibly be necessary to point this out? — is my seat, the seat belonging to Chet the Jet and only to Chet the Jet, end of story. But this was Charlie, so I was cool with it.

"I'm a butterfingers, Dad," Charlie said.

"Who told you that?"

"Timmy."

"Who's Timmy?"

"The counselor."

"The counselor called you a butterfingers?"

"It means I can't catch."

"I know what it means," Bernie said, "but it's a load of . . ."

"Bullshit, Dad?"

"Don't say bullshit."

"Cause it's a bad word?"

"Well, that depends on . . . yes, it's a bad word. At least for now."

"When does it get good?"

"When you go away to college," Bernie said. "First we're going to clear up this catching thing. Reach under the seat —

201

there should be a tennis ball."

"Isn't it Chet's?"

"He won't mind."

Charlie turned to me. Our faces were very close. His eyes were so clear. His skin was so soft. His breath smelled like egg salad. Nothing bad was ever going to happen to this kid. That was my promise to myself.

"Chet?" he said. "Okay if I take your ball?"

No! Absolutely not! It was my ball and belonged to me. All the balls in this car — and there were way more than one, by the way — were mine and mine alone. Also any balls I happen to pick up on my daily rounds are mine. Balls bouncing somewhere on their own, across a field or a tennis court? Those are called in play, amigo, for a reason.

Charlie reached under the seat, came up with a tennis ball, a fairly fresh one, still bright yellow and nappy, the way I like them. He held it up.

"Okay, Chet?"

Perfectly fine. No problem at all. We got out of the car, which was when Bernie told Charlie about his hands already knowing how to catch.

"Make your hands into a cup," Bernie said.

"Like this?"

"A softer cup," Bernie said. "There we go. Now all you do is watch the ball. Your hands will do the rest."

"Really?"

"Eyes on the ball."

Bernie held up the tennis ball. Charlie watched it. The ball arced through the air and landed plop in Charlie's little hands. They closed around it.

"Hey!" Charlie said.

"One more time. And again. One last time."

Arc and plop. Arc and plop. Arc and plop. By now Bernie's tosses had become a bit off line, kind of a puzzler, since he was the most accurate thrower I've ever seen. Once he hit a sidewinder in the head with a Wiffle ball, a sidewinder right in mid-sidewind! Fun for all of us, although maybe the sidewinder missed that aspect, judging from what happened next. But the point I'm making is that Bernie's throws started getting wild. Charlie even had to run a few steps to get his cupped hands under the last one. Plop.

"Okay," Bernie said. "Let's hit the road."

Whoa! Wait! Bernie had been tossing a ball around and I hadn't made a play for it, not even once? What had gotten into me?

"How come Chet's panting, Dad?"

"Probably thirsty."

Out came a bottle of water and my portable bowl. I turned up my nose.

High Chaparral Estates was the fanciest part of the whole Valley and Leda and Malcolm's place — a McMansion without the Mc part as Malcolm once said, possibly some sort of joke — was in the fanciest part of High Chaparral Estates. They had a big green lawn of the kind we didn't like, me and Bernie, and lots of flowering bushes. Domingo the gardener was watering one of the bushes as we came up the path, and Malcolm was supervising.

"Hi, there," he said. "Hey, Domingo, make a rainbow for Charlie."

Domingo moved the hose around until a rainbow appeared in the spray.

"See that?" Malcolm said.

"Yeah," said Charlie.

"Okay," Malcolm said, "now make the pot of gold."

Domingo looked a little confused, but Malcolm laughed — not the best laugh I'd ever heard, maybe needing some oil, if that makes any sense — and Domingo started laughing, too.

"Pot of gold," Domingo said. "That's funny."

Malcolm turned to Bernie. He was taller than Bernie and very skinny, like an enormous weed, with long narrow toes sticking out over the fronts of his flip-flops. "I got back ahead of schedule, but thanks for picking him up."

"Anytime," Bernie said.

"How was camp?" Malcolm asked Charlie.

"Great!"

Malcolm looked surprised. He opened his mouth to say something, but at that moment we had a visitor. Well, not a visitor I suppose, since he lived here. I'm referring to Shooter, a troublesome character in my life. Shooter, still a puppy but now on the largish side, had something to do with the events that followed the sound of she-barking from across the canyon on a long-ago night. Let's call that fact one, as Bernie likes to say. Fact two is "spit and image," something I've heard way too much, as in "He's the spit and image of Chet!"

No time for any more facts, even if they exist, because Shooter had come zooming around the house and was bearing down on me, ears straight back from a wind of his own making and eyes wild, as though he actually intended to —

Oomph!

And a much bigger oomph than the last time we'd gone through this, fairly recently, as I recalled. Not a big enough oomph to knock me off my feet, or even to budge me at all — goes without mentioning. But now it was my duty to show him what could really be done in the world of oomphing, which I proceeded to do. It never occurred to me — and I still don't understand how this happened, although it was Shooter's fault for sure — that Domingo would lose his grip on the hose and that Malcolm would end up getting soaked from head to toe, which he didn't appreciate one little bit.

"Shooter!" he yelled. "Stop this right now! Lie down! Play dead!"

Then came the biggest surprise of this visit. Shooter dropped out of the oomphing game at once, sank to the ground, rolled over, played dead.

Shooter knew how to play dead? I wasn't happy about that. Playing dead was my trick, in fact, my only trick. I lay down and played dead, lying down, just by chance, right beside Shooter. He looked at me out of the corner of his eye. Did he think he could play dead longer than me? Shooter had a lot to learn.

"God in heaven," Malcolm said. "I need a

drink." He glanced at Bernie. "Um, care to join me?"

Bernie's eyebrows rose. Have I mentioned that his eyebrows have a language of their own? Right now they were all about surprise.

"Well," he said. "Sure. Thanks."

"I've got a little bar downstairs," Malcolm said. We were in the kitchen, Malcolm in new clothes, Shooter upstairs with Charlie in Charlie's media room — Charlie had his own media room here in High Chaparral Estates — and me and Bernie with Malcolm.

"I didn't know that," Bernie said.

"Not much of a bar," said Malcolm. "It's actually just a corner of the wine cellar, fixed up with bar paraphernalia."

"Wine cellar? Know much about wine?"

"Wouldn't call myself an expert."

"Ever heard of Mourvèdre?"

"The varietal? Sure. Want to sample some?"

Not long after that we were several floors down from the kitchen in a big wood-paneled room with leather chairs and couches, a bar at one end that reminded me of the small upstairs bar in the Ritz where we'd once spent a very short evening, and wine bottles lining all the walls and in cases here and there on the floor. Malcolm walked around eyeing the bottles, picked out one, then another, and another, grabbed some glasses from a hanging rack, and brought everything to a high-top table in one corner.

"Leda says I have a way of going on and on," Malcolm said.

Those eyebrows of Bernie's rose, but before he could say anything Malcolm . . . kept going on. Some humans like the sound of their own voice. Do I get that? But yes! Sometimes I bark just to hear the sound. Barking can be . . . how to put this? Its own reward? Close enough.

"So stop me if you already know all this. Some wines are made from a single grape species — Burgundies, for example. Others, like Bordeaux, are blends." Malcolm took a corkscrew from the table, started opening bottles. "Mourvèdre was never considered a noble grape, instead got used in blends." He poured some into a couple of glasses, handed Bernie a glass. "Here's a Spanish take, fifty percent Mourvèdre, which they call Monastrell over there."

Malcolm swirled his wine around in the glass.

"You really do that, huh?" Bernie said.

Malcolm nodded. "Frees up the aromas."

Not my favorite dude, but Malcolm was on the money on this one. Frisky little smell waves started coming my way, one after the other: flower-scented — particularly the purple kind Suzie likes, called violets perhaps; pepper-scented; plus sagebrush, red meat, and even a hit of sheep poop. Wow!

Bernie and Malcolm swirled and sipped. Malcolm set a small silver bucket between them.

"You can spit in this, if you like."

"That's all right," Bernie said, making the right choice, in my opinion. I wasn't a big fan of spitting, pretty much a human male thing, in my experience, and indoor spitting was the worst kind.

They swirled and sipped. "Picking up any violet?" Malcolm said.

"Well, flowers, maybe," Bernie said.

"How about pepper?" Malcolm said.

Bernie shook his head. I took a moment to check out Malcolm's nose — long and narrow, in no way as mighty as Bernie's, and yet . . . and yet . . . I didn't want to go any further, so I stopped, which is my MO in this sort of situation.

Meanwhile they'd emptied their glasses and Malcolm was pouring from another bottle.

"This is French, Bandol specifically. Eighty percent Mourvèdre."

More swirling. More sipping. No spitting.

"What do you think?" Malcolm said.

"Kind of, um, astringent," Bernie said.

"More tannic, no question."

"But I actually like it better."

Malcolm smiled. Had I ever seen him smile before? Not that I remembered. It almost made him look like someone else.

"Then have some more." Malcolm refilled their glasses with the French one. Following that they sampled bottles from Australia, California, Washington, and maybe a few others I missed.

"Now," Malcolm said, collecting and opening some more bottles, "let's see what a few brave vintners have done with this big boy all on his own."

Lots more swilling. Lots more sipping. Still no spitting. Things were going well, in my opinion. Malcolm went to the bar and returned with a plate of sliced sausages. How was it I'd lived all this time without wine tastings?

Malcolm drained his glass. "Remind me which ones we haven't tried."

Bernie pointed to a bottle. "That one, I think."

"Ah, Turkey Flat." Malcolm poured. "I'm

guessing you'll like this."

They both seemed to like Turkey Flat and had started in on a second glass when out of nowhere Malcolm said, "Charlie's a great kid."

Bernie stopped sipping in mid-sip, looked at Malcolm.

"Leda doesn't want any more kids, as you may already know."

"I didn't," Bernie said.

"Interesting," Malcolm said, gazing into his glass. There was a long silence. Then he took a deep breath and started opening another bottle. The cork was half out when he paused and said, "I opened a college savings account, if that's all right with you."

Bernie put down his glass. "For Charlie?"

Malcolm said, "Didn't you hear what I just said? About no more kids?"

"Yeah, but . . ."

"In fact, it's fully funded," Malcolm said.

He went back to uncorking the bottle. Bernie gave Malcolm a long look, the expression in his eyes very complicated, not quite like any I'd seen from him before.

"This is practically from our backyard," Malcolm said. "One hundred percent Mourvèdre." He poured and put the bottle down. Bernie glanced at the label, and then again.

"Gila Wines?"

"Heard of them?"

"Yes."

"Nice little winery," Malcolm said. "An associate of mine and I tried to buy it a few years back."

"Yeah?"

"Well, more accurately I considered it. Water's the X factor in any agricultural enterprise out here so I hired a hydrologist to check things out. His report was negative — even for an unthirsty grape like Mourvèdre — so we backed off."

"Was it Wendell Nero?"

"The hydrologist? No. His name was Hoskin Phipps. A big-timer in his field — he's based out here now but he was head of the geology department at Veritan."

"Veritan University?"

"That's what people are referring to when they say Veritan, Bernie." Malcolm took a sip. "You must have played them when you were at West Point."

"Only in an exhibition game."

"Who won?"

"Only an exhibition game and a long time ago."

Malcolm leaned forward. "But it was Veritan. Can't say I know you, but at least I know you well enough to be willing to bet

212

you remember the score — and every single detail if you won."

There was a pause. Then Bernie started laughing. Malcolm joined in. They laughed and laughed. Did a little wine get spilled? Possibly, but that was when I got distracted by the sound of footsteps clattering down the stairs.

Unnoticed by the wine tasters, Leda entered the room, a bit sweaty, wearing a cycling outfit, complete with helmet and those odd cycling shoes, which were making her lean slightly backward. "What the hell's going on?" she said.

Sixteen

The next morning Bernie drank a whole pot of coffee. Also he shaved with a new blade and took a cold shower. I knew it was a cold shower from the sounds he made, like "Yikes!" and "Yow!" and "Yiy!" His face was still pinkish as we drove away from the house. "No Mourvèdre today, big guy — that's one thing for sure."

There, just another example of Bernie's brilliance. The day hadn't even started and we already had one sure thing in our back pocket. I barked at a little old lady waiting for the bus, couldn't contain myself.

"The unknown unknowns aren't what frustrate you, Chet," he said as we went by the rail yards, the auto mile, the new auto mile, and into the part of town that was strip malls and nothing but. "By definition," he continued, "you don't know they're there. It's the known unknowns that keep you awake at night."

Whoa! This was going by way too fast. The part about me not feeling frustrated? Bernie had nailed that one. I hardly ever felt frustrated. When was the last time? Maybe that day I'd been home alone while Bernie went to the dentist — where I'd once tried waiting in the waiting room, but the drill sounds had ended up being too much for me — and a squirrel had spent the whole time keeping busy in the front yard, with me trapped inside and barking my head off to no effect. Was the squirrel an unknown unknown? I had no idea. As for something or other keeping me awake at night? Nope! I gave Bernie a close look.

He glanced at me. "I know what you're thinking — what does all this philosophizing have to do with the case? Answer: Why did Wendell want to see us? That's the known unknown, has been from the beginning, and we've gotten nowhere on it. See why it's so irritating?"

I thought that over from several angles, which took practically no time, and settled on thinking about it from no angle at all, my usual MO. But even after such a big effort, I couldn't get to even the beginning of irritation. Poor Bernie! I pressed my paw on his leg to make him feel better. We sped up big time, which had to mean he was feeling better already.

"CHET!"

Bernie slammed on the brakes. Honking started up all around us. So much road rage! I myself am a lover of the open road.

"What gets into you?"

Me? I couldn't have been more chill if I tried. And how would trying even help with that? I looked at Bernie. He looked at me.

We pulled up in front of Butchie and Mom's Tuxedo World, a strip mall shop we've visited before, although not recently. In the front, Butchie Dykstra's mom ran a tuxedo rental business and had a stock of extremely interesting shoes called pumps. In the back Butchie ran some businesses of a different kind.

A bell tinkled as we opened the door. I love being welcomed like that, and made what Bernie calls a mental note to be on my best behavior. I didn't even think about the pumps, which stood in gleaming rows on a rack over on one side. Maybe I leaned a little that way, but I kept going in a straight line, a total pro, and on the job.

Butchie's mom stood on a stool, tying the bow tie of a very tall pimply kid wearing black tuxedo pants and a frilly white shirt.

"So much classier than a clip on, Wesley.

You'll thank me in the end."

"But you won't be there, Mrs. D."

"Of course not," said Mrs. D. "It's the junior prom."

"Then how am I gonna get it tied?"

"That's what I'm teaching you. Just remember dapper."

"Huh?"

"The letters, Wesley. Here we go. *D*ifferent lengths. *A* simple knot. *P*inch a bow. *P*ull and pluck. *E*nter the loop. *R*efine. And that spells dapper." Mrs. D. patted Wesley's chest. "Look in the mirror."

They looked in the mirror, which was when Mrs. D. spotted us. "Now you just practice for a bit while I deal with these rough customers." She hopped down from the stool, her skirt, perhaps on the short side for a woman her age — just based on what I see around town — flapped up. Wesley moved closer to the mirror. Mrs. D. smoothed her skirt and came over to us.

"Well, well, the two most handsome guys in the whole Valley! When was the last time you wore a tux, Bernie? And please don't say at your wedding."

Mrs. D. was one of those very fast-talking women, and fast-moving, too. Somewhere in the middle of that whole stream of words she slipped me a biscuit, so quick and smooth I almost didn't know it was happening.

"Um, actually —"

"I knew it. Now you come right over here. How can a man stand out in this day and age? By wearing a tux even if there's no special event, that's how! And lots of the leading lights in town are starting to do just that. Here — try this one, just for size."

"What leading lights?" Bernie said.

Meanwhile Mrs. D. was somehow getting a tuxedo jacket on him even though he was resisting. "Arnie Gilchrist, for one."

"Isn't he the advertising guy?"

"And Zeppo Frias."

"He owns nightclubs, for god's sake."

"You're making my case. Now just take a gander at what could be you."

We all gazed at Bernie in the mirror, even Wesley, who'd turned to watch. The tuxedo jacket was a huge success in my view, going very nicely with his Hawaiian shirt, the one with the dancing coconuts, some of the coconuts wearing bras and the rest in tank tops.

"Women," said Mrs. D., "and I'm talking about the best kind of women, like elegance in a man."

"Why?" Bernie said.

Mrs. D. gave Bernie a narrow-eyed look.

"I hope you're not listening to this, Wesley," she said.

"No, ma'am." Wesley turned away quickly and returned to fumbling with his bow tie.

"He's a lost cause. Don't you be a lost cause, Wesley."

"No, ma'am."

Mrs. D. helped Bernie out of the tuxedo jacket, hung it on the rail. "I suppose you're looking for Butchie," she said. "He's not in yet."

"When do you expect him?"

"An hour ago." Mrs. D.'s eyes shifted. All at once she didn't seem quite as lively. "Is there a problem, Bernie?"

"Not for Butchie," Bernie said. "I might be in the market for some electronics."

"Yeah? You can wait in back if you like, look around."

We went through a curtain and into the back of the store. What a place! I'll only mention the mechanical bucking bronco — I'd seen a similar one in action with Bernie in the saddle, briefly, but just long enough to win a C note — and a rocket launcher, which I knew from a video game of Charlie's that Bernie had sort of lost before his next visit.

Were laptops and cell phones electronics? I thought so. Butchie had a few of each.

Bernie picked them up, checked them out, put them down. "Not here, big guy. Does that mean Butchie already unloaded them? Or is it possible . . . ?" He went silent and headed through the curtain to the front of the store. Wesley was gone and Mrs. D. was counting a big wad of money.

"This is only passing through," she said. "We just get to touch it, if you know what I mean."

"All too well," said Bernie.

Touching money? That had never occurred to me. What a shame! I have two basic ways of touching — with my paws and with my tongue, both good, although I get a lot more information from my tongue. How would a wad of money feel on my tongue? A great question, and one I should have been asking long ago. I sidled over toward Mrs. D.

"How about I text him?" Mrs. D. said, at the same time dropping the wad of cash into a drawer and closing it tight. She pressed a button on her phone. A moment or two later it pinged. Mrs. D. checked the screen.

"Good god," she said, "fishing again?"

"Butchie's into fishing?" Bernie said.

"Just recently. A customer brought in one of those inflatable boats. Butchie decided to try it out before we put it on the market.

Today will be the fifth tryout, unless I lost count."

"Where does he go?"

"Geronimo Lake."

"There are fish in Geronimo Lake?"

"So he says."

We hopped in the car, cranked 'er up, and —

"Chet? What you got there?"

What in heck did I have, anyway? It appeared to be, my goodness, a pump. Bernie took it from me gently and went back into the store, where a brief conversation took place between him and Mrs. D., money possibly changing hands. I quickly lost interest and didn't tune back in until we were past the airport and out of town, headed toward Mount Limon, where the sun comes up every morning. It was later in the day now, so the sun had moved on, the way the sun does. I'm also the type that likes to keep moving, so I understood perfectly. I'd gone past Mount Limon before — whenever we worked cases in New Mexico, a very dangerous place when it comes to speeding tickets — but never driven up it. Imagine my excitement when Bernie turned off the freeway and started on the mountain road.

"Chet?"

The air got cooler on Mount Limon and everything around us got greener. The smell of water came drifting down the mountain, and then we rounded a corner and I caught a flash of blue. Not long after that, we parked in front of a small wooden dock by the shore of a lake.

"Actually a reservoir," Bernie said, "but a lake in my book."

Same. A nice round lake, smooth and shining, and smelling lovely, very different from the water that comes out of taps. This water was alive and smelled it, if you know what I mean. There was only one other car around, a jeep hitched to an empty boat trailer. Bernie checked the license plate.

"B-U-T-C-H-I-E," he said. "Would we have our names on the plate if we were in the stolen goods business?"

I didn't know the answer to that one, didn't even understand the question.

"Maybe it's the right approach," Bernie said. "Got to advertise yourself, as my mother would say."

Uh-oh? Bernie's mom was back in the picture? I tried to find room for her somewhere in the case and failed. Also the case itself turned very shadowy in my mind, almost darkening completely.

Bernie shaded his eyes from the sun and gazed out at the lake. There was only one boat on the water, small, wide, grayish, not going anywhere, simply floating in a way that made me want to do the exact same thing, meaning simply float. The air was so clear I could see a fishing rod hanging over the side, the line like a streak of silver vanishing into the blue.

Bernie cupped his hands to his mouth. *"Butchie! Butchie!"*

No answer. No movement on the boat. What had happened was pretty clear. All this peace and quiet had put Butchie — possibly tired from a late night — to sleep, and he was catching some *Z*'s on the deck, out of our view.

"Butchie! Butchie! Butchie!"

Not far from the boat, a little fish jumped out of the water and splashed back in. Then came more silence.

Bernie's face darkened. He kicked off his flip-flops, took off his shirt and pants, so he was wearing just his boxers, and said, "Remember how to swim, big guy?"

But I was already in the lake. Who could forget how to swim? All you had to do was trot through the water, nothing simpler.

Bernie's a fine swimmer, does the crawl, a very splashy kind of swimming. I did the trot right next to him, as close as close could be. Once he turned and said, "Are you trying to drown me?" He really does have the best sense of humor in the world.

We reached the boat in practically no time, one of those inflatables with long — what did they call them? Pontoons, maybe? — springy roll-like sides. We raised ourselves up on one of them and peered into the boat.

No Butchie. There was nothing on the deck but a box of worms, some of them wriggling their way out.

We treaded water, side by side, looking all around. Were we looking for Butchie? That was my guess. I waited for Bernie to call his name again, but he did not. Instead he put his face in the water. I did the same.

It was blurry down there, but the lake wasn't very deep, not at all like a bay I'd once been in, down in bayou country, a bay with gators, including one particular gator name of Iko. But if we had gators here in the desert, I'd never seen one, and I didn't see them now. There was nothing on the mossy bottom but a few beer cans and a whitish something, plus a pair of cargo shorts and a yellow T-shirt. For some reason I didn't understand what I was seeing right away, namely that someone was wearing those shorts and that T-shirt, someone whitish. By that time Bernie was diving down to the bottom. I hurried to catch up. Together we got hold of this whitish person by the waistband of his shorts and hauled him toward the surface, Bernie doing the actual gripping of the waistband and hauling, and me helping as best I could.

We came up into air, took a few deep breaths. Just me and Bernie on the deep breathing part. This someone — in fact a man, a man I knew, namely Butchie, his handlebar mustache all droopy — wasn't taking any kind of breaths. Bernie had Butchie in his arms now, almost like he was hugging him, with Butchie sort of looking over Bernie's shoulder, his eyes empty, and facing me. That meant Bernie couldn't see what I was seeing: Butchie's throat was cut from ear to ear.

I barked.

SEVENTEEN

A fish jumped, out in the middle of Geronimo Lake.

"Was that a fish?" said Captain Stine, our old buddy from Valley PD. He had a harsh, hoarse sort of voice, like he partied every night, but when you saw his face you knew he wasn't the type. "Never used to be fish out here. My dad and I came up on Sundays when I was a kid. I learned how to swim in this lake." He squinted out over the water. "Looks smaller to me now, like it shrank. Funny how that works."

"It looks smaller because it is smaller," Bernie said. "It's drying up."

"Try not to spoil my day," said Stine.

I was happy to hear him say that. Didn't it mean that the day was still unspoiled? I'd started to worry about that. The lake had been so peaceful when we'd first arrived, just the two of us. Now we had lots going on: a couple of PD dinghies out in the lake,

226

with a PD diver in the water; squad cars parked by the shore; cops searching the woods; the ME and her assistants; an ambulance with Butchie's body inside; and me, Bernie, and Stine on the dock, looking out at the lake, the surface now all choppy. But if Stine was right, we were still AOK. I considered plunging in for a quick dip, decided I didn't feel like it. Didn't feel like a swim? That was odd. I lay down.

"You need to talk to Beasley," Bernie said.

"Makes twice you've said that," said Stine. "I've never understood why this isn't county jurisdiction."

"It was all about long ago real estate corruption, if you're really interested," Bernie said. "But in the here and now we have two murders, both throat cuttings, one Beasley's and one yours. Connected, for sure, meaning they've got the wrong guy locked up, among other things."

"Connected how?" said Stine.

"By a cell phone and a laptop I'm hoping we're about to find down on the bottom."

"And if we don't?"

"Then we have to work harder."

Stine looked at Bernie. "Here's something you don't know — there was an attempted murder last night, same MO, in Rio Vista."

"Throat cutting?"

"That was the intent. A trainer from one of those cycling gyms, no suspects."

Bernie shook his head. "Can't be related."

Stine gestured with his chin — a very good chin for gesturing, not the kind of chin you could miss — at the lake. "But this is?" he said.

Bernie didn't reply.

"Do you ever think," Stine went on, "that in our desire to impose order we see patterns that aren't there?"

"Who's we?" said Bernie.

"Anyone with half a brain."

Whoa! Did that include me? Why hadn't I been paying more attention? Sometimes you can reel a conversation back in. Well, maybe I'd done it once or twice. What were they talking about? Desire? Order? Patterns? Desire I understood no problem, but the rest slipped away. Some of our work at the Little Detective Agency was hard on the brain. You had to be cut out for it, and of course I must have been. Otherwise how could we have been so successful, if you leave out the finances part? I ended up feeling included. I had half a brain and then some.

The diver surfaced beside one of the dinghies. She took out her mouthpiece, slipped off her hood, shook out her hair.

"Anything?" Stine called out over the water.

She turned her thumb down.

Stine and Bernie exchanged a look, sort of a silent argument, if that makes any sense.

"What's stupider," Stine said, "moron or cretin?"

"Not sure," said Bernie. "Why?"

"Just trying to place Beasley on the scale." Stine took out his phone, paused. "In return you get to tell Butchie's mom the news."

"In return for you doing your job?"

"Don't push me, Bernie."

Wait! This was interesting. Was it possible? Why not? Push him, Bernie, push him right into the drink! Which would be just the beginning of all sorts of fun. We'd all of us get nice and wet and start feeling a whole lot better.

But for whatever reason, Bernie did not push Captain Stine into the drink. We got in the car and hit the road. As we drove up to Butchie and Mom's Tuxedo World, Bernie took a deep breath and sat very straight and still. That meant he was steeling himself. For what? I had no idea. I took a crack at steeling myself, but just like all the other times I'd tried, I didn't seem to have the knack.

■ ■ ■ ■

Mrs. D. had another frilly-shirted boy in front of the mirror, this one not quite as tall or pimply as Wesley.

"But I don't know how to dance," he was saying.

"Do you know how to walk?" said Mrs. D.

"Uh, sure."

"Then you know how to dance. Put your arms around her and walk her to the music. That's all you have to do."

Mrs. D. saw us from the corner of her eye and turned.

"We'll wait," Bernie said.

She studied his face, then slowly and carefully, suddenly like an old person, she stepped down off the stool. "Tell me now."

Bernie told her.

I went right over and stood next to Mrs. D. It was all I could think of to do. Bernie came, too, arriving just in time to catch Mrs. D. when her legs gave way beneath her.

We drove downtown, Bernie silent the whole time, and parked in front of the bronze tower. Then we just sat there. After a while, a security guard walked up.

"Hey! You can't — Bernie? That you? And

the Chetster?"

"Ruben? You're working security?"

"Yessir."

"But how is that possible?"

Ruben — who'd hijacked a beer truck that had turned out to be full of empties — leaned in closer. "The powers that be in these parts don't actually know me as Ruben."

"What did you change it to?"

"Rube. Makes it easy to remember. Plan on sittin' here for a spell?"

"Maybe."

Ruben stuck a red card under the windshield wiper. "So's no one'll bother you."

"Thanks, Rube."

"Least I could do. What goes around comes around."

"I've heard that."

Ruben tapped the hood and moved back to the entrance of the bronze tower. Right about then was when the huge doors slid open and Gudrun Burr walked out, Mason, her bearded receptionist with the cauliflower ear, beside her.

"Growling again? You stay here for the time being, big guy."

Growling? Uh-oh. But . . . but Gudrun! When I have issues with someone I never forget, even if I end up forgiving them later, and I was nowhere near that with Gudrun. Meanwhile Bernie was headed toward the small plaza in front of the bronze tower. What was "time being" again? I wrestled with that for a while and —

"Chet?"

— in the course of my wrestling somehow found myself out of the car and on the plaza, right beside Bernie. I got the feeling Bernie had a little more to say to me — something nice, I'm sure — but before he could Mason spotted us and tapped Gudrun on the arm. She turned her head, saw us, and raised her eyebrows, at the same time possibly losing her footing the smallest bit. We went over to them.

"I thought I might be seeing you again," Gudrun said. "If not quite so soon."

"Is there somewhere we can go to talk?" Bernie said.

Gudrun studied Bernie's face, her eyes bright green in the sunshine. Was she about to say, About what? or Anything wrong with right here? which was what we usually got in this kind of situation. Instead she nodded and said, "How about I buy you a drink?"

Bernie nodded. We walked across the plaza and entered another tower, this one silver. Seeing Bernie and Mason side by side, I realized something I'd missed, namely the size of Mason — a little taller than Bernie but much wider, especially across the shoulders and chest.

Inside the tower, we entered a small, dark bar on the first floor. Me, Bernie, and Gudrun sat at a table in an alcove at the back, me more or less under the table — and absolutely not growling, no way I'd make a mistake like that, not if it meant I'd have to wait in the car — and Mason took a spot at the bar.

The waiter came over.

"Welcome, Ms. Burr," he said. "Your usual?"

"Thank you."

"And you, sir?"

"Mourvèdre," said Bernie.

Have I mentioned that the tabletop was made of glass, meaning I could see through it? Right now, seeing through it, I had a good view of Gudrun's face. Some human faces are often in motion. Others are mostly still. Gudrun had the still kind of face. Now it was even stiller.

"Excuse me?" said the waiter. "You're talking about the varietal? I'll bring you the wine list."

"That's all right," Bernie said. "Make it a beer."

"Any special kind? We've got —" And the

waiter got started on a long, long list.

"That last one," Bernie said.

The waiter smiled a smile that was anything but and went away. Gudrun gave Bernie a different sort of smile, maybe amused although mixed with other things I had no clue about.

"I'm beginning to think you're the type who's full of surprises," she said.

"Like?" said Bernie.

"I wouldn't have taken you for a wine geek."

"I'm not."

"But Mourvèdre — isn't that somewhat obscure?"

"I just happened to sample some yesterday," Bernie said. "A little too much, in fact."

"So you just blurted it out?"

Bernie nodded.

"I wouldn't have taken you for a blurter either," Gudrun said.

Bernie shrugged. The drinks came. Gudrun's was a deep golden color, smelling of champagne, sugar, oranges, and some kind of plant. She and Bernie clinked glasses. They sipped their drinks. From my spot under the table I could see they relaxed a little, the way humans do after a drink or two, although more than two can lead to non-relaxing problems. Bernie stretched out his legs a bit. Gudrun slipped off one shoe — the high-heeled kind — and flexed her foot. Her toenails were painted bright red, always an interesting sight, but way more interesting was the smell that arose from her foot. It was a fresh smell — unusual for a human foot except after a shower — a fresh and clean watery smell, and not the watery smell that comes with tap water. Not at all. This was the watery smell that comes from fresh outdoor water, say a lake, for example. Also interesting was the fact that her old smell — dying flowers — was almost completely gone, like . . . like . . . that was as far as I could take it on my own. I gazed up at her through the glass tabletop. She happened to glance down. Our eyes met. Gudrun slipped her shoe back on.

"So what are we doing here, Bernie?" Gudrun said. "Don't tell me this is a social visit."

Over at the bar, Mason shot us a quick glance.

Bernie put down his glass. "You wanted evidence," he said. "I have some."

Gudrun took another sip, this time a big one. "Let's hear it."

And Bernie told a whole big story, all about Wendell Nero, Florian, cell phones, laptops, Butchie Dykstra, and Geronimo Lake. How could he possibly hold all that in his head? But that's Bernie, every time. I got completely lost, but in the nicest way, by the time he came to the end.

Gudrun sat back and shook her head. "What's your IQ, Bernie?"

"I have no idea," Bernie said.

No surprise there. IQ, whatever it was, had never come up before. If I had to guess, it was probably something to do with the Porsche, specifically the mysterious part under the hood.

"That was a high IQ way of telling me your little story," Gudrun said. "Suggesting a narrative but not spelling it out. More than that — arousing the desire."

"Arousing the desire?" Bernie said.

Gudrun cocked her head to one side. "To have it spelled out, of course. So I'll spell it out. Someone — let's call him Person X — killed Wendell Nero. At some point after that, my client entered the RV, discovered the body, and stole a cell phone and a laptop, which he sold to a fence named — what was that name again?"

"Butchie Dykstra."

"I love your milieu," Gudrun said. "My client made this sale and went to bed in his landlocked boat, where you found him.

236

Person X then murdered poor Butchie, presumably in a hunt for the missing cell phone and laptop, which X had for some reason neglected to take from the RV. Conclusion: my client is innocent of the murder of Wendell Nero, and oddly enough in the absence of the cell phone and laptop, quite possibly not guilty beyond a reasonable doubt of the theft as well." She gave Bernie a direct look, at the same time stirring her drink with her fingertip. "Did I miss anything?"

"No."

"Leave anything out?"

"No."

Gudrun stopped stirring her drink, licked her fingertip. "Then surely you see the problem."

"I see lots of problems," Bernie said. "But there's enough here for you to drop the plea deal idea and go to trial."

"Nice try," Gudrun said. "Among other things that would mean putting Florian on the stand to testify about the cell phone and laptop, uncorroborated testimony that the DA would blow up before lunch time, day one. Try to imagine Florian in the witness box and a jury looking on." Gudrun rose. "With that IQ you couldn't possibly not know what I need, Bernie." There was a slight pause before she continued. "Bring me the cell phone and the laptop. Then we'll talk."

Bernie rose, too, and so did I. When he moves, I move. Things work out better that way.

"Or," Gudrun went on, "we could go out to dinner some time and not talk about any of this."

Bernie gazed at her, said nothing.

"Your call," said Gudrun.

Over at the bar, Mason was signing the check. His writing hand went still for an instant, then moved on.

EIGHTEEN

"Hoskin Phipps," Bernie said. "Typecasting people by their names is something we need to stay away from in this job — and in life, big guy — but what are the odds his family came on the *Mayflower*?"

What happens when the smartest human in the room raises his game? No one around him understands a thing. At least that was what happened to me. Other than the name Hoskin Phipps ringing the faintest of bells, I was clueless. There he was, my Bernie, not talking himself up in the slightest, steering us along with just two fingers on the wheel. Can you imagine? I gazed at him in awe. His eyes were on the road, golden in the late-afternoon light, both the road and his eyes. Were we crushing it? I thought so.

We drove through the East Valley, toward the huge wooden cowboy who stood over the Dry Gulch Steakhouse and Saloon, six-guns in both hands. They had a patio out back where the nation within was always welcome. The scraps on that patio — don't get me started. Slow down, Bernie, hit the turn signal. But he did not, and soon we were in Pottsdale, passing Livia's Friendly Coffee and More, the more part having to do with the house of ill repute in back — where the goings-on were unclear to me, although I'd formed very positive opinions of the two employees I'd met, Autumn and Tulip, both excellent patters — and pulled into an office park on the next block.

Bernie parked in front of a small adobe building and read the sign on the glass door: "Phipps Consulting." The glass was the dark-tinted kind, and just as Bernie started to open the door, a convertible driving by got reflected in the glass. Bernie whipped around and stared at the car, driven by a ponytailed woman and now turning onto a cross street and disappearing from sight.

"Was that Suzie?" he said. He gave his head a little shake. I loved when he did that and was pretty sure he'd learned it from me. "I must be losing my mind." Which was impossible — a mind that big would be found immediately. Couldn't have been Suzie, of course, since she was in London and London was far away, the distance maybe being the start of the whole problem between them. So Bernie wasn't losing his mind. It was just playing tricks on him. At that moment, something funny happened: I smelled those little yellow flowers, the kind you sometimes see on the banks of a dry wash. There were no dry washes in sight, no little yellow flowers, but the smell of those little yellow flowers reminded me of Suzie's smell. I had a thought I'd never had before, somewhat disturbing: Was my nose playing tricks on me, the same way Bernie's mind was playing tricks on him? Could that even happen? One of my back paws slipped on the floor as we entered Phipps Consulting. A paw slipping? How embarrassing! But Bernie hadn't noticed, so —

"You okay, Chet?"

How embarrassing!

We were in a small reception area — desk, file cabinets, no receptionist. Through an open door we could see a room where a man with his back to us was writing on a white board. Bernie didn't speak, or cough, or clear his throat. Sometimes when there's a chance to simply watch, that's what we do. We're really pretty good, in case you're still wondering.

All at once, the man's posture changed just the littlest bit. Right away, Bernie said,

"Hello?"

The man turned, not one of those quick turns you see from an alarmed human. "Hello?" he said, smiling a friendly smile. "Can I help you?"

He had a pinkish face, fair hair graying at the sides, wore khakis and a button-down shirt and tortoiseshell glasses, pushed up on top of his head. I've come across more than one tortoise out in the desert, harmless dudes and oh so slow. That would just kill me! Did you know that if a tortoise somehow tips over onto its back the little fella has a tough time getting back up? Bernie told me to knock that off and pronto, and what Bernie says I do, right away if possible. As for this guy in the tortoiseshell glasses, I made him out to be harmless from the get-go. Funny how the mind works.

"Hoskin Phipps?" Bernie said.

"C'est moi," said the man, losing me completely. Hoskin Phipps, yes or no? It was a simple question. At this point I picked up a scent flowing on an AC current from his direction toward us — specifically the scent of cat. Harmlessness? Did I have to rethink that already? I've never enjoyed rethinking.

"My name's Bernie Little," Bernie said. "And this is Chet."

Since we were continuing with the inter-view — if that's what this was — I assumed the smiling man was in fact Hoskin Phipps. And I was also assuming this was an inter-view. Uh-oh. Back in the time after the saguaro case — oh, the horrible saguaro case — when Bernie was in Valley Hospital and I was staying with our buddy Rick Tor-res who worked missing persons at Valley PD — some perp we'd collared said, "I as-sumed I had permission," and Rick said, "Assumed? Assume makes an ass of you and me. Know what an ass is, pal? A donkey." And that particular perp had resembled a donkey in some ways, although that's not what I'm trying to get across, which was that I'd had some experience with donkeys in my career and had no desire to be one.

"I'm a private investigator looking into the murder of Wendell Nero," Bernie went on.

"A terrible thing," said Hoskin Phipps. "I was sick when I heard the news."

"You knew him, then?"

"Not well. We weren't friends or anything of that nature, had met once or twice at conferences. But I stood — I stand — in profound admiration of his work."

"Any idea what he was working on?" Ber-nie said.

"That's no secret," said Hoskin. "Wendell was creating a hydrological summa of the Great American West during the entire Quaternary up to present day."

"Um," said Bernie. "Was that what he's been doing recently?"

"Recently and always — it was his life's work," said Hoskin. "May I ask how your question relates to the murder? Didn't I read that the murderer is in custody?"

"There's a suspect in custody, yes."

"Do I hear a but?"

How many times had that come up, people hearing a but from Bernie when there hadn't been a but? Maybe if you couldn't bring much to the table in the hearing department — a human thing, not your fault, please don't feel bad — you sometimes imagined sounds that weren't out there. That was as far as I could take this problem on my own.

"I wouldn't say that," said Bernie.

Of course not! It wouldn't have been true, and no one was truer than Bernie.

"It's just that we like to get as complete a picture of a case as we can," Bernie continued.

Hoskin nodded. "I understand that sentiment completely. It's the essence of good science." He smiled. "Sure you're not a scientist, Mr. Little?"

"Very," Bernie said. "And call me Bernie."

"May I see your business card, Bernie?" The smile stayed on Hoskin's face, broadened, if anything.

Bernie looked surprised but he went over to Hoskin and handed him our card, with Suzie's flower design.

Hoskin glanced at it and laughed. "I would have expected a pistol of some kind." He made his hand into a gun and went *"Pow pow"* right at Bernie. He laughed some more, then shook his head. "Sorry," he said. "Sometimes I get carried away. The bookish life will do that to you."

"The bookish life?" Bernie said. "Are you still at Veritan?"

Hoskin reached up, lowered his tortoise-shell glasses down over his eyes. "Completely retired from academe," he said. "But you've done your homework on me."

"Not really," Bernie said. "Your name came up."

"In what context?"

"Hydrology. I'm trying to get a handle on that aspect of Wendell's life."

"Hmm," said Hoskin. "Didn't you already ask me about that? Didn't I answer, to the best of my ability, I hope?"

"But you were both doing the same thing

in the same place — hydrological consulting here in the Valley."

"Well, the embarrassing truth is I'm just keeping my hand in. Did some surveying for the light-rail project last year, for example, but I'm really not a businessman. Plus I've spent most of my life back east."

"At Veritan."

"That's right. I haven't built a network here."

"There must be a lot of Veritan alums in the Valley."

"Oh, sure — and in every big city. Some like to socialize at the Veritan Club, over on Ponce Street, and some — like me — don't. And here's a secret. Promise not to tell. I spent my undergraduate years at Yale." He laughed again. Laughter always carries a handy breath sample, in this case revealing that although Hoskin's teeth were nice and white, there was something rotten going on.

"Your secret's safe with me," Bernie said. "What's more, I'd like to hire you."

"My goodness," Hoskin said. "To do what?"

I was with him on that. Had we ever hired anybody in our whole career? Well, yes, there'd been Vitoriana de Castilla y Leon, a famous international fashionista, whatever that was, exactly, who'd helped us with the design of our Hawaiian pants and according to Bernie was worth every penny of the home equity loan, whatever that was, the actual selling of the Hawaiian pants turning out to have been a bit of a problem, and Vitoriana herself turning out to be Bonnie Dorfman from Key West, where she probably was now if she'd served her time. But other than that we've hired nobody. Why would we? We've got me and Bernie.

"Are you familiar with Dollhouse Canyon?" Bernie said.

"Only on the map."

"I'd like you to come up there and walk us around, hydrologically speaking."

"May I ask why?"

"That's where Wendell was working when he was killed."

"I'd be happy to," said Hoskin.

"How's right now?" Bernie said.

"Perfect. And there'll be no charge." Hoskin went to a shelf where a few laptops lay in a stack. He took the top one. "Ándale."

Out in the parking lot, there was an attempt to get us all in the Porsche, me, Bernie, and Hoskin, but it just didn't work out, so Hoskin ended up following in his car. Hoskin's car was actually something of a surprise, a Porsche, in fact, and not new, although not as old as ours, and also lacking the martini glasses decoration on the front fenders. Bernie checked the rearview mirror way more than I'd ever seen him do, all the way up the West Valley freeway and onto the two-laner. Traffic thinned out as we entered the hills and then with a *ROAR* that would have made me jump, if I was the jumping type, Hoskin pulled out and zoomed past us like . . . like . . . we were slow! And that's so wrong! We're the fastest, now and forever. Nothing more irritating had ever happened in my whole life.

Bernie! But before I could even think that thought — meaning *Bernie,* although I did think it anyway — Bernie said, "Well, well," and floored it, pedal to the metal. Now we were going to show this . . . this professor! A professor, of all things. Time to teach this professor a lesson. Wow! Had I made a sort of joke? There really was no stopping us. Now we were doing some roaring of our own, wheels hardly touching the ground, which was certainly what it felt like, getting closer and closer to . . . and if not a whole lot closer, then at least somewhat. Had to be. We were the fastest. Case closed.

Hoskin's Porsche, a black one, came to the big red rock, swerved onto the dirt road, fishtailed wildly and spun off — but no. In fact, no fishtailing or spinning off, not even much of a swerve. And neither did we — no swerving, no fishtailing, no spinning, not that you'd notice, and we would certainly have shot past Hoskin in the next moment or two, but before we could, a dust cloud came down on us and we couldn't see a thing. Bernie took his foot off the pedal. That dust cloud was raised by Hoskin, of course. Cheating? You tell me.

Hoskin, parked by a lone cottonwood, was leaning on the hood of his Porsche. "What fun!" he said, as we parked beside him. Our Porsche was all dusty. His was not. We were dusty, too. I gave myself a good shake, but Bernie just didn't know how. He patted his pants a bit, and his shirt, but what about his eyebrows and his hair? They remained dusty.

"You're an excellent driver, Bernie," Hoskin said. "We'll have to do this more often."

"That would be . . . nice," said Bernie.

We walked around Dollhouse Canyon. "A classic box canyon, of course," Hoskin said, "and what is a box canyon if not a type of valley?"

I had no answer to that question. If only Hoskin had asked, "Has a javelina been by lately?" The answer to that was a big yes. You really can't miss their smell, mostly skunky but with some piggy mixed in, and this one was especially smelly. Just to be doing something, I followed the smell around the cottonwood, and toward a little jumble of rocks.

"Hydrogeologically speaking," Hoskin was saying, "we're always interested in valleys. Gravity attracts water, Bernie, meaning all water would flow to the center of the earth, if it could. But what stops it? Impermeability, that's what. Have you noticed we've got a few cottonwoods growing here?"

Bernie nodded.

"Cottonwoods are a good sign," Hoskin said. "Willows even better. It suggests, but does not prove, that we've got water somewhere down below." Hoskin flipped open his laptop. "So let's go to the map, in this case the last USGS survey, dated 1977. And what do we find?"

Bernie and Hoskin huddled over the laptop. Bernie pointed. "Is that the aquifer?"

"An aquifer, Bernie. We have more than one."

Whoa! Impossible! How many times have I heard Bernie say we've only got the one aquifer? Way way more than two times, two being the highest number I can work with, although once on an amazing day I somehow jumped from two to four. Maybe that would happen again. You can always hope and I always did.

"In this case we have what I'd call a small, perched aquifer, overlaid on a granite base at about five hundred feet," Hoskin went on. "The water down there is probably seven thousand years old — as you can see from this footnote re tritium and carbon-fourteen analysis. But the key point is the small volume. And that was in 1977. Let's take a look at that cottonwood."

They walked over to the cottonwood tree. "Note the dead branches at the top," Hoskin said. "The dead leaves." He picked at the bark. A strip came right off. He handed it to Bernie.

"The tree's dying from lack of water?" Bernie said.

"And so is that one, and those over there," said Hoskin, pointing to the other cotton-woods. "How much rain has fallen out here since 1977? Thirty inches? Forty? Whatever the number, it's not close to replenishing a small aquifer like the one we've got here."

"What about the vineyard?" Bernie said.

"Vineyard?" said Hoskin.

Bernie gestured at the steep slope at the closed end of the canyon. "Just on the other side."

"I was unaware of that," said Hoskin. "But grapes won't be growing over there much longer."

Bernie was giving Hoskin a close look, which Hoskin, snapping the laptop shut, didn't see. I went back to what I was doing, namely sticking my nose into a tiny space in the jumble of rocks, where I knew for sure that — *OUCH!*

"So what was Wendell doing out here?" Bernie said.

"Probably just what we're doing," said Hoskin. "Getting depressed about the water situation in the American desert."

I licked the end of my nose, which stung a bit. Normally that does the trick, but for some reason my tongue was dry.

NINETEEN

"Searching down deep for perched aqui-fers," Bernie said. "A pretty good metaphor for what we do, big guy. So why aren't I feeling good about the case?"

I knew the answer at once: metaphors. Don't think for a moment that I know what metaphors are exactly, or even roughly, but metaphors entering the conversation always means we're off track. Right now we hap-pened to be in the Old Town part of Potts-dale, meaning Old Town was off track. Ber-nie parked on the side of the street opposite a solid and fancy-looking pink adobe build-ing, with potted flowering plants lining broad stairs up to a huge wooden door. Then we just sat there, Bernie thinking and me feeling him think.

"Where did he learn to drive like that?" Bernie said.

I wondered who he was talking about, but I didn't wonder very hard. I reserve my best mental efforts for when we're on track. When we're off track I ease off the gas a bit. Take a tip from a pro.

Bernie laughed to himself, a quiet little laugh that's half-snort. I loved that snort part, wished he'd do it more often. "Malcolm was right about one thing." Bernie patted his pockets. That meant he wanted a cigarette, must have forgotten that he'd quit. Bernie's a champ at quitting smoking — sometimes he smokes one and throws the whole rest of the pack away. Now he gave up on the patting, took a deep breath. "That exhibition game against Veritan. It was at the old ballpark in Vero Beach. We did win and I remember. Well, not everything, but my inning, yeah." Bernie got a look in his eyes that I'd never seen and suddenly he was a college kid, at least to me. "Spring training, each of the pitchers got an inning. I started, so I had the top of the order." He rubbed his hands together, then looked at the palm of his pitching hand. "This was before the elbow problems. Nine pitches — eight heaters and then the slider. A slider, which I didn't even have, except for that one time." He pointed at the fancy old building across the street. "The Veritan Club, Chet." The look in his eyes changed and college kid Bernie vanished, just like that. "How about we go inside, check out the elite."

The elite? A new one on me, but if Bernie thought it was a good idea then I was on board, case closed. He reached for the door handle and paused to watch a taxi pull up in front of the Veritan Club. A passenger got out. It was Suzie. Bernie's heartbeat changed. I heard it happen, clear as clear.

The taxi drove off. Suzie stood on the sidewalk. She glanced one way, then the other. It was so good to see her. She looked great, standing so straight, the sun on her face, her dark hair longer now, her eyes shining and black like the countertops in our kitchen. She glanced both ways down the sidewalk, then checked her watch, put on sunglasses, and just stood there.

Bernie got out of the car. Me, too, goes without mentioning. We crossed the street. Suzie wasn't looking our way, not until we stepped onto the sidewalk.

"Bernie!" she said. "Chet!"

"Hi, Suzie," Bernie said.

Meanwhile I was saying hi myself, up close, sniffing up her smell, one of the nicest human smells I'd ever smelled, all about those little yellow flowers that grow by the dry washes, and she was bent forward and stroking my head like she'd really missed me. Well of course! I'd have missed me, too, if that makes any sense. I'd have missed me big time. Right around then was when I spotted Bernie's reflection in Suzie's sunglasses. His hands were half-raised like he was about to hug her.

Suzie straightened and raised her arms like she was going to hug him back, but that wasn't quite what happened. Instead she gripped his upper arms in her hands — diamonds flashing in the sun — and gave him a squeeze, although keeping a space between them.

"You look terrific," she said.

"Right back at you," said Bernie. "Times ten."

She grinned. "How you talk!" And then she lowered her hands. The sun again caught the diamond ring on her finger. Bernie saw it and his heartbeat changed once more. And, in his eyes, what was this? The tiniest flinch, there and gone. You'd have to know Bernie really well to catch something like that, and I did.

Suzie noticed him noticing. She took off her sunglasses, and there were those eyes of Suzie's, the real deep kind.

"He's a good man, Bernie," she said.

For a moment, I thought she was saying Bernie was a good man, true for sure, but why even bother saying it in a tight little group like this? Then I began to maybe see what was happening.

Bernie smiled, at first not a very happy smile, but then it changed and seemed a bit happy, and then it changed some more and ended up being actually happy.

"I'm happy for you," he said. "You deserve the very best."

And now Suzie did put her arms around him and gave him a hug. He hugged her back, but a brief kind of hug. Then he stepped away.

"How long are you in town?" Bernie said.

"Well, I have news on that front," said Suzie. "I'd love to tell you all about it. We'll have to meet for —"

At that moment, a long black car drove up. A uniformed driver got out and opened the door for a salt-and-pepper-haired man in a dark suit. He had a squarish face with strong features, not at all the face of someone who gets bossed around, more like the opposite. He saw Suzie and waved. She waved back.

"That's him?" said Bernie in a low voice.

"Good grief," Suzie whispered. "Don't be a dope."

The man came up, shook hands with Suzie.

"Sorry to keep you," he said. "Damn traf-fic."

"No problem," said Suzie.

The man glanced at Bernie. Maybe he was the type of human — and there were some — who didn't seem to even be aware of the nation within. Here's a strange thing: I'm extra aware of those very types! What's that all about?

"Loudon," Suzie said, "I'd like you to meet my . . . old friend, Bernie Little. Ber-nie, this is Loudon DeBrusk."

Loudon DeBrusk's eyes — the very light blue kind that remind me of the sky when night is barely gone — seemed to shift for the briefest instant. He and Bernie shook hands.

"Nice meeting you," DeBrusk said.

Bernie nodded. He has many nods. This one meant nice meeting you, too. Plus a little something else I couldn't quite grasp.

DeBrusk turned to Suzie and gestured toward the big and heavy wooden door of the Veritan Club, a door with metal studs, like doors you see on some old ranch houses in these parts, except fancier.

"Shall we?" he said.

"I'll be in touch, Bernie," Suzie said, and then she and DeBrusk walked up the stairs and entered the Veritan Club. We stood on the street, Bernie gazing at the closed door, me gazing at Bernie. After what seemed like a bit too much of that, I moved closer and gave him what you might call a little push.

Bernie was very quiet. We left the Old Town part of Pottsdale, left Pottsdale totally, got into a traffic jam at Spaghetti Junction where all the freeways come together, and ended up in South Pedroia, Bernie not saying a word the whole time. It was almost like he was somewhere else. This was a bit disturbing. When you're here you're here! I sat up very straight, on high alert even though there was nothing to be alert about. It was just to remind Bernie we were here and nowhere else. Anytime now he'd be giving my head a quick scratch and I'd know he got the message. Except he did not.

We came to the street with all the self-storage places, one big garage-like building after another, all of them with many doors. Bernie parked in front of our door, pressed a button on his phone. The door slid up. Humans have lots of tricks like that. Does it make things more fun for them? I took a glance at him. He didn't seem to be having fun. We went inside and did something we hadn't done in a long time, namely check out our Hawaiian pants.

Racks of hanging Hawaiian pants. Shelves of folded Hawaiian pants. Boxes of boxed-up Hawaiian pants, stacked floor to ceiling. A beam of light came through a small high-up side window, a light beam full of swirling dust. We walked to the back where a stool stood against the wall, a single pair of Hawaiian pants draped on top, the legs slumping down to the floor. Bernie picked them up and held them against his body, like he was thinking of trying them on. *Try them on, Bernie, try them on! They'll look great!*

But he did not. Instead he folded them very carefully and was about to put them back when he noticed an open pack of cigarettes lying on the stool.

"Hey," he said, the first word he'd spoken in some time. Moments later, he was sitting on the stool, lighting up, taking that first drag, letting it out with a long, slow breath. "Pot of gold," he said. Someone else had said that very thing and not long ago. I came very close to remembering who. Chet the Jet, on fire! Or at least heating up. Smoke rose into the light beam and mixed with the dust motes up in the golden air. There's all kinds of beauty in life.

Bernie took another drag. "There's what you can control and what you can't," he said. "Which everybody knows. There's also what you think you can control but can't, which some people know. But what about the things you think you can't control but actually can? See where I'm heading with this?"

At first I did not but then from out of nowhere it came to me. We were going to burn our self-storage to the ground, let all the Hawaiian pants go up in smoke! Wow! What a brilliant idea! I did a fast trot to the door and back, just letting Bernie know I was totally on board.

"Getting antsy, big guy?"

Ants? Something about ants? There were certainly ants down under the floor, ant smell one of the most common smells around, but no ants were actually on me. In fact, that had never happened. Ants and fleas are very different, but there was no reason Bernie would know that. I cut him some slack. I'd cut all the slack in the world for Bernie.

He took one more drag, ground what was left of the cigarette under his heel, and rose. "A theory of the case, yes, we always need that," he said. "But bending facts to fit the theory?" He shook his head. "Not so fast, right, Chet?"

Not so fast? I didn't like the sound of that,

not one little bit. We walked outside, closed the door, and drove away, burning absolutely nothing to the ground. My head felt somewhat tired inside. I curled up on the shotgun seat. Bernie made a phone call. I heard some back and forth between him and Captain Stine. Whatever this was, it made no sense at all. I didn't even try. The sound was enough, more than enough. Bernie and Stine put me to sleep.

"Ride Your Butt Off," Bernie said.

I opened my eyes.

"Spin Classes, Road Racing, Mountain Biking," he went on.

I sat up, saw the Rio Vista Bridge not far away. We were parked by a storefront with a bicycle hanging over the door. Bernie was reading the sign.

"Start Feeling Good Today."

We hopped out of the car, me actually hopping. I felt good today, but I hadn't just started feeling good. When had it begun? I thought back and back but never came to the beginning of me and feeling good. Meanwhile we were on our way into Ride Your Butt Off, if that was the name of this place. True, I already felt good, but what harm could it do?

A desk stood in the entrance. Behind it

was a big, dimly lit room with a whole bunch of people pedaling stationary bikes. The bikes formed a circle around a single bike, pedaled by a sweaty woman wearing one of those mouthpiece plus earpiece things. All the bikes had screens on them, and all the bikers were glued to their screens, except for the sweaty woman who was watching the bikers and shouting, "Ramp up, ramp up, one twenty, one twenty-five, one thirty, give me your best, give it, give it!" What else? Everyone was sweating — I'd never smelled so much human sweat in one place in my life, an ocean of human sweat, really a special treat for me, but at the same time some of the faces of the riders reminded me of a perp we'd taken down long ago name of Fats Sezura, specifically how Fats's face had looked just before his heart attack. All in all, I was ready to be out of there.

A dude at the desk said, "Help you?"

"We're looking for Eva Rome," Bernie said.

He pointed to the sweaty woman leading the ride, if that's what she was doing and if a ride to nowhere could still be called a ride.

"That's her," he said. "They're almost done and her next class isn't till Wednesday. Or I can hook you up with another instructor if you like."

"We'll wait," Bernie said.

The dude looked at me.

"There's a dog on the internet who rides a bike," the dude said.

"We'll wait outside," Bernie said.

Whoa! But —

Eva Rome came outside, wiping her face with a towel. Some humans — actually very few — move like they're not touching the ground. Eva was that kind. She had a teenage body but an older face and her eyes were older still.

"You wanted to see me?" she said.

"I'm Bernie Little and this is Chet."

"Is this about the other night? You're with the police department?"

Bernie handed her our card. "We're working on a case that's probably not related to what happened to you. I just wanted to rule it out for sure."

Eva rubbed the side of her neck, very lightly. "What happened to me was the scariest thing in my whole life," she said. "You want me to tell you?"

"Please," said Bernie. How polite of him! He really is the nicest human in town.

"I was walking home after the ten p.m. class — that's our last one — when someone grabbed me from behind," Eva said. "This was at the Super Low Gas on the corner." She pointed down the street. "It was closed and this guy was really strong. He dragged me behind the station, got a knee in my back and a hand over my mouth. I couldn't move at all. A woman came up. She wore a bandanna over her face, right up to her eyes, and had a knife with a real long blade. She held it right in front of my eyes. Then she said, 'Where's Dewey?' And I said I hadn't seen him in three weeks, had no idea where he was."

"Who's Dewey?" Bernie said.

"This guy I used to know. Sort of a boyfriend. I broke it off. That's the truth and it's what I told her. She pressed the edge of the blade against my throat, right here, and said, 'Prove it.' "

"Prove that you hadn't seen him in three weeks?" Bernie said.

"Like, how do you do that?" said Eva. "But then I thought of a way. Check my phone. That's what I told her. It was in my pocket. She took it out, went through the phone. That was that."

"They let you go?" Bernie said.

"There were texts and calls from Dewey, but not for the past three weeks. The woman told me to lie facedown and not move. I lay down by a trash barrel and didn't move. I thought I heard them going away but I still didn't move. At last I got a grip and took a look. They were gone. I got up."

"Jesus," Bernie said.

"I know," said Eva.

"You told the police all this?"

"I'm not sure they believed me."

"What makes you say that?"

"Or maybe it's just that I didn't give them much to go on. You know — disappointing them."

"Did they ask you to describe the knife?"

Eva nodded. "It had a red handle."

"Did you see the face of the man?"

"No."

"What about the woman's eyes?"

"They didn't ask me that."

"But you saw them."

"Yeah."

"And?"

"They were real real smart," Eva said.

"Did you notice the color?"

She shook her head. "Just that they were real real smart. Scary smart." She thought for a moment. "Am I in danger?"

"No," said Bernie. "Not from those two."

"How do you know?"

"Because you're still here," Bernie said. "What does Dewey do?"

"For a living?" said Eva. "He takes short-cuts."

"Such as?"

"I never wanted to know the details."

"Has he done time?"

"I think so."

"What for?"

"I don't know. Nothing violent — I made sure about that."

"Why did you break up with him?"

"He was part of the old me. I've finally — finally — decided to get past the old me. I'm . . . I'm killing her off on the bike."

Bernie gave her a long look. She dabbed at her face with the towel. "What's Dewey's last name?" Bernie said.

"Vaughan."

"Do you have a picture of him?"

Eva's phone was tucked in the waistband of her tights. She took it out, tick-tacked at it with the tip of her fingernail, turned the screen so Bernie could see. Bernie went still, although not that anyone would notice, other than me.

It just so happened that I could see the screen, too. And there was my Dewey, with his surfer hair, his beachboy grin, and the little round bullet scar on his cheek. I looked forward to our next get-together.

"Did Dewey ever mention the name Wen-

267

dell Nero?" Bernie said.

"No."

"Did he ever talk about an uncle?"

"I don't think he had any uncles. He was fostered most of his childhood, going from one family to another. That's how it started, the two of us. I felt sorry for him."

"Maybe not the best foundation," Bernie said.

"I know that now," said Eva. She looked my way for the first time, gave me a quick little smile. Then she turned back to Bernie. "Do you know what they want with him?"

"No," Bernie said.

"Are you looking for him, too?"

"I wasn't. But now? Yes."

"What's he done?"

"Nothing I'm aware of. It's possible that we can end up protecting him, me and Chet. But the real reason is that he knows things we need to know."

"About what?"

"Two murders," Bernie said. "And he'll also know who attacked you the other night."

"You mean they could be arrested?"

"And put away."

Eva gazed up at the sky. A balloon had gotten loose and was rising higher and higher. "Dewey has a friend — well, maybe an associate is how to put it — down in Campo Pequeno. I've never met him."

"Do you know his name?"

"Dewey calls him Mig."

TWENTY

"Could artificial intelligence solve this case right now?" Bernie said.

I didn't think about that for even a single second. Sometimes Bernie talks in his sleep, just a bunch of words, all jumbled, not meaning anything. This was like that, except he was awake, and driving up and out of the Valley on a road I knew well. Soon would come the souvenir stand with the giant sombrero-topped flamingo, and then a nice long nap, and after that you're in Mexico.

"Or how about this?" Bernie went on. "Would an AI version of me still have Suzie? I don't mean have. That's the kind of thing I've got to stay away . . ."

His voice trailed off. It's not that I was happy about that — who wouldn't be happy, just hearing the sound of Bernie's voice? — but I wasn't exactly unhappy. Meanwhile the giant flamingo appeared in the distance.

270

I shifted around a bit, kind of circling on the shotgun seat, trying to find the perfect napping position, and while that was going on Bernie slowed down and exited onto a crossroad. We weren't headed for Mexico after all? Too bad. I had some fond memories of Mexico, starting with a chance encounter behind a cantina with one of my own kind, her name turning out to be Lola. The females of the nation within are sometimes in the mood and sometimes not. It's easy to tell. Is that how it goes in the human world? Perhaps not.

"I mean would AI me still be with Suzie," Bernie said. "But what if Suzie was AI Suzie?"

The day was taking a bad turn. We entered a dusty little town. "Campo Pequeno," Bernie said. "Coronado came through here. The Zunis weren't impressed."

So far I was with the Zunis, whoever they might be. We drove down the main street, the dusty little town being the kind with one main street and . . . and a few back streets. Was there something familiar about this place? My sleepiness vanished, just like that. I sat up straight, on high alert, a total pro ready for total pro action. The first action I thought of was biting. That was odd. Biting never came first, not even with the perpiest perps. That wasn't my MO.

A diner stood between two boarded-up buildings. One of the best things about humans is all the different kinds of restaurants they've got going. Steakhouses are the best and all-you-can-eat vegan is the worst. Somewhere in the middle are diners, which are mostly about eggs, in my experience, and I've got no complaints about eggs, but where diners really shine is in the sausage department.

We entered the diner. I didn't smell sausages or even eggs, the main aroma in this place being stale coffee. There was no one around except one apron-wearing woman at the counter, chewing gum and scrolling through her phone. Maybe not a promising start, but then I remembered that gum was important in this case! And because of me! I'd found a wad of cherry gum out back of Wendell Nero's RV and that had led us to Florian Machado, now in an orange jumpsuit, case closed! Wow! Was this what it felt like to be Bernie? He had it made in the shade! Then I thought, uh-oh, maybe he didn't know that he had it made in the shade, and after that, wham, from out of nowhere, came another troublesome thought: If the case was closed, what were we doing in this crummy diner? Did I mention the fat flies slowly circling one of those sticky flypaper strips hanging from the ceiling?

The woman looked up from her phone, raised an eyebrow. Maybe she was the strong silent type, except for the strong part, since she was on the short and roundish side.

"Coffee, please," Bernie said, "and a bowl of water for Chet, here."

The woman cracked her gum. "Gotta charge you a quarter for the water," she said.

Bernie nodded one of his nods. This nod meant yes and also sent some sort of message. Soon Bernie was sipping stale coffee and I was sipping water from a bowl with a dead fly lying on the bottom, or, on second look, maybe not quite dead. No complaints. You toughen up in a job like mine, and I was toughened up to begin with. Whoa. Just then came another memory — what was with all these memories all of a sudden? — a memory of when I was very small. Had I ever had a memory of when I was very small before? Not that I remembered, but in this memory I lay in straw in the corner of a shed, and a big man with big boots walked up and —

And lucky for me that memory broke into pieces and disappeared. Whew. Because otherwise maybe I'd have found out that I wasn't toughened up to begin with, and then what? But now we didn't have to go down that road. What a life!

Bernie took another sip, made a bit of a face, put the cup down. "Know anyone in town named Mig?" he said.

The woman turned her phone over, laid it on the counter. She had rings on every finger, and the thumbs. Not the kind of thing you see every day, although I had seen it before. We've cleared a lot of cases, me and Bernie. "Mig who?" she said.

"Just Mig is all I know," Bernie said.

"You from around here?" she said.

"The Valley."

"Thought so."

Then there was a silence, except for the buzzing flies. Was it Bernie's turn to speak? That would have been my opinion, but he kept quiet. It hit me: he was letting the flies do the talking! A new technique. But that was Bernie. Who else would even think of putting flies to work?

"Folks in this town like their privacy," the woman said at last.

"I'm the exact same way," Bernie said. "I don't want to invade Mig's privacy the slightest bit. I just want to talk to him."

The woman cracked her gum again.

"About what?"

"If I told you," Bernie said, "I'd be invading his privacy."

The woman's head went back a little. I could feel her thoughts, thoughts very unlike Bernie's, heavy and slow. "There's more than one Mig in town," she said. "I'd have to think."

"Maybe this will help." Bernie laid some money on the counter; I hoped not a lot. But this was something we had to do from time to time. Some folks think better when money changes hands, just one of the many human quirks out there. Human grooming, for example, is . . . how would you put it? A gold mine of quirks? Something like that. But no time to go into it now.

"The Mig you probably want," the woman said, sweeping the money off the counter and into an apron pocket so fast and smooth I almost missed it, "lives over on Pershing Street. There's no signs — take the last turn on the east side, last house, and you didn't hear it from me. Enjoy your day."

We drove down an unpaved and rutted back street that seemed familiar, but at the same time strangely hazy. This whole town seemed strangely hazy, even the smells. What was up with that? No answer came before we pulled into a driveway at the last house on the street, a small house with no neighbors and a shiny new pickup in the dirt driveway. The haze started to clear a little, like a breeze was stirring in my mind.

The side door of the house opened and a man came out, a short wide man. He was wearing nothing but shorts, the kind that came down almost to the ankles, and had shaving cream on his face.

"Yeah?" he said, looking at Bernie and then at me and only me.

The haze in my mind cleared completely. We got out of the car.

"We're looking for Mig," Bernie said.

"Yeah? Who's we?"

"I'm Bernie and this is —" He turned to me. "Chet?"

Uh-oh. Was I growling? Pawing at the driveway a bit? That kind of thing can happen when the mind clears and you start to get a grip on what's what. Not that I actually had a grip on what's what. It was more of a feeling. But I dialed everything down. I'm a pro, in case you've forgotten.

"Are you a cat person by any chance?" Bernie said.

What a strange question! I'd never heard Bernie even speak those words. Cat person? Had he come up with a new technique that

276

would end up working wonders in ways I couldn't yet see? That had to be it.

"Cat person, dog person, people person," said Mig.

"Everybody likes you," Bernie said.

"Damn straight."

"Except Chet, here."

"So what?" said Mig. "He's a dog."

Bernie's eyes, which had held no expression at all, now flashed Mig a look I wouldn't want flashed at me, but it was there and gone before you would have known. "But the point is you've got lots of friends," he said.

Mig raised his hands in the gesture that means *what can I do.* Then he said, "What can I do?" just in case we were slow on the uptake. Get ready for your own uptake, buddy boy. That was my thought, but I kept it totally inside, meaning the quick look Bernie shot me was about something else.

"We're interested in one of your friends in particular," Bernie said.

Then came a silence. Was Mig waiting for Bernie to speak first? If so, he was going to lose. And at last he said, "Like who?"

"Dewey Vaughan," Bernie said.

Mig's mouth opened, closed, opened again. Was it waiting for his brain to catch up? You see that in humans from time to

277

time, although never Bernie, of course.

"Dewey, huh?" said Mig. "Wouldn't call him a friend, exactly."

"What would you call him?" Bernie said.

"More like . . . an acquaintance."

"A business acquaintance?"

"Sure. A business acquaintance."

"And what sort of business are the two of you in?" Bernie said.

"You first," said Mig.

Bernie handed him our card.

"A real private eye, huh?" said Mig. "Let's hope and pray Dewey's done nothing wrong."

"I'll only know after we find him," Bernie said.

"Can't help you there," said Mig.

"Why not?"

"Don't know where he is. Why else?"

"I could think of many reasons," Bernie said. "But instead let's play pretend."

"Huh?"

"Pretend you were me, looking for Dewey. Where would you start?"

What was this? Mig being Bernie? This case was not going well.

"That's a tough one," Mig said. "How do you even start?"

"How about with the last time you saw him? Where and when?"

Mig thought about that. A tiny gleam shone in his eyes, then vanished.

"Come with me," he said. "I got something to show you."

We followed Mig around his house to a sort of wooden barn at the back, old and a bit lopsided. A padlock hung on the door. Mig took a key ring loaded with keys from his pocket and unlocked the door. We followed him inside. There were windows in the barn, all of them tarpapered over, but in the gloom I could see a couple of pickups, shiny and new like the one in the driveway.

"Stay right there for a sec," Mig said. "I'll switch on the light."

He went over to the workbench, reached up, and pressed a button on the wall.

All at once, Bernie shouted: "Chet!"

But too late. The floor fell away right out from under us.

TWENTY-ONE

Falling, falling, falling, and then: *Boom*. A soft boom. That was me landing. I'm a soft lander, as long I can get my paws under me, as I did now, no problem. There was also another boom, this one more of a *BOOM*. That was Bernie, perhaps not a soft lander, the *BOOM* being followed by an *"Ooof!"* Then came some gasps, like he was fighting for breath. Poor Bernie. He'd gotten the wind knocked out of him. The same thing happens in the nation within, so I knew the wind always comes back, which it did with Bernie, pretty quick.

"Chet? You okay?"

Totally okay, except for being down at the bottom of this hole or whatever it was. We both looked up. Yes, a hole under the floor of Mig's barn, but the floor hadn't fallen out from under us. Instead a sort of square door had opened, a door that now hung to one side of the hole. Oh, no! A trapdoor?

Once I'd heard Bernie and Rick Torres talking about what to do if you fall through a trapdoor. I'd heard but — possibly due to a Rover and Company cookie — I hadn't listened, and so was no further ahead. Not my fault but that was no help now.

It was dark and shadowy up in the barn, but darker and more shadowy down in the hole. Bernie grunted, tried to get up, grunted again, and this time rose to his feet. If he'd been taller, say as tall as one Bernie stacked on top of another Bernie — wow, one of my best ideas — then he could have reached the edge of the hole and pulled himself up. Then it hit me: Hadn't we been working on wall climbing, me and Bernie? Weren't the hard earth sides of this hole like walls? Had I ever climbed a wall this high? Maybe not, but Bernie thought I'd been doing great. "Amazing, big guy, amazing!" was what he said the last time we practiced. Who wouldn't want to hear that?

Here's how to climb a wall. First, wait for Bernie to say "Up, Chet!" Then run your very fastest straight at the wall and keep running till you reach the top. Then scarf up a bowl of steak tips from Dry Gulch Steakhouse and Saloon, ordered special. That's all there is to it! I'm sure you could do it if you tried.

Was now the time? Bernie's mouth opened. Up, Chet! was coming next, I just knew it. But before it could, I heard footsteps from above. Mig appeared at the edge of the hole. He still wore only his shorts, but he'd wiped the shaving cream off his face. That was the first thing I noticed, before the gun in his hand. Funny how the mind works.

Mig gazed down at us. Some humans have this ugly look that's close to a smile but is not about friendliness, not one little bit. Smirk, maybe? Mig was smirking, big time.

"Smart guy, huh?" he said. "How smart are you feelin' now?"

Bernie didn't answer.

Mig gestured at me with the gun. "That's my goddamn dog," he said. "Think you can just steal from me, no consequences?"

"What the hell are you talking about?" Bernie said.

"Think about it, smart guy." Mig stepped away. Then came a little squeak and the trapdoor slowly closed, thunking down in place and putting us in total darkness. I see pretty well in normal darkness, at night, for example, but I don't have much experience with total darkness.

Bernie touched my back. "No worries, Chet. We're okay."

How nice to hear that! I'd come close to being a little concerned.

I sat in the dark, thinking about nothing much. Was I hungry? No. Thirsty? No. I was okay. We were okay. Perhaps being down in this hole wasn't a perfect situation, and that smirk was very bothersome, but things could be worse. I was trying to think how things could be worse and coming up with nothing, when I heard Bernie moving around at the other side of the hole, making sounds that reminded me of digging. Digging? I listened carefully. Yes, digging for sure. Humans are good at digging with shovels, and they are really amazing diggers when they use earth-moving equipment — I have no problem admitting that — but watching them dig with their hands can be a little frustrating. Of course, I wasn't watching Bernie dig on account of not being able to see a thing. Instead I was listening to him dig, which turned out to be even more frustrating. How interesting! There's so much to learn in life. My impression is I'm making very good progress. I was thinking to myself, Good boy, Chet, when it hit me that we were down in a deep hole and yet Bernie was digging even deeper. What was up with that? I waited for the answer, and . . . and it came! He was trying to find the aquifer. Wow! Perhaps a little unusual at a time like this, but we think outside the box at the Little Detective Agency. And weren't we in a sort of box at the moment? So thinking outside of it was the way to freedom! My goodness! Do not mess with us, my friends.

The digging sounds stopped. I heard Bernie crawling my way, felt him giving me a pat. "No worries," he said in a low voice. Very nice of him to say that but totally unnecessary. We were thinking our way to freedom.

Another squeak. The trapdoor fell open with a bang, letting in some light. Mig stood at the edge of the hole again, his gun in one hand and a coil of rope in the other.

"How's life treating you?" he said.

Bernie didn't answer. Was he about to say, Up, Chet? And then I'd leap way way up there, grab Mig by the pant leg, and drag him back down in the . . . well, perhaps not that. I got a little confused.

"Here's what's gonna happen," Mig said. "I'm lowering one end of the rope. Got a clamp on it. You're clampin' it onto the dog's collar. Then I'm pulling him up. Any funny moves and I shoot the both of you. Got it?"

Bernie didn't answer.

Mig pointed the gun right at Bernie, a big gun, bigger than our .38 Special, locked in the safe at home. "You lookin' to die?" he said.

Right then I knew bad things were in store for Mig. Otherwise what kind of world were we in?

"No," Bernie said.

"Then say you got it," said Mig.

"I'm not going to clamp him by the collar." Bernie's voice was quiet and calm, but there was anger in it, too, way underneath. You had to know him to hear it, and no one knows Bernie like me. "That'll choke him."

"Like in a damaging way?" said Mig. "Investment-wise?"

Bernie's eyes got so hot at that moment, like a fire had started up inside him. "Lower the rope," he said, his voice maybe shaking the slightest bit.

Mig knelt down and lowered one end of the rope. The little light there was gleamed on the metal clamp as it came down. Bernie reached out and grabbed it. Then he took off his belt and wrapped it around my chest, tying the ends together over my back. He looked at me. Was this possible? Bernie was about to clamp the rope onto the belt and let Mig haul me up to the top? Alone?

Without him? But what would happen to Bernie, down in the hole and all on his lonesome? I backed away.

Bernie bent over me. Our faces were very close, almost touching.

"Who's a good boy?" he said, his voice low, almost a whisper.

I'm a good boy, of course. I'm *the* good boy, but —

"No worries," he said, even quieter.

But — but . . . but if Bernie says no worries, then that was that. I stood still. He clamped the rope to the belt. Then he stroked the top of my head, maybe the nicest pat he'd ever given me. He looked up.

"All set," he said, raising his voice. "Real easy now."

"You're not giving the orders," said Mig.

He started pulling on the rope. There was a lot of grunting and sweating but not much action. Slowly and jerkily, I rose into the air, first my front paws and then all of me. That felt very bad although it didn't hurt at all. But my paws belonged on the ground. How else could I take care of myself?

"We're good," Bernie said, so low this time it might have been in my head. I'm used to that. Bernie's voice is often in my head, just one of the many fine things about my life. *We're good, we're good, we're good.*

And almost before I knew it, there I was almost up top, just about level with the barn floor. Mig bent his knees for one final pull on the rope. He had a real nasty look on his face. I almost remembered something Bernie had said about a certain kind of man who only cares about winning, but before it came to me, things speeded up.

First, I heard Bernie moving around in the hole. I glanced down and saw him reaching into his pocket and taking out a rock, baseball-size but not perfectly round, in fact somewhat jagged. Then, with a real big grunt, Mig yanked the rope one more time. I came up to the top of the hole and started to swing toward him. "Ha!" he said, his eyes gleaming and a big smile starting to spread across his face, when *CRACK!* The rock hit him smack in the middle of the forehead. Crack! Smack! We have some lovely sounds in our business. Mig's eyes rolled up. He went down, and as he fell he let go of the rope. I landed softly on the barn floor. The other end of the rope dropped down into the hole.

My first inclination was to take Mig by the throat and see what came next. But where was the sport in that? Mig lay on his back, out cold. I moved to the edge of the hole and looked down. Bernie had the free end of the rope in his hands. How much things had changed out here in Mig's garage, and how quickly!

"Hey, Chet, how're we doing?" Bernie said.

My tail got going, big time.

"Going to need you to brace yourself for a few seconds."

Brace myself? What was that? Bernie pulled on the rope. Wow! Was he strong or what? I slid right to the edge of the hole. But of course I dug in and stopped right there. I'm pretty strong myself, amigo, and games of strength are what I live for, and if that's not quite true, at least I enjoy them. Now Bernie had his feet against the side of the hole and was — rappelling? Was that the word? I kind of remembered it from the day we took Charlie to the rock-climbing wall, where unluckily I'd become a little too excited and had to spend most of the time outside in the car. But did Bernie really think he could out-strength me, rappelling or no rappelling? I have this way of making myself immovable, so that's what I did. Bernie gave up right away, scrambling out of the hole and dropping the rope.

He gave me a huge hug. "Thanks, buddy." What a good loser he was!

■ ■ ■ ■

Bernie hoisted Mig onto his shoulders and carried him into the house, a very messy house, the kitchen, as so often in messy houses, being the messiest part. Just for one example, there was an open pizza box on the counter with a single slice remaining. And then it wasn't. Sausage and pepperoni, if you're interested.

Soon we'd splashed lots of nice cold water in Mig's face and got him sitting at the kitchen table, eyes open, if a little glassy.

"Wha," he said. "Wha the hell happened?"

"You know what they say about curiosity," Bernie said.

Oh, no, not the killing-the-cat thing again? What was curiosity? How do you get some? I needed to know, and had wondered about this so many times, always coming up, like now, with zilch.

"How come," Bernie said, taking a seat at the table and brushing away an ant headed for the sugar bowl, "you think Chet here is your dog?"

"Huh? You serious?" Mig winced, rubbed his forehead, checked his hand. "I'm bleedin'."

"Just superficially." Bernie went to the

counter, found a balled-up sheet of paper towel, not too dirty, and dabbed Mig's forehead.

"Ouch," said Mig.

"Mig — step it up, for god's sake. Answer the question."

"How come it's my dog?"

"He."

"Huh?"

"How come he's my dog. Chet's not an it."

"Christ. How come he's my dog? On account of I paid for him, cold hard cash."

"How much?"

"It's not the amount," Mig said. "It's the principle of the thing."

Bernie sat back. "How so?"

Mig spread his hands. "You pay for something and you don't end up owning it? What's so hard to understand?"

"Who did you pay?"

"What the hell kind of game are you playing? You already know."

Bernie was still for a moment. Then he nodded. "Dewey Vaughan?"

"Hell, yeah. I paid the bastard six hundred and fifty bucks."

"When was this?"

"I dunno. The other night."

"Tuesday night?"

"Yeah, must have been."

"Where did this happen?"

Mig gestured with his chin. "Out in the driveway."

"Dewey brought Chet here?"

Mig nodded. "We . . . negotiated. Settled on six fifty, which I handed over in good faith. Then things went haywire."

"How?"

"Goddamn dog," Mig began, and then caught the expression on Bernie's face and tried again. "Chet took off. That was on Dewey, a hundred percent. A pretty boy, nobody home upstairs, if you know the type. Then after all hell . . . in the confusion, Dewey took off, too."

"With the money?"

"You got it."

"You must have gone after him."

"Bastard's disappeared."

Bernie leaned forward. "Chet and I are a team, Mig. Understand that?"

Mig nodded.

"Chet doesn't belong to Dewey and never did. Therefore Dewey was trafficking in stolen goods — except Chet's not a good, he's a living, conscious being."

I wasn't good? Was that what Bernie had just said? I couldn't believe it, so I didn't, instead moseying over to the empty pizza box and giving its insides a lick or two.

Meanwhile Bernie was saying ". . . Dewey was trafficking in living, conscious beings. You see how serious that is?"

"Um," said Mig. He gave his forehead a gentle rub.

"Did you do much thinking on how and why Dewey had Chet in the first place?"

"I try to stay in my lane," said Mig.

"You're way way out of it now," Bernie said. He didn't raise his voice or make any threat, but Mig's eyes darted around a bit. That's a sign of fear that no one could miss.

"I got no actual info," Mig said.

"But?"

"But Dewey does some contract work from time to time."

"Who for?"

"Dunno."

Bernie gave him a look.

"Come on, man," Mig said. "I'd tell you if I knew. Why'd I want to protect Dewey?"

"How do you know about the contract work?" Bernie said.

Mig shrugged.

"Think," Bernie said, not raising his voice, more like lowering it, if anything.

Mig thought. After a while he said, "Surfing. That's how he met her."

"Met who?"

292

"The lady who pays him for the contract work. They met surfing. Maybe he was giving lessons. Something like that."

"Did he mention her name?"

"Nope. And I didn't ask."

"Where were they surfing?"

"Hawaii, maybe?" said Mig.

"Which island?"

"Hell, might not even have been Hawaii."

"Did he say anything about this lady who hires him?"

"She's a hard-ass bitch. That stuck in my mind. There are more hard-ass bitches in charge these days — ever notice that?"

"It depends on the definition," Bernie said.

Mig blinked.

"What else about her?" Bernie said.

"Nothin'," said Mig. "I'm reaching as it is."

Then we just sat there for a bit. Far far away I heard that train whistle again, somewhere in the desert.

"What are we going to do with you, Mig?" Bernie said.

"How do you mean?"

Bernie didn't answer.

Mig glanced at me, then back to Bernie. "Got an idea," he said.

"Go on," said Bernie.

"I know some guys down in Mexico," Mig said. "And Chet here's a special dog. These guys have a thing for special dogs. They pay serious money — I'm talkin' fifteen grand, maybe twenty. I could handle the transaction for you, no sweat. How does a fifty/fifty split sound?"

I had no idea what they were even talking about, but it must have sounded bad to Bernie. Had I ever seen him move so quick? In a flash he was on his feet, looming over Mig, arm drawn back like he was going to smack him, not a backhander, which I'd seen him do once or twice, but an open-handed slap across the face, which would be a first from Bernie, in my experience. His hand whipped forward, so fast it made a breeze I could hear, and Mig cried out and flinched, and Bernie slapped the hell out —

But no. At the last second, or even later, Bernie slammed on the brakes. His hand trembled in the air, so close to Mig's face there was no daylight in between. But he didn't touch him.

TWENTY-TWO

"Not all questions have answers," Bernie said. "Demand exceeds supply. Does that mean the cost goes up? And if so, is it the cost of the knowledge itself that's rising, or the cost to the well-being of the seeker?"

Bernie went silent. I was glad of that, especially if it meant his mind was taking a little rest. He'd been asking so many questions lately. Not when we were getting the 411 from witnesses — that was business as usual — but in times like this, on the road, just the two of us. And it wasn't just how many questions, but how hard they were. The cost of knowledge? Good grief.

"But," he went on, patting his pockets and finding no cigarettes, "here are three that must have concrete, findable answers. One: Where is Dewey? Two: Who is the quote hard-ass bitch who employs him? Three: Who is looking for him — besides us, I mean?" He glanced my way and gave me a look. I gave him a look back. "And that leads to all the subquestions: Did Dewey break into Bo's room at the hospice and . . . kidnap you? How the hell could he have managed that?"

What was this? Me kidnapped? That didn't make a whole lot of sense. Meanwhile we seemed to be driving along a road that bordered a vineyard. I tried to settle into the world of smells and smells alone, a very interesting world where . . . whoa! Where all the questions have answers! What a thought! I hoped no more like it came around anytime soon.

"But somehow he did manage it," Bernie went on. "Did he have help? From the quote hard-ass bitch, maybe? Was he working for her? What would her reason have been?" He gave me an elbow, not at all hard, the way good buddies do. "A lot of loose strings to pull on, huh? Better than having none."

We were good buddies, me and Bernie, and also more than that. But there were no loose strings in the Porsche, or any strings at all, for that matter. I hoped he wouldn't be too disappointed. At the same time I had the strange feeling I already knew the answers to some of his questions. Me, Chet! Maybe they would come to me. In the meantime, I let myself get lost in the sweet

sweet smell of grapes under a hot sun and was even considering a brief nap when Bernie pulled over to the side of the road.

A gentle hill sloped down from the roadside, planted with rows of vines. Off in the distance on the valley floor stood a few adobe buildings. Had I seen all this before, but from a different angle? Bernie turned and gave me the quiet sign, finger across his lips. I loved the quiet sign, hadn't seen it in way too long.

We got out of the car. No way you would have heard us if you'd been there. Well, no way you'd have heard me. A few rows over — oh, those smells so lovely, if I hadn't been a total pro I might have had trouble concentrating on the job — a man knelt on the ground, eyes closed and hands pressed together in front of his chest, a sweat-stained cowboy hat lying beside him. Some humans prayed from time to time. This was how they did it. As to what it was all about, I wasn't sure. None of the humans I knew well did any praying — not Suzie, Eliza, Charlie, Leda, Malcolm, Rick Torres, Captain Stine — although more than one of our perps had sort of . . . prayed to Bernie, falling to their knees, pressing their hands together, and saying, "C'mon, man, cut me a break." Whoa! So maybe I did know what prayer was about: getting cut a break. Yes? No? Maybe? I guess I really didn't know. But I've left out something important: I'd once seen Bernie pray.

This was back on the horrible broom closet case, the only missing-kid case we didn't solve. Well, we did solve it, but too late. The little girl's name was Gail. We were on our way, pedal to the metal, bringing the wind, the night moonless but full of stars, both of us hunched over, when Bernie took his hands off the wheel, pressed them together in front of his chest and said, "Please don't let us be late."

I didn't know who he was talking to and in the end we were late. Later we took care of justice on our own. There. That was all I knew about prayer.

This old praying man, dressed like a field worker in dusty denims, was someone we knew. Last time he'd been real angry at us, maybe because Bernie had eaten one of his grapes. Whoa! Was that a clue? Hadn't I heard Bernie say clues were important in my business? Yes! And now, I, Chet the Jet, had come up with a clue all by myself! Not only that, but I knew exactly how to put this clue in action. The time had come for me to eat a grape or two myself. I was sizing up a big purply cluster hanging from the nearest vine, when the old man, Diego Torrez, if I was remembering right, opened his eyes. He saw us, looked alarmed, then confused, and finally angry.

"Praying for rain?" Bernie said, his voice gentle.

Diego gazed at Bernie in silence. Then he nodded a small nod, hardly any movement at all. "You a pastor?" he said.

Bernie shook his head.

"But I've seen you before. In church, maybe?"

"No, sir," Bernie said. "I'm the one you caught eating your grapes."

Diego gave Bernie a closer look. "Now why'd you go and do a thing like that?"

"I guess I was trying to educate myself," Bernie said.

"About what?"

"Mourvèdre, it turns out."

"You know something about Mourvèdre?" Diego started to get up, had some trouble. Bernie gave him a hand.

"Not really."

Diego faced Bernie. A bowlegged old man, maybe trembling a bit. I liked him. "But you've drunk some?"

"Yes."

"Such as?"

"Turkey Flat, for one," Bernie said.

"Goddamn Aussies," said Diego. "Tried mine?"

"Yes."

"And?"

"I liked it."

"Liked it? How's that going to help me? What was your impression, man? How did it strike you?"

"I don't know much about wine language."

"Screw wine language! Wine language has scared off more potential drinkers than you can shake a stick at."

Sticks were in the conversation? A welcome development. I perked up.

"Want a better starting point?" Diego was saying. "All wine is masculine, feminine, or a mix. So what's Mourvèdre?"

"On the masculine side," said Bernie.

"There you go." Diego tilted his head sideways, like he was trying to see Bernie in a new way. Then he reached out to one of the grape clusters, plucked a grape and handed it to Bernie. "Try this."

"You're sure?"

"It's mine," said Diego. "If I want to give it away I can give it away." He put his hand to his chest. "Mine, plus the sun's and the earth's," he added.

Bernie put the grape in his mouth. What

about me? Was I getting a grape? It didn't look that way. We were partners, me and Bernie, perhaps something Diego wasn't clear on.

"Chew slowly," he said.

Bernie chewed slowly.

"Taste," said Diego.

Hello? Couldn't I chew slowly? Couldn't I taste? Yes to both, with the possible exception of the one about chewing slowly. I began to think that I actually wasn't going to be included in this grape tasting. Fine. No problemo. I moved down the row a bit and marked a perfectly placed cluster of grapes, for no particular reason.

"Well?" Diego said.

Bernie swallowed. "The truth is it's maybe not much of an eating grape."

"Of course not! It's the raw material, for god's sake. What else?"

"I'm not sure I can really —"

"What about juicy? Is it juicy?"

"Yeah," Bernie said. "Juicy for sure."

"You got that right," Diego said. He toed the hard ground with his dusty boot. "Juicy as ever. Maybe even more so. But how is that possible?"

"I don't understand," Bernie said.

"Eighty percent of an average grape is water and these are higher than that. So what's going on?"

"Are you talking about the lack of rain?"

"Not just that," said Diego. "Ever heard of aquifers?"

Bernie nodded.

"We got an aquifer right under our feet," Diego said. "Been feeding vines up here for centuries. And now it's drying up, squeezed out like a sponge. So how come my grapes are so juicy?"

"How do you know the aquifer's drying up?" Bernie said.

"Seen the report," said Diego.

"What report?"

"Scientific report on the aquifer."

"Who prepared it?"

"Couldn't tell you," Diego said. "But it's been kickin' around for a few years." He gazed over the vineyard. "And I'm an old man, so these decisions aren't up to me. Worse thing you can do — try to dictate what happens after you go. But . . . but that's not the same as prayin', is it?" He turned to Bernie. "So yes, sir, I'm praying for rain."

He looked up at the sky, clear blue, not a cloud. But I actually didn't need to see. I can sort of feel when rain is coming. There wasn't going to be a single drop, not for quite some time.

"What decisions are you talking about?" Bernie said.

Diego spread his arms real wide, like he was getting ready to hold something big. "Gila Wines," he said. "What to do with it, the whole future."

"But what's the future if the water's drying up?" Bernie said.

Diego shot him an angry look. "You been talking to my son?"

"No," Bernie said. "Well, yes, but not about this. He invited me to the monthly tasting."

Diego stuck out his chin. "Slippery answer if I ever heard one. You a slippery customer, by any chance — what's your name again?"

"Bernie Little. And this is . . ."

He looked for me at his side, but as I've already mentioned I'd wandered off slightly and now it seemed I'd wandered some more and was now . . . marking another grape cluster, meaning I'd saved a spurt or two for marking purposes without even having to think about it. So nice when the body takes over sometimes and does the thinking for you.

". . . Chet," Bernie finished up.

Diego gazed at me. I gazed back, not much else I could do, what with one back leg raised up like it was.

"Sorry," Bernie said, "he —"

"Nothing to apologize for," said Diego. "Tell you a secret. The night before every harvest I come out here by myself and piss on a vine. For luck, you understand. My daddy did the same thing, and his daddy before him. It's a family tradition."

What a great family! I started feeling very good about the case. As for what it was about, exactly, those details would come to me soon, or later, or not at all. But the important thing was that we were cooking, me and Bernie.

"You got any family yourself?" Diego said.

"A son," said Bernie.

"How old?"

"Almost seven."

"The easy days. My Jimmy's forty-five. The not-so-easy days."

"You're having disagreements about the winery?"

Diego's eyebrows, white and shaggy, rose. "How'd you know that?"

"You pretty much told me."

"I did?" Diego's eyes got an inward look. He took a deep breath. "We got an offer to sell out. Not a bad offer. Decent, in fact. Jimmy wants to take it. Makes sense, I can see that, with the aquifer being squeezed dry."

"Who's the buyer?"

He shrugged. "Some outfit. Swiss, maybe. Can't remember the name."

"But isn't there some sort of discovery attached to the sale?" Bernie said.

"Sure," Diego said. "We showed them the report. They didn't blink an eye. Who knows? Maybe they want a tax loss. Maybe they're wine hobby types. Jimmy says who cares."

"But it's hard to let go," Bernie said.

"Not just that. The thing is . . . Bernie, was it?"

"Yup."

"The thing is, Bernie, the grapes are so juicy. That's been bothering me. I even mentioned it to Wendy."

"Who's Wendy?"

"An old friend from grade school. Haven't kept up at all, but when you go way back like that there's always a connection. So I looked him up."

"Wendy's a he?" Bernie said.

"Nickname for Wendell — what the kids used to call him. Wendell Nero — he went into hydrology. I only learned that recently. Bottom line: we talked and he seemed interested, interested enough to start looking into things in Dollhouse Canyon, just over the rise. Then a terrible thing happened

— maybe you heard about it?"

"Tell me," Bernie said.

"He got murdered in an armed robbery," said Diego. "They caught the bastard, thank god. I felt so bad."

"Why?"

"Because he was there on account of me, doing a favor."

"You're not responsible," Bernie said. "Unless you were involved in the murder."

Little splotches appeared on Diego's face. "What the hell? Who are you anyway, asking all these questions?"

Bernie handed him our card. Diego held it at arm's length and peered at it. "What's it say?"

This was interesting. Most grown-up humans can read, in my experience. Was Diego trying to pull a fast one? I moved closer and kept an eye on him. Meanwhile Bernie went into some long explanation, not so easy to follow.

". . . asked me to meet him the night before," he was saying. "Any idea why?"

"No," said Diego, now calming down.

"Who knew you had been in contact with Wendell?" Bernie said.

"Nobody."

"Not Jimmy?"

"Kept it under my hat. No point in stirring things up prematurely."

"What exactly was Wendell doing in Dollhouse Canyon?"

"He didn't tell me."

Bernie studied the rise that led over to Dollhouse Canyon. I saw movement up there, possibly a goat. Yes, a goat for sure. Actually a few, including a little one. I could head on up there and try to do some herding. Or not, goats and herding being the kind of combo it was.

"You keep goats up here?" Bernie said.

"Some," said Diego.

A cloud passed over the sun. The goats bounded away and out of sight.

"I want you to keep your hat on about this conversation," Bernie said.

"Why?" said Diego.

"Because of the grapes," Bernie told him.

"Their juiciness?"

Bernie nodded, one of those nods that was all about agreement. The only problem was Diego's hat, not on his head but still lying on the ground. *Pick it up, Diego. Put it on. Get with the program.* But he did not, instead just stood there watching as we walked back to the car and drove away.

TWENTY-THREE

"Do you realize," Bernie said, as we crossed the Rio Vista Bridge and took the exit that meant we were headed home, "that someday — and probably soon — every single word spoken by everyone at any time will be recorded and preserved?"

Oh, no. Poor Bernie. This kind of thing was happening to him more and more. Was it about the case? Hadn't we solved it, what with Florian Machado locked up and all? Was there some other case I didn't know about? Ah. I sat up straight, ready for anything, especially action and lots of it.

"A terrible prospect," he went on, as we turned onto Mesquite Road, where right away the smell of me was in the air, faint but there, "except it would be useful at times. For example, did Hoskin Phipps really tell us he was unaware that there were vineyards just east of Dollhouse Canyon when he himself had prepared a hydrological study of Gila Wines for Malcolm and his buddies? I'd like to dial into — what would you call it? Big Brother's Spoken Record Control? And just hear Hoskin's exact —"

The phone buzzed. I was very happy to hear it. Whatever came next had to be easier on the brain.

"Bernie?"

Oh, good. It was Suzie. There was so much to like about her, including the fact that she was always easy on the brain, or at least my brain.

"Hi, Suzie," Bernie said. Just his normal voice saying a very normal thing, but all at once I saw the flash of the diamond ring on her finger. Hey! I realized my eyes were closed! How do you like that? It just goes to show you can give your eyes a nice break from time to time and still stay in the picture — if you have a nose and ears like mine. Which you most certainly do not, so forget this part.

"You busy at the moment?" Suzie said.

"Well . . ."

"I'd like to see you. But if now's no good how about —"

"Now's okay," Bernie said. "Or good. Okay or good or . . ."

There was a silence. Silence on the phone can be stronger than silence not on the phone, if that makes sense. This was one of those strong silences.

"Do you know Mudville?" Suzie said.

"Sure."

"Meet in an hour?"

"All right."

They clicked off, click click.

Bernie turned to me. "Mudville? We never went there, not once." We drove home. Bernie showered and changed — very unusual in the middle of the day — and we got back in the car. "Is that the point?" he said.

Poor Bernie. Maybe we should go deep in the canyon and shoot spinning dimes out of the sky. That was the only fix I could think of.

Mudville turned out to be a bar that was all about baseball! Why had I never been here before? Baseball was my favorite game, the ball itself being the most interesting of all balls, so fascinating when you get inside, which is why you hear humans talking about inside baseball, although I've seen a human actually chewing on a baseball only once or twice. The lacrosse ball is second, by the way, with mouth feel like no other. But back to Mudville, with its baseball photos and baseball bats all over the walls, plus old beat-up baseballs in plastic display cases —

one glance told me those display cases would be no problemo! — plus flags and banners and even a real batting cage, although no one was in there taking hacks at the moment.

Suzie sat at a table by the window overlooking the patio, empty on account of the heat. She smiled as she saw us coming. Suzie! I'd missed her. When I've been missing somebody I like to give them a big hello. And if her drink got spilled it was only water, and the waiter mopped it all up lickety-split.

"He hasn't changed," Suzie said when we were all sitting in our places, Suzie on one side of the table, Bernie on the other, and me between the table and the wall, a cozy but comfortable spot that "would keep him out of trouble," as Bernie may or may not have said.

"Maybe he's just gotten more," Bernie said.

"Like more of everything?" said Suzie.

"Yeah."

Suzie laughed. Bernie smiled. The thought of whoever they were talking about seemed to make them happy. I wondered who it was.

The waiter came back, gave me an odd sort of look and took the orders: beer for Bernie and Suzie, water for me. As the waiter walked away, back turned to us and at some distance, he muttered something under his breath. I hear all those under-the-breath mutterings, just so you know. "Spill it right on the floor for him or can he handle a bowl?" was the waiter's actual muttering, the meaning not clear to me.

Suzie looked around, got a very pleased expression on her face.

"What?" Bernie said.

"It's so American," she said. "That's why I wanted to come here."

Weren't we all Americans — me, Bernie, Suzie? I didn't get it.

"You, uh, miss being here?" Bernie said.

"For sure," said Suzie. "It's not that I don't like London. That old line about whoever's tired of London is tired of life is true, Bernie, although I'm really starting to hate nifty little sayings like that."

Bernie laughed. "And the people who make them up?" he said.

Now Suzie laughed, too. This was nice. Would we soon be going home for one of our little lie downs, me by the front door, Bernie and Suzie in Bernie's bedroom? That was my guess.

The drinks came, the waiter placing my bowl on the floor, just out of reach. A moth was floating in my water. The waiter gave me a look. Did he think I'd be bothered by a moth in my water? He had a lot to learn about Chet the Jet. I gave him a look back.

Bernie and Suzie clinked glasses and drank.

"How are you doing, Bernie?"

"No complaints."

"What are you working on?"

"It's complicated, but basically a murder case that wants to stay open even though we closed it."

"Tell me more."

"First you," Bernie said. "How long are you here for?"

"Quite some time," said Suzie. "Semi-permanently, you might say."

Bernie put down his glass. "You're on assignment?"

"Kind of. But not for the *Post.* I resigned."

"Whoa!" Bernie said.

My reaction was the same as his, and not for the first time. Suzie was a reporter, back when we first met her for the *Valley Tribune,* and then with the *Washington Post,* a real big deal, Bernie said, but it meant she had to live in Washington — where we once paid her a visit and got all involved in a strange case about a bird that actually turned out to be a drone, my first experience with drones and last, I hope — and later they moved her to London, far far away and kind of upsetting for me and Bernie, and now? Here she was? Back in the Valley? So complicated, and there was a real good chance I'd gotten it wrong.

Humans get a bit flushed when they're excited about something. I saw that flush on Suzie's cheeks. "I liked working for the *Post* and they treated me well, but more and more I got the feeling I was coming in at the end of something and I'm more interested in whatever's next."

"Like a Pony Express rider on the day they're laying down the first rails?" Bernie said.

"Oh, Bernie, that's perfect!" Suzie said.

Perfect? With ponies involved? Weren't ponies a kind of horse? I've had bad luck with horses, prima donnas each and every one.

Now Bernie flushed, too. He took a sip of beer, maybe more of a gulp. "So what's your railroad train?"

"We're still in the blueprint stage, but it's all about the marriage between a professional, well-funded, and technologically sophisticated platform and the spirit of citizen journalism."

"What's the spirit of citizen journalism?" Bernie said.

"Uncorrupted, unherdable, dogged," Suzie said.

Dogged? Right then I knew that Suzie was going to be a huge success.

"And," Bernie said, "who is we?"

"I was coming to that," Suzie said. She sat up straight, put her hands on the table. "There's a partner. His name is Jacques Smallian. He's a half-French, half-American investor."

Bernie thought for a moment or two. "He's the well-funded platform and you're the spirit?"

"No." Suzie frowned. "I wouldn't say that at all."

"My fault," Bernie said. "I didn't mean it to come out like that."

"You didn't?"

Bernie laughed. "I guess I did."

Suzie laughed, too. What was funny? I didn't know. They stopped laughing, each took a sip of beer.

"When's the wedding?" Bernie said.

"Next month," said Suzie. "Just a small wedding, maybe in that little garden at Rancho Grande. Jacques's out looking at houses right now, but he's coming here to meet you, if that's all right."

"Meet me why?" Bernie said.

"Because you're the most important person in my life," said Suzie.

"After him," said Bernie.

Suzie nodded.

"Well," Bernie said, followed by "uh" and then "um," and finally, "could be worse."

"Oh, Bernie." Suzie smiled and shook her head. The waiter returned, took Bernie's empty glass.

"Another?" he said.

"Make it bourbon," Bernie told him. The waiter went off and Bernie turned to Suzie. "You're going to be living here?"

"Our beat's the American West," Suzie said. "Everything about it."

"Jacques's from here?"

"He was born in Austin. His dad was American but his mom's French and he grew up mostly in France, except for college. He actually played baseball, just like you."

"What college?"

"Cal Tech."

"They have baseball?"

"That's not very nice," Suzie said, but she was laughing as she spoke.

That was when a man came up to our table and put his hand on her shoulder. Suzie turned to him and her face just lit up. No one could have missed it and Bernie didn't.

"What's so funny?" the man said.

"Jacques," said Suzie, "I want you to meet Bernie. He was just registering his surprise that Cal Tech has a baseball team."

"Thank god they do," Jacques said. "I wouldn't have gotten on the roster anyplace else."

Bernie rose. He and Jacques shook hands. Hey! Their hands looked kind of alike. What was up with that? Jacques's hand was a bit smaller, and the knuckles weren't swollen like Bernie's — meaning . . . meaning . . . meaning he didn't have Bernie's sweet uppercut. Wow! I'd figured out a meaning, and all by myself. But no time to pat myself on the back now — something I actually can't do although it sure would be nice — because the point I was trying to make was about the shape of their hands being pretty much identical. And not only that! While Jacques was a bit smaller, they seemed to have the same body type, plus there was a lot of similarity in their faces. Even their noses — although Jacques's didn't seem to have been broken much, if at all, and also wasn't quite the size of Bernie's — looked alike. But the kicker was their smells. I'd never come across a man who came close to smelling like Bernie, but Jacques did, if a little less powerfully, perhaps, and certainly not as strong on the funky side. So much to think about. I didn't even know where to start, and before I could, Jacques was turning to me.

"And this must be Chet," he said, squatting down in front of me so we were at head level. "Heard a lot about you, big guy."

Whoa. No one called me big guy except for Bernie. Plus wasn't this dude Suzie's boyfriend? Didn't Bernie want to be Suzie's boyfriend again? And here he was, this new boyfriend dude, his face so close I could bite it right off.

Oh, no! What a terrible thought! I got busy unthinking it and pronto, but wasn't quite finished when Jacques said, "Will he let me pat him?"

No way! Absolutely not! Out of the question!

"Sure," said Suzie. "That's one of his things."

Oh, really? Getting patted by random strangers was one of my things? What an outrageous suggestion! The fact is I'm extremely picky about who . . .

Around then was when I realized that Jacques was giving me a nice pat, and perhaps had been patting me for some time. He turned out to be pretty good at it! How about moving on to the spot between my ears and — oh, my, he already had. He'd found that special spot. Try digging in your fingers and — and . . . and just like that. Well, well. Perfecto.

Yikes. Perfecto? Impossible. Bernie was perfecto. This dude — important to get the name right, bear it in mind — this dude Jacques couldn't be as good as Bernie. That was off the table. What he could be was second best. That was on the table.

"Look at that tail," Jacques said.

"I think he likes you," said Suzie.

Bernie laughed a very small laugh. My tail dialed it down, all on its own.

Not long after that came more drinks and baseball talk, and the next thing I knew Bernie and Jacques had stepped into the cage and were fiddling with the dials on the pitching machine.

"Where should we start?" Bernie said.

"Seventy-five?" said Jacques.

"Five cuts each?"

"Sure."

"Keep score?"

"Sounds good."

"Hey, Suzie, come over here," Bernie said. "You keep score. Anything that looks like a hit counts one. Fouls count zero."

"Swings and misses are negative one?"

said Jacques.

"You bet," Bernie said. "This is America."

"Oh for god's sake!" said Suzie.

But Jacques thought whatever Bernie had said was funny and laughed and laughed. Then they started taking their cuts. *Whack whack whack!* How exciting! I wanted to be in that cage so bad, chasing those balls around and —

"Chet?"

Oops. Did I seem to be standing up, front paws on the cage? In the air hung the sound of recent barking, perhaps coming from the parking lot outside. I went and sat beside Suzie. You wouldn't have noticed me.

Whack! Whack! Whack! They turned the machine up to eighty, eighty-five, ninety, numbers far beyond two, or four, the number that comes after two, which I'd recently learned when Bernie happened to get down on all fours. These codes can be cracked, my friends! Never lose hope.

But the important thing was the blur of those baseballs and the whacks of the bats and the laughter of Bernie and Jacques. Two guys having fun is always a nice sight. Up went the dial to ninety-five. Jacques whiffed on all his pitches. Bernie hit every one of his. What a sweet swing! It reminded me of his uppercut. Hey! I'd learned something new about Bernie.

"Wow," Jacques said. "Can you handle one hundred?"

"Nah," said Bernie, and switched off the machine. They shook hands again. This handshake was different from their first one, hard to explain how. Did it mean something? That was as far as I could take it on my own.

Back in the car, Bernie was in a real good mood. He didn't say anything, had no particular expression on his face. I could just feel it, like he'd gotten lighter inside, could just unbuckle his seat belt and float up into the sky. Although ignore the seat belt part since we didn't have seat belts in the Porsche, not if we meant seat belts that worked. But anyone could have seat belts that worked. Not everyone could have beautifully painted martini glasses — Nixon Panero of Nixon's Championship Autobody at his very best — on the fenders. I was feeling very cheerful about . . . well, pretty much everything, when I began to sense a change in Bernie's mood, a darkening, none of it on the outside but I knew.

We sat at a red light. "I guess it's not so bad," he said. "In the context of . . ." He took a deep breath, let it out slow. "Must've been the star of the team at Cal Tech. Can't help but . . ."

He took another deep breath. The light turned green.

"Do we just blunder around stupidly until we're done?" he said.

Someone honked an angry honk. I was kind of with them, except for the angry part. We moved on, and were soon in Pottsdale, zipping by Livia's Friendly Coffee and More.

"Work is the answer, big guy," Bernie said. "Let's start with the little blip in Hoskin's story."

We came to the small adobe building with the tinted windows. Hoskin Phipps's shiny new black Porsche sat outside. Bernie slowed down, almost pulled over, then kept going, hung a U-ee, and parked on the other side of the street, a little way down.

This was called sitting on somebody, in this case Hoskin, who might have fooled himself into thinking he'd beaten us in a car race, an impossibility, of course. Sitting on dudes was one of our specialties at the Little Detective Agency. Sometimes you had to sit forever and ever, but at other times —

The door to Hoskin's office opened and out he came. But not alone. There was another dude with him, a salt-and-pepper-haired dude in a dark suit, with the face some men get after years of bossing around others. Hey! Hadn't I seen him before? Outside that club with the studded wooden door? Meeting Suzie? Wow! Was I on fire or what?

They got in Hoskin's Porsche and drove away. After them, Bernie! Floor it! Burn rubber! Make them eat our dust!

But we just sat there. Bernie got on the phone.

"Suzie?"

"Oh, hi, Bernie, that was so much —"

"Who is Loudon DeBrusk?"

"Loudon? I don't understand. He's not a friend or anything like —"

"But who is he?"

"Bernie? Is something wrong?"

Bernie came close to raising his voice. "Just tell me."

"Loudon DeBrusk is a financial manager. He runs the Veritan University Endowment Fund."

"What's that?"

"All wealthy colleges and universities are sitting on piles of money, which they invest, with all kinds of tax advantages. Veritan's is one of the biggest — one hundred billion dollars and rising."

"You're doing a story on endowment

funds?" Bernie said.

"Partly."

"Veritan's in particular?"

"Partly."

Silence from Bernie.

"Well, mostly," Suzie went on. "Sorry to be so vague, Bernie. Too soon to talk about it, that's all."

"Uh-huh," said Bernie.

"But what's your interest in Loudon?" she said.

"Too soon to talk about it," said Bernie. He turned the key and pulled onto the street.

"Oh, please don't —" Suzie began, but then the phone did one of those fadeouts. "Bernie? I'm losing you." And then there was just fuzziness, more fadeouts, and silence.

TWENTY-FOUR

Late that night while we were sleeping —
Bernie in his bed, and me by the front door
where I can keep a nose on things, if that
makes any sense, and I hope it does since
keeping a nose on things has worked very
well for me my whole life so far — the
phone rang. Late-night phone calls happen
sometimes in our business. It's the same
ring but it doesn't sound the same as the
ring at any other time. I trotted down the
hall and into Bernie's room. He was sitting
up in bed, moonlight gleaming on his eyes
and the phone in his hand.

"Hello," Bernie said.

"This Bernie Little the PI?" said a man
on the other end. Here's something you
should know about me: I can usually hear
the other end of a phone call whether it's
on speaker or, like now, not on speaker.

"Who's this?" Bernie said, maybe asking a
question he already knew the answer to. I

sure did.

"Name's Dewey."

Bernie said nothing, just swung around and got his feet on the floor.

"We met," Dewey said. "Over at the college, kind of a surprise at the time. I was Uncle Wendell's nephew."

"And now who are you?" Bernie said.

"Dewey. I already told you."

"But in what role, Dewey? That's the question."

"Role? Like, um . . ."

"Have you and Mig kissed and made up?" Bernie said. "Let's start there."

"Huh? What do you know about Mig?"

"Wrong answer," Bernie said.

Silence on Dewey's end. Bernie rose, headed down the hall and into our office, where we've got a rug I love. It has an elephant pattern. Once we'd had a case involving a real elephant, name of Peanut. She's never been in the house, of course — what a nightmare that would have been — but ever since that case our office smelled of elephant. How do you like them apples? As for apples, Bernie and I eat them together, he taking care of the outer part and me the cores.

Dewey spoke at last. "How come you're making all this trouble?" he said. "I'm trying to do a deal."

"What kind of deal?"

"I've got something you want and I'll listen to offers."

Cradling the phone with his chin and shoulder — perhaps a difficult move and never one that shows the human face to best advantage, in my opinion — Bernie removed the waterfall painting from the wall and set it on the floor.

"What is it you've got?" he said.

Behind the waterfall painting is the safe. Bernie spun the dial and took out the .38 Special. What a nice sight! Hadn't seen the .38 Special in way too long. Was there some way Bernie could shoot Dewey over the phone? Whoa! What a strange thought, and totally impossible, I supposed, although could you ever count Bernie out on anything? There's only one answer.

"Something with your name on it," Dewey said.

"The page you cut out of Wendell Nero's appointment book?" Bernie said.

"Uh, yeah. How'd you know that?"

"What do you want for it?"

Dewey laughed one of those little laughs possibly called a chuckle. "How much is it worth to you?"

"That depends," Bernie said. "How many

players are involved?"

"Players?"

"Have you got partners, Dewey?"

"You talking about Mig again? Him and me are done — which you'd know if you really knew anything."

"What about the hard-ass bitch?"

"Who the hell are you talking about?"

"The woman who hires you for contract work."

Dewey went silent. We left the office, went back to the bedroom. Bernie laid the .38 Special on his pillow — a sight that bothered me for some reason — then pulled on a pair of jeans and tucked the gun in his waistband. I felt much better.

"What do you know about her?" Dewey said.

"Not much," said Bernie. "Who is she?"

Another silence, not as long, but long enough for Bernie to slide his feet into sneakers, new ones I couldn't even smell, at least not from outside the house.

"You don't know?" Dewey said.

"Why would I be asking?"

"If it was a trap, that's why," said Dewey. "And you were working for her."

"You're not making much sense," Bernie said.

"No? Then how's this? You can have her

name, too, as well as the appointment thing — a twofer. That's the kind of guy I am. Basically."

"What's the number?" Bernie said.

"Let's make it a low low low ten K," said Dewey.

"Five," Bernie said.

Ten K? Five? Low low low? All of it puzzling. I settled on the low low low part, which went best with our finances. Bernie could be a very good negotiator, a fact maybe not widely known.

"Nine five," said Dewey. "Final price."

"I need proof you've got the page."

"Why else would I go to all this trouble?"

"Do we have time for all the possible answers?" Bernie said. "Take a picture of the page and send it."

"Think I'm stupid? If I do that, you wouldn't need the page!"

For a moment I thought Bernie would smile, but he did not, didn't even come close. "Crop it," he said.

"And then we're on for nine five?"

"If the picture looks right."

They clicked off. Bernie finished getting dressed. "Drink some water, big guy."

I have many water bowls around the house. I chose the one in the front hall, the biggest and also usually the coolest, what with the tiny breeze always coming through the crack under the door. Then we went out and sat in the car.

Ping!

Bernie checked his phone. He held it up, eyeing the screen this way and that. I saw what appeared to be a sheet of paper with writing at the top and the back of a man's hand resting on the bottom, the writing disappearing under his thumb. " 'A.M.,' " Bernie read. " 'Bernie Little, friend of the Rusks, re Little C and Big C' something or other. The next word starts with 'a.' " Bernie turned to me. "A is for aggravating, big guy."

Uh-oh. A tricky one. I tried to get my head around this whole new thing but it kept kind of sidestepping me, and then it was gone completely, except for the *big guy* part. So we were good to go!

Bernie peered more closely. "What's this between Dewey's fingers?"

Whoa! Those were Dewey's fingers? That was Dewey's hand? Bernie had figured that out all by himself? At that moment I knew one thing for sure: we were going to be rich. Maybe not soon, but one day. What a great feeling!

"It kind of looks like the top of a cup or something like that, and then the top of

something next to it, like a spout or . . ."
He flipped open the glove box, found a crumpled envelope and a pen, started in on a drawing, greenish in the glove box light. The phone rang.

"Well?" said Dewey.

"It's a deal," Bernie said. "How about we meet in Dollhouse Canyon?"

"Where's that?" Dewey said.

Bernie's eyes shifted toward me, like he was including me in something. I had no idea what, but still, how thoughtful of him! "Don't know Dollhouse Canyon?" he said.

"Never heard of it," said Dewey. "And I'll name the place, thanks just the same."

"Then name it."

"You know the old fire lookout tower off Franco Road?"

"Yeah."

"Meet you there in an hour. Nine five. Cash."

"It'll take me longer than that to get there," Bernie said.

"Not at this time of night," said Dewey. "I googled the drive time." He did that chuckling thing again. "Way ahead of you, buddy." Click.

Ah, night. Night with the moon, the stars, the open road, and us, me and Bernie.

Don't forget about our ride, the oldest Porsche we've ever owned. It's the kind of car that anyone with an ear for picking up new sounds would love, and I happen to have two ears just like that. Right now, for example, there was a tiny *thweep thweep* coming from the engine and a *croomph croomph,* even tinier, from somewhere below, both appearing for the first time. I wondered what Mindy Jo was up to tonight.

We climbed up above the Valley, huge and all lit up below. Was everyone asleep? How could they be, with all those lights on? Humans need their sleep. That's one of the most important things you learn about them. I like just about all the humans I've ever met, including most of the perps and gangbangers, but I like them better when they've had a good night's sleep.

We switchbacked up a steep ridge over to the other side, and all those lights disappeared. Sometimes Bernie says you can drive backwards in time. I was in the mood to hear him say it again, but instead he said, "He googled the drive time. Is it possible, Chet, there's a law that says as technology gets smarter people get stupider?"

That didn't have the sound of an easy question. We were on the side of the law, of course, me and Bernie. But wait. Didn't I remember Bernie telling someone we were on the side of justice? I even remembered who it was — Deputy Beasley! Hadn't seen him in some time and didn't miss him a bit. Now all I had to do was tie this together and —

And then Bernie said something I knew I'd never forget. "Let's call it Chet's Law."

Chet's Law? Chet's Law! Had I ever heard anything so wonderful? I let Bernie know exactly how I was feeling, big time. We did a three sixty, maybe two of them, but ended up not going off the ledge, the road having turned into a sort of track with sheer drop-offs on both sides while I wasn't paying the closest attention.

Up and up we climbed, higher and higher, and at last a spindly watchtower rose before us in the moonlight. Right away I caught the aromas of booze and weed, but neither of them recent.

"They were supposed to tear it down last year," Bernie said.

Was that why we were here? To tear down the old watchtower? Did that kind of job pay well?

A motorcycle stood at the base of the tower, moonlight gleaming on its chrome. We parked beside it, got out of the car, looked around. There wasn't much to see

— a small, flat table of land with those steep drop-offs on all sides and distant lights shining here and there, dim in the desert darkness.

A man called from above, a man I wasn't a fan of, namely Dewey. "Come on up."

"You come down," Bernie said.

"Dude. Got you in my sights. Up."

Bernie's gaze went to the stairs leading up the tower to the little boxy room on top, a rickety-looking staircase with no rails or risers, and some treads missing, and then to me. He crouched down, took my face in his hands, and said, "I need you to stay, Chet. Hear me? Sit down, now, and stay. I'll be right back."

I stayed on my feet. Not because I didn't understand. I understood perfectly. Also not because I was refusing to cooperate, although maybe I was. But who could blame me? Staying down here while Bernie went up the tower on his own? What kind of teamwork was that? We were a team, me and Bernie, had always been a team — except maybe for the time before we met — and would be a team forever.

Bernie smiled. "Counting on you for backup, big guy. Just sit and stay for a few minutes, okay?"

I was backup? That was different, backup

being an important job in our line of work. I sat. I stayed.

Bernie started climbing the stairs, the moonlight glinting on the hammer of the .38 Special, tucked in his belt at the back. Up and up he climbed, and what was this? I seemed to be up myself, at least up on my feet, rather than sitting. But I was not moving even the slightest bit, just staying in place, and wasn't staying the whole point of the sit stay? Sitting, standing, what's the difference? As long as you're not moving! Anyone can sit, my friends, but not everyone can stay, far from it. I heard Bernie's voice in my head: *What a good boy!* How nice of him! I kept on staying, staying better than I'd ever done. Don't forget I'm a pro.

Bernie climbed the stairs, not fast, not slow, but just right. We were in control, baby. I didn't see or hear any movement on the little roofed platform on top, but I could smell a man up there, specifically Dewey. Once I smell someone it's forever. I could also pick up the scent of the .38 Special, even though Bernie hadn't fired it in some time. What else? Mesquite, no surprise there, plus one of those cute little tortoises, so much fun to flip them on their backs and —

Whap whap whap.

What was that?

Whap whap whap. Very faint, but out there in the night: the sound of a helicopter. I scanned the sky, saw no moving lights. There were only the moon and stars. They moved, too. I hadn't known that for the longest time. Then all at once, on a night stakeout, it had come to me. The moon and stars are on the move, but very very slowly. It actually makes me uneasy, hard to explain why. I'd rather not have known.

As for the helo, the sound faded and faded, almost down to nothing. But not quite nothing. I stayed.

TWENTY-FIVE

Bernie grunted once or twice as he climbed the stairs. From the platform above came Dewey's voice. "Got you in my sights."

"You already said that," Bernie told him.

"Just giving you fair warning. I like to be straight up with people."

"What about with dogs?" Bernie said. He reached the edge of the platform and for a moment the whole of Bernie was silhouetted against the moon. I wanted to be right there with him! Why couldn't I be? Then I remembered: I was backup. I stayed where I was, although actually I wasn't quite where I'd been, at the foot of the stairs, but possibly up a step or even two.

"What's that supposed to mean?" Dewey said.

"Think back," said Bernie, as he stepped onto the platform and disappeared from view. But at that last instant, and moving so quick, the way he can when things are getting exciting, Bernie reached behind him and whipped out the gun.

CRACK! A gunshot, fired in the darkness up there, specifically the .38 Special. I know the sound of our own gun, goes without mentioning. Then came the clatter of something heavy, possibly metal, falling on the platform floor.

"Ow," cried Dewey, "you sneaky bastard!"

"Let's see that hand," Bernie said.

"You shot me!"

"Just a graze, if that," Bernie said. "I was aiming for your gun."

"Who the hell do you think you are? Some kind of trick shot?"

Well, of course he was! Better that Dewey learned that a little on the late side, rather than never at all. He was sitting on the floor — by now I seemed to be up on the platform myself — holding one hand in the other, and Bernie was crouching over him. Was there some reason I shouldn't be here? None that came to me. I spotted a gun — had to be Dewey's — lying on the floor, snapped it up and brought it to Bernie. He glanced at me, kind of in surprise, which made no sense. It was me, Chet the Jet. His mind must have been elsewhere, but he got a grip at once.

"Good boy, Chet." He took Dewey's gun

— just a little thing, hardly what you'd call a real gun, and stuck it in his pocket.

"Ow," said Dewey. "Jeez, it hurts."

We gazed at Dewey's hand, me and Bernie. Was there a drop of blood on the edge of the thumb? I couldn't quite make it out.

"You're going to be fine," Bernie said.

"The hell with you. I thought you were one of the so-called good guys."

"That's it exactly," Bernie said. "I'm taking you in."

"In where?"

"To the cops," Bernie said. "Theft, two counts. Count one, the page from Wendell Nero's appointment book. Count two, which shouldn't be theft at all in my book, but kidnapping, was the abduction of Chet."

Dewey's eyes shifted my way. More or less just for fun, I showed him my teeth. He looked somewhere else real quick.

Whap whap whap.

I'd almost forgotten about the helo. Was that whap whap whap getting louder? Maybe a bit.

Bernie held out his hand.

"What about the nine five?" Dewey said.

"You're asking me to pay for stolen property?" Bernie said.

Dewey glared at Bernie, like he actually didn't like him.

"But I'll make a deal," Bernie went on. "If you give me that page nicely, I'll forget about count one."

Dewey reached into his pocket.

"And," Bernie went on, "if you give me the name, I'll forget count two."

Dewey paused. "What name?"

"The woman who hires you. A hard-ass bitch — you met her surfing in Hawaii."

"Don't know what you're talking about," Dewey said.

Bernie gazed down at him. "You're afraid of her."

"Me? Afraid of some woman?"

"No shame in that," Bernie said. "Just means you're a realist about life. Not all conflict comes down to physical confrontation."

"Ha!" said Dewey. "Shows what you know — she's a fuckin' nightmare when it comes down to . . ."

"Go on," Bernie said.

Dewey shook his head.

"Did she order you to slice the page out of Wendell Nero's appointment book?" Bernie said.

"I don't take orders from anybody," Dewey said.

"Suit yourself. Did she hire you to do it?"

Dewey gazed up at Bernie. There was fear

in his eyes, and plenty of it in his smell. "Mig didn't know about this. Where are you gettin' your information?"

"It's out there," Bernie said. "Can't you feel the momentum? Time to save yourself, Dewey."

Dewey peered into the night. I heard the whap whap whap, now faint again, almost dialed down to nothing.

"I don't feel nothin' — except for my hand, what's left of it."

"For god's sake, man," Bernie said. "Focus."

"On what?" said Dewey.

"The appointment book. Did she tell you to slice out the page with me on it?"

Dewey looked into the darkness again and nodded a small nod.

"But didn't she also want you to give it to her when you were done?"

Dewey nodded again.

"What did you tell her?"

Dewey smiled a smile of the crafty kind, never a good human look. "I misunderstood and destroyed it."

"How?"

"How I destroyed it? I didn't — that's the point."

"I'm aware of that," Bernie said. "But she must have asked how."

Dewey shot Bernie a quick glance. "Know something? You're like her."

Bernie showed no reaction, but he reacted inside. I felt it. He was starting to be a lot less fond of Dewey. And maybe Dewey felt it, too, because he quickly added, "I told her I burned it. Burned it in my sink — always good to add a detail like that."

"You played her like a violin," Bernie said.

"Kinda," said Dewey. "I thought it might be valuable someday — nine point five valuable."

"No one's perfect," said Bernie.

"How about a grand?" Dewey said. "One lousy K. Call it expenses."

"The negotiations are closed." Bernie held out his hand. Dewey pulled a small envelope from his pocket and gave it to him. "But," Bernie went on, "the name is worth a grand."

"And you'll let me go?"

Bernie nodded.

"How about two?" Dewey said.

"Nope."

"One point five."

"The name," Bernie said.

"Money first."

"Name first." Bernie's eyes got a sudden inward look, the way they did when some new idea popped up in that amazing brain of his. "Did she also order you to kidnap Chet?"

"Told you," Dewey said. "I don't take orders from anybody. I'm my own boss, maybe something you're missing even though you're the know-it-all type of —"

WHAP WHAP WHAP! WHAP WHAP WHAP!

Oh, no. From out of nowhere and so fast, the helo was right on us! Right on us although I still couldn't see it. But I could hear it, all right. I heard that helo and nothing but, a roar that filled the whole sky, shook the fire tower and made me start jumping around and . . . and going crazy! Stop that whap whap whap! Stop it now! That was all I could think.

As for what I could see, we had Dewey, eyes and mouth opened wide, possibly screaming, even if I couldn't hear the screams. We also had Bernie, moving real quick. Before I even knew it, he'd scooped me up and flung me over his shoulder — me, a hundred-plus pounder — crossed the platform and started down the stairs, coming pretty close to running, like he didn't have a wounded leg after all. He even turned his head and shouted something to Dewey, maybe "Come on, Dewey!" But I couldn't hear a word. No other sound could penetrate that whap whap whap.

343

WHAP WHAP WHAP. A whap whap whap that tilted and circled around us and then came a bright flash and Bernie leaped the rest of the way, me leaping, too, off his shoulders and into the night.

BOOM! A tremendous boom, and then a sound like splitting matchsticks, but huge, and the whole tower flew apart in many pieces. By then I was on the ground, with Bernie lying over me. Little fires were breaking out here and there, and the whap whap whap was fading fast. I followed the sound with my eyes and glimpsed a helo silhouette crossing the moon. And then it was gone, both the sound of it and the sight. The little fires made crackling sounds. Those seemed so tiny to me, and at the same time so clear.

Bernie went pat pat pat along my back. "You okay, big guy?"

Sure! Maybe not tip-top, what with a strange muffling in my ears, but I was good to go. We rose and hurried over to Dewey, a still shadow on the ground where the tower had stood. He lay on his back. We looked down at him. There was nothing we could do. His face was undamaged — in fact all of him looked undamaged, except for that tiny smear of blood on his hand that he'd been fussing about, but the — what would you call it? Inner Dewey? Something like

344

that. The inner Dewey was gone. It can happen very fast.

We got busy stamping out the fires, Bernie doing the stamping and me trying not to get too close whenever Bernie said don't get too close. Stamp stamp stamp "not too close," "back off a bit," "Chet!" We worked our way across the little plateau, stamping and not getting too close. The wind came up and sent some small burning thing across our path. Bernie went to stamp on it, stopped himself at the last second. It was the envelope Dewey had brought, maybe the whole point of tonight's meeting. Bernie reached for, grabbed a corner, but too late. Flame shot up and the envelope turned to ashes in his hand. He shook them off. The wind caught them and blew an ash or two onto Bernie's face. He rubbed them off, leaving a black smear on his forehead. That bothered me. I wondered about licking his forehead, making everything all better. Perhaps later.

"To top it off," Bernie said, "we're in Beasley's jurisdiction."

"Hell of a mess," said Deputy Beasley.

Dawn was breaking all around us on the little plateau, a lovely sight that reminded me of one of Charlie's finger paintings.

Once we'd finger painted together, just me and him, me using my paws of course, Charlie helping to dip them in the paint pots, the whole thing his idea. A brilliant kid, but that was to be expected. I'd learned so much that day, including the facts that in finger painting it's best to keep the paint on the paper and not let it wander off onto other things — for example, a white couch — and that not all people were fans of finger painting — for example, Leda.

We stood in a circle around Dewey. Beasley had a huge mug of coffee in his pudgy hand. He took a sip. The two officers with him took sips of their coffee. Bernie had run through our story, answered some questions, run through it again. Beasley had said "Hell of a mess" a few times. Were we getting anywhere? I didn't know.

"Can't even think why the goddamn thing was still standing in the first place," Beasley said. "Wasn't it s'posta come down years ago?" He turned to the officers. They glanced at each other. One shrugged. The other one hesitated for a moment and then he shrugged, too. I was getting hungry.

Beasley turned back to Bernie. "Tell me the helicopter part again."

Bernie told him the helicopter part. The sky got even wilder — like paint pots were

346

getting spilled all over the place — but there were no helicopters, nothing flying at all except a lone black bird.

"No lights," Beasley said.

"Nope," said Bernie.

"No identifying features."

"I didn't really see it, except for a second, silhouetted against the moon. But I sure heard it."

"Silhouetted," said Beasley, saying the word real slow.

"Correct," Bernie said.

"You guys check out aviation traffic, three-mile radius, last six hours," Beasley said. "Herm — take civil. Nestor — military."

The officers went to their squad cars, got on the phones.

Beasley took another sip of coffee. He toed a broken length of wood from the tower.

"You mentioned a grenade," he said.

"Fired from the helo," said Bernie.

"Got any experience with grenades fired out of helos?"

"Some."

Beasley squinted at Bernie over the rim of his mug. "Possess any grenades yourself?"

"What kind of question is that?" Bernie said.

"Just gathering information." Beasley

pointed down at Dewey. "Any chance our friend here had possession of grenades?"

"No idea," Bernie said. "And I don't see the relevance."

The officers got out of their squad cars, came over.

"Civil," said Herm. "Negative."

"Military," said Nestor. "Same."

Beasley took off his hat, scratched his head. A few flakes of dandruff drifted off, got lit up by that paint pot sky. There's all kinds of beauty in life.

"We got a problem," he said.

"One way of putting it," said Bernie.

"See," Beasley went on, "we deal in facts, don't we, boys?"

For a moment I thought Herm and Nestor were about to do their shrugging routine again, but they nodded instead.

"Facts," Beasley said, "is like this guy De-wart —"

"Dewey," said Bernie.

"— whatever, picks a place like this to sell you some alleged page from an alleged book, now burned to ashes, so not a fact, that part. Then we got facts of lots of noise and an explosion. What I'm thinking is you're lucky to be alive."

"True," Bernie said.

"So you're agreeing he set you up?"

"No," Bernie said. "Or if he did, he didn't realize he was being set up, too."

"By who?" said Beasley.

"Whoever sent in the helo," Bernie told him.

Beasley sighed. "We're trying to stick to facts."

"So?"

"So the helo is not a fact," Beasley said. "Maybe someday it will be, and if that day comes, why then we'll have to . . . what's the word I'm looking for?"

"Reboot?" said Herm.

"Apologize?" said Nestor.

Beasley glared at Nestor. "Reboot," he said. "If and when that day comes. But for now what we have" — he stuck his chin in Dewey's direction — "is this five-and-dimer with a setup that went wrong. Blew up in his face, you might say."

Herm laughed. Nestor did not.

"Summing up," Beasley said, "the department thanks you for calling this in. We'll take over from here."

Bernie's eyes caught all the dawn colors, became two eye-sized blazing skies. "What the hell are you talking about?"

"I'm not blaming you," Beasley said. "Goes with your job. Complications are good business. But it don't go with my job.

349

Florian Machado killed Wendell Nero. Case closed."

This all had been hard to follow, right to now. But sometimes at the very end is when understanding comes. Cases are closed by me, grabbing the pant leg. Deputy Beasley had gone off the rails.

Twenty-Six

The sky settled down as we topped the hills and headed into the Valley, but Bernie's eyes did not. They kept blazing away until we hit the morning traffic jam near the airport and came to a stop. Then, when all the drivers around us were ramping up inside, Bernie started ramping down. He turned to me.

"You must be famished, big guy."

Bernie, on target as usual. Was there a stronger word than famished? If not, then we needed one. *Food! Now! Food! Now! F—*

The phone buzzed.

"Hello," said a man, an old man with a scratchy voice, an old man I knew. "Is this Bernie? Bernie Little?"

"Hi, Diego. This is Bernie."

"Oh, good. You gave me your card. I'm calling the number."

"What can we do for you?" Bernie said. "You sound upset."

"I am upset," said Diego.

"About what?"

"Can we talk in person?" Diego's voice sank to a whisper. "I don't trust the phone."

"Where are you?" said Bernie in a normal voice.

"My office," said Diego, still whispering. "Can you drive?"

Diego's voice rose back up, maybe now on the high side of normal. "Of course! Been driving since I was eight years old."

"That's not what I —" Bernie stopped himself, started over. "Come to our place. We're on Mesquite Road." Bernie gave him the house number.

"Mesquite Road on the west side of Settler's Canyon?"

"Yes."

"Family name of Little used to own that whole stretch."

"A long time ago," said Bernie.

We drove home. There was a package on the front step. Bernie picked it up and we went in. He carried the package into the kitchen and started unwrapping it. I walked to the corner by the fridge and stood over my food bowl. You can stand over your food bowl in a way that no one notices. I chose the opposite kind of way. Bernie stopped what he was doing.

"How does kibble mixed with Slim Jim slices sound?" he said.

Yes!

"Or would you prefer — ?" Bernie started laughing, possibly because I had shifted position slightly, was now standing on my hind legs, front paws on his shoulders. "I get it," he said, and got that kibble poured out and the Slim Jims sliced up and pronto. Bernie could be something of a tease at times. The fun we have!

Bernie went back to the package, opening it and taking out a bottle of bourbon. "Heard of this one but never sprang for it." He read the note. " 'Bourbon reminds me of Billie Holiday. This particular make reminds me of her at her very best, singing "If You Were Mine," for example. We should catch some music one day — Gudrun.' "

Bernie glanced up. Billie Holiday singing "If You Were Mine" was our favorite, although the very best part came at the end, when Roy Eldridge started up on his trumpet, doing things to my ears I can't possibly describe. But right now there was a look on Bernie's face I'd never seen before. Confusion was part of it, and surprise, and other things I didn't have a chance to understand, because all at once I was very sleepy. That can happen when you're up all night, as you learn pretty quick in a job like mine.

A knock on the door. A knock on the door, and I hadn't even heard anyone coming! Me, Chet, in charge of security! Asleep on the kitchen floor? I bounced right up. My tail drooped. I forced it back up and ran to the door, ready to do who knows what to whoever was there. Who knows what to whoever — I kind of liked that. Was there a way to add it to our card?

Bernie came down the hall, rubbing his eyes. He opened the door. This wasn't anyone I'd even consider doing who knows what to, just Diego, an old man, anxious and upset, reminding me for some reason of a child, despite him being so wrinkled and bent.

Bernie led him by the hand. "Come in."

Diego entered the house, took a look around. Bernie was taking a look around, too, but at whatever was going on up and down the street, which happened to be nothing at all. Except . . . except old man Heydrich had his sprinklers on? In the middle of a hot hot day? Bernie glared at all that sparkle and shut the door.

"Nice place you got here," Diego said.

"Nothing fancy," said Bernie.

"That's what I'm saying," said Diego. "It's connected."

"Connected?"

"To the land it's sitting on. A common thing at one time, not so common now." Diego licked his lips. "I'm a bit thirsty, if you don't mind."

Thirsty and not too steady on his feet. We got Diego settled at the kitchen table, a glass of water in front of him. He sipped, closed his eyes, sipped again.

Diego opened his eyes, put down the glass. "You have good water here."

"Regular city water," said Bernie.

"I'm making allowance for that," Diego said. "Did you know that in the old days we'd toss pennies and dimes into the water barrels?"

"Because the ions kept the water fresh?" said Bernie.

"Fresh and clear," Diego said. "Although we didn't know the reason at the time. We just did it because that was always the way." His eyes got a bit watery. He took a deep breath and they dried up. Diego had a nice smell, reminding me of old saddles, minus the horse part. "Everything changes, no matter what you do. I wouldn't wish death on myself, Bernie — that's a sin — but if the changes just could have waited till I was gone I'd have been thankful."

"Are you talking about specific changes?" Bernie said.

"Yes, sir. We're selling out. Jimmy and I had a long talk last night. Did you know we bought the land in 1806?"

Bernie nodded.

"But the fact is there were Torrezes working it for two centuries before that, even more." Diego took another sip of water.

"So it's not an easy decision," Bernie said.

"Yes and no," said Diego. "That land is part of me, just like my arm or my leg. Yet a land without water is dead, like a body with no blood running inside." He looked about to say more, but did not, gave his shoulders a little shrug instead.

"I get that," Bernie said. "But is there any hurry?"

"The very question I asked Jimmy. How can I argue with the answer? It's a good offer — better than good — and no offer may ever come again, not with the aquifer squeezed out dry."

"Which hasn't happened yet," Bernie said.

"But the scientists say it's certain to," said Diego.

"What scientists?"

"The ones who wrote the report."

"The report was written by Hoskin

Phipps," Bernie said. "Have you ever met him?"

"No."

"Has Jimmy mentioned him?"

Diego shook his head.

"Why don't you trust your phone?" Bernie said.

Diego hung his head. "I didn't really mean that. We're family. But Jimmy doesn't want me interfering in things, messing up the deal."

"Is your phone tapped?" Bernie said.

Diego looked up, more than surprise on his face, maybe even shock. "Oh, no, never. He's my son."

"Drink some more water," Bernie said.

Diego picked up his glass and drank more water.

"Who's the buyer?" Bernie said.

"Some Swiss outfit — didn't I tell you?"

"You didn't say the name."

Diego thought. "It'll come to me," he said.

We waited. Hot summer days could be very quiet on Mesquite Road. I heard the faint swish swish of Heydrich's sprinklers.

Diego rose, went to the window. "Did I tell you I was going to walk away with enough money to live comfortably for the rest of my days?" he said.

"Good to hear," Bernie said.

Diego turned. "Jimmy ran the numbers. He —" Diego broke off, distracted by something on the fridge door. He went over and peered at the photo of Wendell and the girl with the goat sitting on her feet. "What's this?" he said.

"It was on the wall in Wendell's RV," Bernie said. "I took it after the police investigation was over."

"Why?" Diego said.

"No reason," Bernie told him. "I just liked it."

"You don't know Tildy?"

"She's the girl?"

Diego — his back to us, his eyes still on the photo, nodded. "But what's going on? It looks like they knew each other."

"Why would that be a surprise?" Bernie said.

Diego leaned closer to the photo. "Well, I suppose it makes sense if . . . ."

"If what?"

"If this photo was taken in Dollhouse Canyon."

"That's where Wendell had the RV."

"I guess that explains it," Diego said.

"Not to me," Bernie said. "Who's Tildy?"

Diego turned. "A fine kid. Her family helps out from time to time."

"Meaning they work for you?"

358

"Seasonally, more or less. Harvest, pruning, plus caring for the animals. Tildy loves animals. She's very good at teaching the goats to stay away from the grapes."

"How does she do that?"

"She just talks to them in Spanish — now, now, no grapes, none of that you little scamps — and for some reason they get the idea."

"Can she speak English?"

"Perfectly. But she talks Spanish to the goats."

"I'd like to see her," Bernie said.

Diego shook his head. "They were supposed to be here for most of the summer, but we got a tip last week and they went home."

"Home to Mexico?"

"Sonora," Diego said. "Her and her mom. The dad stayed down there this year — too sick to travel."

"Where in Sonora?" Bernie said.

"I don't know, exactly."

"Who would?"

"Juana — she's the cook."

"We need to talk to her," Bernie said.

"Sure," said Diego. "I can set that up."

"Now would be good," Bernie said. "And not at the winery — somewhere else."

Diego gave Bernie a long look. Then,

under his breath, maybe to himself, he said, "The grapes are still juicy."

"Stall," Bernie said. "Stall for as long as you can." He took the photo off the fridge.

Outside Diego got in his pickup and we hopped in the Porsche, ready to follow him, unless there was some other plan I'd missed. But before we could get started, a commotion got going over at the Parsons's house, Mr. Parsons shouting, "No, Iggy, back!" and Iggy doing his yip yip yip. Their front door opened a crack and somehow Mr. Parsons squeezed out backwards, blocking Iggy with his walker. I caught a glimpse of Iggy trying to dart his way through. Once Bernie said, "Imagine if Iggy was Chet's size." I realized now what a scary thought that was. Then the door closed and Mr. Parsons came stumping over.

"Bernie! Been trying to catch a moment with you — you haven't been around much."

"Is there a problem?" Bernie said.

"On, no, no problem. Edna just wanted me to ask if this is true." He took a rolled-up newspaper from his back pocket, straightened it out. "Right here above the fold, as they say. Prominent Valley Journalist to Wed."

Bernie took the paper. There was a pretty big picture of Suzie and Jacques, holding hands and smiling. Bernie gazed at it. I gazed at Bernie.

"Says they plan on starting some new venture out here," Mr. Parsons said.

Bernie didn't answer. His eyes stayed on the picture.

"Is it true?" said Mr. Parsons. "Bernie?"

Bernie turned to him. "Is what true?" Perhaps he spoke a little sharply. He said, "Is what true?" again, this time more gently, which was how he usually spoke to Mr. and Mrs. Parsons.

"About the venture?" Mr. Parsons said.

"It is," said Bernie.

Mr. Parsons sighed. "Well, I wish them luck, of course."

"Me, too," said Bernie, handing back the paper.

We got in the car but were hardly out of the driveway when Charlie called.

"Dad! I made a shoestring catch! In a real game!"

"Good job!"

"But it's not on video."

"No problem. Just remember it in your mind."

"Okay. Dad?"

"Yes?"

"What's chin music?"

Bernie's eyes got an inward look. "It's when a pitcher throws high and tight to back you off the plate. Why?"

"Timmy — that's the counselor in case you forgot —"

"I —"

"— stood in the batter's box and we all got a chance to pitch to him. He said I was throwing chin music."

Bernie laughed. Had I ever seen him look so happy? They said goodbye. Bernie stopped looking happy, glanced at me. "But what's the response to chin music, big guy?"

Wow! The toughest question that had ever come my way. I waited for the answer. It seemed to be taking a long time. Then, quietly, maybe to himself, Bernie said, "You hit the next one out of the park."

I'd never have guessed.

"My goodness!" said Juana. "What a big dog!"

"If you're uncomfortable," Bernie said, "I could put him —"

Juana interrupted before I learned where Bernie was planning to put me. Would it be better to think of it as trying to put me? Possibly, but we never got that far. "Oh, no,"

Juana said, "I'm fine with dogs."

No news to me. I'd known Juana was a fan of me and my kind from the moment she'd stepped down from the cab of her pickup, an older, bigger one than Diego's, and not dusty, like his, but sparkling and polished. Human fear has a smell — actually a number of them, depending on things we can't go into now — that I don't miss. Juana, a short, wide woman with one of those very smooth skins you see on female humans from time to time, was mostly about kitchen smells, particularly sausages frying in the pan. I liked her from the get-go.

We sat at a shady picnic table behind the big truck stop off the highway on the South Pedroia side of town, Diego and Juana on one side, me and Bernie on the other. Bernie laid the photo on the table.

"I understand you know this girl," he said.

"Sure," said Juana. "It's Tildy. And that's the poor man who got killed."

"You knew him?"

She glanced at Diego. "Mr. Diego says you're a private detective?"

"I am," Bernie said. "A suspect is in custody but there are some loose ends."

"You can trust Bernie," Diego said.

"Okay, then," said Juana. "I did not know

the man but I met him once."

"When?" Bernie said.

Juana pointed to the photo. "Then."

"You took the picture?"

"Sí."

"How did that come about?"

Juana folded her hands on the table, very nice-looking hands, in my opinion. "It began with some goats, I think, going over the ridge into Dollhouse Canyon. Tildy went to get them and so she met Doctor Wendy. That's what she called him. She kept going there, helping with his work, she said. Then one day Dr. Wendy called Pepita — that's Tildy's momma — and said what a bright girl Tildy was and when the day came he would make sure she went to college. I thought, well, maybe I should meet this gentleman. Tildy is a smart kid, very responsible, but . . . twelve years old."

"You didn't trust Wendell?" Bernie said.

"And I did not not trust him. I just wanted to be sure. And he was a very nice man, no problem, teaching her all about the land."

"What did she mean by helping with his work?"

"That's what she told Pepita."

"What do you know about the roll of papers under her arm?"

364

"Nothing."

"Diego says she and her mom went back to Sonora because they got a tip," Bernie said.

Juana turned to Diego. "Tip?"

"Isn't that the usual thing?" Diego said. "A warning about *la migra*?"

Juana shook her head. "Pepita was worried the sheriff would learn Tildy had been helping Dr. Wendy."

"And would come to question her?" said Bernie.

"That's right," Juana said.

"Amounts to the same thing," said Diego.

"We need to talk to her," Bernie said.

"Because of the loose ends?" said Juana.

"It's more than that," Bernie told her. "They've got the wrong man."

Juana thought about that but stayed silent.

"And possibly," Bernie added, "Diego can keep the vineyard."

Juana turned to him.

"Maybe you don't know," Diego said, "but there's a water problem so we're going to have to —"

"I know," Juana said. "We all know." She took a notepad from her bag, wrote on the top sheet, peeled it off, and gave it to Bernie.

TWENTY-SEVEN

Bernie spun the dial on the safe. But why? Didn't we already have the .38 Special? I squeezed in closer for a better look, perhaps even getting my front paws up on the wall, practically at the level of the safe. Had I ever stood so high before? Not that I remembered. Was it possible I was getting taller? What an exciting idea, and I'm not the type that gets excited easily. Or am I? And if I was would that be a problem? Maybe it's even better to be —

"Chet?"

I eased myself back down to the floor, stood silent and still. You wouldn't have noticed me. Bernie felt around in the safe. "Here we go — my passport, your papers."

Passport and papers? That meant Mexico. Have I mentioned Lola? She and I met in an alley behind a cantina, on a night I'd found myself not very sleepy, and wandered away from our hotel in a dusty little town, possibly leaving through the open window. Would we be visiting that dusty little town on this trip? I trotted down the hall and parked myself at the front door, my nose just about touching it. Bernie came up, reached around me, laughing softly as if at some joke, and turned the doorknob.

His phone buzzed. His hand withdrew from the doorknob.

"Hello?"

"Hello, Bernie. It's Gudrun."

"Um. Hello."

"Did I catch you at a bad moment?"

"Uh, no."

"Are you in town?"

"For the moment."

"On your way somewhere? Somewhere interesting?"

Say goodbye, Bernie. Let's roll. But he said nothing and we didn't roll. I remained where I was, nose to the door.

"The reason I ask," Gudrun went on, "is that I wondered if you were free for dinner tonight, say around seven at my place?"

"Thanks," Bernie said, "but —"

"I think you'll want to say yes," Gudrun said over him. "I've got something to show you."

"Like what?"

"It's a message of sorts — from Florian

367

Machado."

"What's the message?"

"I prefer to show you in person," Gudrun said.

A long pause on our end. I could feel Bernie's thoughts, dark ones, moving fast. "All right," he finally said.

"Last house on Upper Camino Royale," Gudrun said. "The guard will let you in."

I went on standing by the door for some time, even though I knew it was hopeless. Funny how the mind works.

"Haven't been up this way for a while," Bernie said.

I myself had never been here before, way up in the faraway hills that blocked the sun at the end of every Valley day. And we were getting latish, the sun orange and kind of flabby, poking out from behind a slope from time to time and then disappearing behind another one, casting a shadow over us. Way down below the Valley went on and on, mostly in shadow, too, except for the tops of the downtown towers, which looked like they were on fire — but no smoke, so no worries about that — and planes rising up from the airport and turning to gold, or starting out as gold and blackening as they came in to land.

We were rising, too, up and up on a high curving ridge that led to a tall metal gate. A man's voice spoke, although there was no one to see.

"Welcome, Mr. Little. Drive on through."

The gate swung open. We drove on through. A bird rose off the gate post, circled up into the golden light higher and higher, and disappeared. Bernie took a deep breath. "Nice air," he said.

That was interesting. Did it mean Bernie found some air nice and some not nice? What made this air nice to him? I took a casual sniff, breathed in a river of scents, way too many to even get started on now. But there was lots of piñon pine aroma, a bit like chestnuts roasted at Christmas — before the fire extinguisher comes out — and also the smell of hot asphalt, rising from the Valley floor. So Bernie liked that mix, piñon pine and hot asphalt? I'd have to remember that.

"What's with you?" Bernie said.

I found I was giving him a close look. Nothing was on my mind. Zip, zilch, nada. I yawned a big yawn.

"Don't tell me you're sleepy?"

Sleepy? When we were on the job? Or even if we weren't? I got that yawn under control and pronto, not so easy with yawns. The sun sank away for good, taking most of the colors with it.

We followed a driveway of smooth, polished pavers toward a tall dark house that looked like an arrangement of boxes, some of them seeming to hang over the edge of a cliff. Outside lights flashed on and I saw that those boxes were mostly made of dark glass. Then an inside light went on in one of the higher boxes and I could see right inside. There was Gudrun, looking out at us. The inside light went out and she vanished. We parked and walked to the door.

Bernie started to knock but Gudrun was already there, opening it, so Bernie knocked only air.

"Welcome," she said, smiling at Bernie. Then she noticed me and her smile sort of got stuck. "Ah," she said. "You've brought your formidable friend."

"Is that a problem?" Bernie said.

"Not at all," said Gudrun. The sun might have taken away the colors, but it had missed her eyes, somehow still very green. "I love dogs," she said.

Lots of humans love me and my kind. Some don't. Gudrun was in the second group. I always know right away. As for me and Bernie being friends — true as far as it went, which wasn't nearly far enough.

Gudrun led us into the house, lights going off behind us and going on in front. We ended up in a glass box that really was hanging over the cliff. Only Bernie and Gudrun actually went all the way in. I kind of hung back in the part that seemed like it still had land underneath.

"Quite a place," Bernie said. "I assume something's holding it up."

"I hope so," said Gudrun.

Bernie turned to her and laughed.

"Care for a drink?" she said.

"I thought you had something to show me."

"Oh, I do," Gudrun said. "But your hands will be free."

Bernie looked a bit . . . oh, no. Flustered? Was that it? A certain type of woman sometimes got him flustered in a certain kind of way. Was Gudrun that certain type? I hadn't thought so, but now I realized that she was, plus a lot more. Bernie's smell changed slightly, which was the proof. And her smell, what you might call a matching smell although very different, changed, too.

"Bourbon's your drink, I believe?" Gudrun said, moving toward a glass cabinet that seemed suspended in midair. I did not like this house, not one bit. Bernie followed her over to the cabinet. I entered the room.

The floor was made of stone, and strangely cold. The chairs were white, the couch black, and there was a tall metal sculpture of a man who was way too skinny. Worst of all was a small cage hanging from a hook in one corner, and in that cage a hamster, run-run-running on a wheel. Why? Why are you doing that, little hamster?

Gudrun poured bourbon into two glasses, gave one to Bernie.

"It is my drink," he said. "And thanks for the bottle. But how did you know?"

"A little bird told me," Gudrun said.

I made the connection right away — don't forget I'm a pro. Gudrun was talking about the bird that had flown off the gate post and vanished in the evening sky. Some birds can talk, of course, but this was the first time we'd had one working with a human. And not just any human — this human was no friend of mine. The case, all about . . . well, who even knew, exactly, had taken a bad turn.

They clinked glasses and drank. The sky darkened and a star blinked on, then another, and another. Bernie had explained the stars to Charlie and I'd paid close attention. Did you know that they were just giant balls of . . . something or other? Charlie had watched Bernie's face the whole time. I could still see the look in his eyes. He loved Bernie. And so did I! We really were a lucky little bunch.

"Did the same little bird mention Billie Holiday?" Bernie said.

What a brilliant question! Who else but Bernie would have even dreamed of asking it? I think you know the answer.

"Maybe, maybe not." Gudrun smiled. She had very white teeth, perhaps on the small side, but sharp-looking, for a human. "It's also possible we have similar tastes."

Bernie's eyebrows rose slightly. Have I already mentioned they have a language of their own? Right now they were saying something about getting interested in Gudrun.

"For starters," she went on, "we've got bourbon and Billie. Just staying with the B's for now, we can add baseball. I understand you were a pretty good pitcher in college. No little bird necessary — baseball stats never die."

Bernie's eyebrows got a little more interested.

"And I myself," Gudrun continued, "was a catcher."

"Never played softball myself," Bernie said, "but I've always thought it's just as —"

"I'm talking about baseball," Gudrun said. "High school baseball."

"With the boys?"

"I had my own locker room, but otherwise yes — with the boys. Now you're going to ask if I started or rode the pine."

"You're wrong about that," Bernie said. "I was going to ask what high school."

Those green eyes shifted the slightest bit. "The Screaming Eagles of North Malvern High."

"Near Pittsburgh?"

"Correct." Gudrun set her glass on the sideboard and, real smooth, got into a catcher's crouch, kind of right in front of Bernie, a bit of a strange sight. She put a hand between her legs, lowered one finger. "Fastball." Then two. "Curve." Then one more finger. Hey! Could that be three? The whole number thing was suddenly clear to me, or just about. "Changeup," she said, "although none of the boys had one." She rose, again real smooth, and picked up her drink. "Did you have a changeup, Bernie?"

"Um." Bernie cleared his throat. "Uh, well, no. Never got comfortable with the grip."

"No?" she said, giving him an odd sort of look. It seemed to make Bernie redden. But why? I was getting a bit lost.

He cleared his throat again. "I didn't even have a curve, just a chickenshit slider that tended to stay up in the zone."

"So you relied on your heater?" Gudrun said.

"Heater's putting it a little too strong," said Bernie. "But right now, if it's all the same to you, I'd like to see whatever it was you were going to show me."

"Are you in a rush, Bernie? Going somewhere?"

"No," Bernie said.

That surprised me. Weren't we on our way to Mexico? Lola was on my mind again, and more vividly than ever, for some reason.

"Working on anything interesting these days?" Gudrun said.

"Nothing new," Bernie said. "We're still on the Wendell Nero murder."

Gudrun picked up the bottle, refreshed their drinks. Sometimes humans say, "Care for another?" or "a splash more?" Gudrun just poured.

"Are you one of those guys who lets perfect stand in the way of good?" she said.

A complete puzzler, and maybe to Bernie, too. "Meaning what?" he said.

"Meaning loose ends are part of the human condition, Bernie. You can tie yourself inside them and end up accomplishing nothing, or you can take a bow for a job well enough done and move on."

She took out her phone and pointed it at a screen hanging from one of the glass walls. The screen lit up and a man appeared, a man I knew, specifically Florian Machado. He was sitting on a stool and wearing an orange jumpsuit. First came Gudrun's voice.

"I understand you have something to say."

"Yeah," Florian said. "It's, like, about the deal."

"The plea deal the state has offered?"

"Hell, yeah. Is there some other deal out there?" Florian laughed a laugh that didn't sound happy. He rubbed his hands together. Were they shaking a bit? I thought so. "The thing is," he went on, "I want to take it."

"Instead of going to court?"

Florian nodded.

"And what's your reason?"

Florian shrugged. "Death penalty. I wanna live."

"Even if it means in prison?"

"Yeah. You never know. Maybe they'll change the law. Make it more . . . what's the word." There was a long pause and then Florian said, "Humane. They'll make it humane."

"So that's your whole reason?"

376

"Mostly."

"What's the rest of it?"

"Well, there is the part about me doing it."

"Doing what?"

"The thing that happened to what's his name."

"Wendell Nero."

"Yeah. The old guy. I never meant any harm."

"But?"

"But he, uh, surprised me. All's I wanted to do was grab some stuff — electronics, things like that. I thought there was nobody there. That was the surprise. And the stupid bastard came right at me. I couldn't believe it. A scrawny old dude coming right at a . . . specimen such as myself."

"And what did you do?"

Florian sat for what seemed a long time, first looking right at us, and then down at the floor. He took a deep breath. "Ah, hell," he said. "I cut his throat." He closed his eyes. The screen went dark.

Gudrun turned to Bernie. "Come on upstairs," she said.

Bernie no longer looked flushed; in fact, he was pale. "What's there?"

"The best view in town," Gudrun said. "It washes all the ugliness away."

Bernie rose but didn't say anything. He had a blank look on his face. I'd never seen that before. It scared me.

"Would Chet prefer to stay here?" Gudrun said. "I've got some snacks for him and it's not really dog safe up there."

Bernie didn't answer, his face no longer blank but dark and deep in thought.

"Bernie?" Gudrun said.

He gave himself a tiny shake, the exact same thing I would have done at that moment. I stopped being scared.

"Sure," he said. "Want to stay here, Chet?"

I didn't see why not, especially if snacks were involved. Gudrun went to the sideboard, opened a cabinet, took out a red box. Yes, a red Rover and Company box, containing the best biscuits in town. I'd even visited their test kitchen, but no time for that now. Gudrun put two giant-sized biscuits on a plate and laid it on the floor. Then she led Bernie across the room and up the spiral stairs.

I trotted over to the plate, took a quick sniff of those wonderful biscuits and snapped one up. And then . . . and then I spat it out. Whoa! Why did I do that? I lowered my head over the biscuit, did some more sniffing. There was something a little strange about the smell. How could that be?

A Rover and Company biscuit not smelling right? That made no sense to me. But also it hadn't tasted quite right either. I had a funny feeling on my tongue. I tried licking away that funny feeling on my paw, and it mostly worked, but there was still a bit of funny feeling left. A cool drink of water would have been nice. I looked around, saw no water bowl. Over in the corner, my poor little hamster was still on the wheel. I started up the spiral stairs.

I'd only climbed spiral stairs once before in my life, chasing a perp about whom I now remembered nothing except that he was wearing boxers and one of his ankles seemed to be bleeding a bit. From somewhere behind me, Bernie had called, "Careful, big guy — spiral stairs are tricky." And I hadn't had the slightest notion! Where would I be without Bernie? I'd carefully leaped right up, hardly touching the stairs at all, avoiding the problem pretty much completely. Now I did the same thing, and in no time popped up to the top, and found myself on a kind of deck, with no walls at the edges, only thin see-through rails. For a moment I felt like I was floating in the night sky. I came close to running back down the spiral stairs. Then I noticed Bernie and Gudrun.

A couch stood at one side of the deck,

facing the edge so that anyone sitting on it would see the view. Bernie stood with his back to the back of the couch, if you get what I mean, and Gudrun was facing him.

"I could use a man like you," she said.

"I'm not a lawyer," said Bernie.

She touched his chest. "What I don't need is more lawyers." Her fingertip moved in a little circle, still touching him. "What I need is someone like you."

Bernie backed away, but not far, being blocked by the couch.

Human anger has a smell, somewhat like sweat, although not the fresh kind, and blood. Now it came off Gudrun in a little wave. But when she spoke, there wasn't a hint of any of that in her tone. In fact she almost sounded sweet.

"You're not attracted to me, Bernie?" she said.

"Uh, that's . . . that's not it," Bernie said.

"You're seeing somebody?"

Bernie shook his head.

"Then what?" said Gudrun. "I'm not asking for a lifetime commitment."

Bernie shifted his weight to one side, shifted back.

"Don't you ever just jump into something?" Gudrun said. "Seize life in the here and now? Maybe I misjudged you."

"It's not that."

"Then what?" The night was silent, except for the faint hum of the city, far below. At last Gudrun spoke. "Are you still not over Suzie Sanchez?"

Bernie's head snapped back, like he'd been hit. And for one terrible moment I thought he was about to hit her back, for real. I'd never seen Bernie hit a woman, or even come close. He never would and never could. Sweat appeared on his forehead, like he was in some awful struggle.

"What do you know about Suzie Sanchez?" he said.

"Not much. We have a mutual acquaintance."

"Who?" said Bernie.

Gudrun shook her head. "I won't say. But she told this mutual acquaintance that, quote, he loved that damn dog more than he loved me."

That staggered Bernie. He reached behind, gripped the couch with both hands. "I don't believe you."

Gudrun shrugged. She looked up at him. He looked over her head into some very faraway distance, but slowly his gaze came down and met hers.

"Believe this," Gudrun said. She took Bernie's face in both hands, pulled him close and kissed his mouth. And kept it there until Bernie started kissing her back, kissing her hard. He wrapped his arms around her and held her tight, even bending her backwards a little. One of his hands slipped up under her shirt. One of her hands did the same to him. Bernie made a sound deep in his throat, a sound I'd only heard from behind closed doors, then lifted her off the floor like she was nothing and started to turn, as though to carry her around to the other side of the couch.

That was when he saw me, watching from the top of the spiral stairs.

TWENTY-EIGHT

The trip down to Mexico was quiet. The night was quiet, the road was quiet, Bernie was quiet. Even the uniformed dude at the border was quiet, speaking softly like he was afraid of waking a baby.

We drove along the main drag of the little border town. Potholes appeared in the road, first one or two, then many, and by the time we hit open country there was no pavement left, the potholes winning out completely. Bernie's pedal foot usually gets heavy in open country, but not on this night. Even the Porsche, usually so loud in the best way, was quiet. The road curved up a long slope, no other traffic coming or going. At the top, Bernie pulled to the side, shut off the engine. Then came pocket patting, glove box checking, under the seat fishing, and finally he found a cigarette, somewhat bent. Bernie tried to straighten it, ended up breaking it in two. He lit up the longer end, breathed out a long smoky cloud that turned silver in the moonlight.

"God help me," he said.

God came up in many human conversations, but he remained a shadowy figure to me. What was his deal, anyway? Where was he? Could he help Bernie? And why would Bernie need help? Weren't we having a pretty good life, except for the finances part? Aha! I started to get where god might be useful.

The cigarette end glowed bright. Bernie blew out more smoke, shook his head. "Saved my bacon, Chet," he said.

He turned to me, his eyes sort of watery, but he wasn't crying. Bernie was not a crier, except for the day we packed up Charlie's room for his move to High Chaparral Estates. What we had going here had to be a trick of the moonlight.

"You know those movies where a house takes off from its foundation? That's me right now."

I was lost. The house thing made no sense to me at all. As for saving bacon, there was none around to be saved or for any other purpose, such as frying up a panful and chowing down. I know when bacon's on the scene, my friends. Trust me.

Bernie put his hand on my head, rested it

there in a way that felt perfect. "If she said something like that, or even close, then . . ."

Who? Saying what? And then? I had no answers, and before they could come, Bernie cranked 'er up and we got back on the road, much faster now. "Let's do some damage, big guy — like a wrecking ball."

What a great idea! Why hadn't we thought of it before? A wrecking ball, doing damage — who could ask for more? You have to be grateful in this life. I knew one thing for sure. We were going to be rich.

I caught a glimpse of a few dim lights at the base of a butte that blacked out a section of the starry sky. "That's where we're headed," Bernie said. "Los Pozos — can't remember what that means."

The road dipped down and the dim lights vanished. Cliffs, steep but not very high, rose on both sides. I heard the crunch of a boot heel somewhere up there and smelled a bit of weed. We came through the opening between the cliffs at the far end. A roofless pickup with a roll bar and two dudes in the front was parked across the road. Bernie stopped the car, took the .38 Special from the glove box, and placed it in the space between his seat and the door.

We sat where we were. The pickup dudes

sat where they were. I felt Bernie starting to relax inside. Most folks would be going in the other direction. Bernie's not most folks, which should be pretty clear by now.

Nothing happened for a while. Then the moon slipped behind a cloud. The dudes got out of the pickup and came toward us. One had a rifle over his shoulder, the other had a handgun in his belt. They were in no hurry. In our business when dudes like these two are in no hurry, it's up to you also to be in no hurry. I sat like I had all the time in the world. Which I did, so it was easy-peasy.

They stood on either side of the car and gave us tough-guy looks. Bernie gave them one of his no particular look of any kind looks, just one of his many techniques. The dude on his side said something in Spanish. I know the sound of Spanish, but hardly any words, just *tocino, cerveza, amigo, perro* — things like that.

"I do better in English," Bernie said.

"Yeah?" said the dude. "What if we don't?"

Bernie shrugged.

The dude on my side kicked one of our tires. "Why you ride a shitbox?" he said.

Bernie turned to him. "There's a law against shitboxes in Mexico?"

386

Silence. Their faces got all stony. Then the dude on Bernie's side started laughing. My dude got into it, too. They laughed and laughed. Bernie's dude had lots of gold teeth. My dude had pretty much no teeth of any kind. Their laughter died down.

"What are you doing here, man?" said Bernie's dude.

"Just visiting," said Bernie.

"Visiting who?"

"A friend of a friend."

"This friend of a friend have a name?"

"Sure," said Bernie. "But I don't broadcast things like that. I try to keep people safe, especially the harmless ones."

"Harmless?" said my dude.

"*Los inocuos,*" said the other.

The dudes glanced at each other over our heads.

"Fifty dollars," said Bernie's dude.

"Each," said my dude.

"Huh?" said Bernie. "Take another look at the car and think again."

The dudes laughed some more, ended up pocketing thirty each. Less than fifty apiece? More? I leave that to you. They moved the pickup off the road and we drove on.

The lights started blinking off in Los Pozos, the little town at the base of the butte. Bernie took a scrap of paper from his pocket, read the writing on it in the dashboard's green glow. We passed a few houses, all dark, and stopped before one that seemed a bit bigger than the others and had blue TV light shimmering behind the curtains. We got out of the car and knocked.

"Sí?" came a woman's voice from inside.

"Pepita?" Bernie said. "Juana gave us your address."

"You're the one with the dog?"

"Yes."

The door opened. A thin woman with dark circles under her eyes gave us a look and motioned us inside. She glanced up and down the street and shut the door.

We were in a small room, neat and tidy, with not much furniture. There were a few card table chairs, a floor lamp, a table, and a bed, where a man, also thin, lay sleeping. His chest went up and down. I smelled his breath, the breath of a human with something wrong inside. A girl sat beside the bed on one of the card table chairs. She'd been watching TV, the sound turned down, but now her eyes were on us: big dark eyes shiny with health. That was a nice sight. This was Tildy. I recognized her from the photo we'd found in Wendell's RV. Only a photo at first, and now here she was in real life. We were cooking, me and Bernie.

"Sit, please," Pepita said.

Bernie sat on the one remaining card table chair. Pepita sat on the end of the bed.

"Explain, please," Pepita said.

"I don't know what Juana told you."

"Just you can be trusted."

Bernie nodded. "I'm Bernie Little and this is Chet." He handed her our card. "Wendell Nero wanted to meet with us. He didn't say why."

"You don't have to speak so soft," Pepita said. "When my husband sleeps like this — and thank god for it — he hears nothing."

Bernie raised his voice a little. "We brought in the suspect but I don't think he's guilty, not of the murder. Something complicated is going on and I think maybe Tildy can help."

"Me?" Tildy said. She sounded very scared. Poor kid. I went over and sat beside her.

"I understand you were helping Wendell with his work," Bernie said.

The kid nodded. She was trembling. I sat on her feet, the only move I could think of. The trembling eased up a bit. Did the fact that I'm a hundred-plus pounder have something to do with it? The thought crossed my mind.

"He was such a nice man," Tildy said. Tears rose in those deep dark eyes and overflowed. She wiped them away with the back of her hand and didn't make a sound.

"He was teaching you?" Bernie said.

"Yes," said Tildy. "About hydrology."

"The hydrology of Dollhouse Canyon?"

"Not just that. The whole Southwest."

Bernie smiled a quick smile, there and gone. "Tell me something he taught you."

Tildy spread her hands, beautifully shaped hands, hard not to stare at. "There were so many things."

"Just one," Bernie said. "Maybe a fact that would surprise an ordinary person."

Tildy thought for a moment. "Earthquakes, even far away, can change the aquifer."

"That's news to me," Bernie said.

"You know about aquifers?" said Tildy.

"Not nearly enough." Bernie rose, took a photo from his pocket, held it so Tildy could see. I saw, too: the picture of Wendell and Tildy standing together, the rolled-up papers under her arm. Tildy gazed at the photo. Her eyes got misty again. I gave her knee a quick lick. This time there was no teary overflow.

Bernie pointed to the picture. "What are those papers?" he said, his voice gentle.

"Diagrams," said Tildy.

At that point I saw how closely Pepita was watching Tildy. There was love in that look, plus a kind of amazement. Her husband's eyes remained closed. He went on sleeping, filling the little room with his sick breath.

"Diagrams of what?" Bernie said.

"Not accurate diagrams based on tests," Tildy said. "They were really just Dr. Wendy's thoughts about the rain clouds below."

"The rain clouds below?"

"That was what he called the aquifers."

"Where are the papers now?" Bernie said.

"I don't know," said Tildy. "He kept them in the RV."

Bernie sat back down. He was quiet for a bit, his gaze on the sleeping man. "All right, Tildy," he said at last. "You be Dr. Wendy and I'll be you. Teach me about the rain cloud under Dollhouse Canyon."

"Rain clouds," said Tildy. "Little C and Big C."

"I don't understand."

"Neither did he at first! That was the whole problem. How come the grapes were still good when the aquifer was almost dried up? Dr. Wendy cudgeled his brain."

"Cudgeled his brain?"

"That's what he said. It means he thought

391

and thought until he wore out his poor brain. But finally it came to him. The earthquake shifted the aquitard! Eureka!"

"Whoa," said Bernie. "What earthquake?"

"The big California one — from Fullerton."

"But that was years ago."

"Slow and huge," Tildy said. "The forces are slow and huge."

Bernie gave her a long look. She rested a hand on my neck. I felt her pulse, surprisingly strong for such a skinny little person.

"What's an aquitard?" Bernie said.

"Any formation that blocks an aquifer," said Tildy.

"Keeping the water from getting to the surface?"

"You're a good student," Tildy said.

"Tildy!" said Pepita.

Bernie just laughed. Then he dug a pencil from his pocket and said, "Can you draw me those rain clouds?"

"Do we have any paper, Momma?" Tildy said.

Pepita turned to Bernie. "Is cardboard okay?"

"Sure," said Bernie.

Pepita went into a back room. I heard a ripping sound. She returned with a big piece of cardboard with one rough edge.

"Perfect," Bernie said.

They pulled their chairs up to the table. Tildy took the pencil. "Here is the surface. Down below — this is not to scale — we have . . ." She stuck her tongue between her teeth, did some drawing.

"That's the aquifer?" Bernie said.

"Little C," said Tildy. "A perched aquifer at four hundred and eighty feet. Perched means it's resting on a bed of hard rock, and don't think of it as a pool of water — it's more like a damp sponge. Or in the case of Little C, an almost dry sponge. And now comes the big surprise." Tildy did some more drawing, the pencil moving all the way to the edge of the cardboard and even off it.

"What's that?" Bernie said.

One interesting human expression is the look of triumph. It's not always a pleasant sight, but now on Tildy's face it was one of the nicest I'd ever seen. "Big C!" she said.

"Another aquifer?" said Bernie. "I don't get it."

"Right! And we didn't either until —" Tildy blushed, glanced at her mom, started over. "Dr. Wendy didn't either, not at first, not even after he studied the bore hole maps all the way to the Arkansas River. But it's true! And do you see this shape here?"

Bernie leaned closer. "Kind of like a spout?"

"Yes! A spout! That's exactly what Dr. Wendy said. A spout squeezing up between these two granite aquitards. You see them?"

"Kind of," said Bernie.

Tildy made some rapid movements with the pencil. "Is this better? See the granite formations, blocking off almost the whole of Big C? Except for the spout?"

Bernie pulled his chair in closer, bent over the drawing. Their heads, his and Tildy's, were almost touching. In the dim glow of the floor lamp, he suddenly looked much younger to me, and I also thought I saw how Tildy would look as a woman.

"Is the spout pouring into the bottom of Little C?" Bernie said.

"Not pouring," said Tildy. "We can't say pouring. But there is contact."

"And before there wasn't?"

Tildy nodded, a lock of glossy black hair falling over her face. "The earthquake shifted things around. There may not even have been a spout before, and Dr. Wendy thinks — he thought — that the whole formation with Big C inside got carried west for miles and up for hundreds of feet."

"Does that mean nobody knew about Big C before this?"

"It was all blocked off."

Bernie sat up, turned to her. There was a real intense look on his face, but he smoothed it out, made it gentle. "So who knows about this?"

"Me and now you," said Tildy. "And my mom."

"I don't know," said Pepita.

"But I told you."

"And I still don't know."

"Oh, Momma."

Bernie took another look at the drawing and pointed. "The vineyard is here?"

"Yes," said Tildy.

"Wendell didn't tell Diego about all this?"

"Diego?" Tildy said.

"Señor Diego," said Pepita.

Tildy shook her head. "First he wanted to do more research, map out the size and shape of Big C. But then . . ." She looked down.

The lamplight flickered, went brownish, then brightened. Over on the bed, Pepita's husband made a quiet little groan. Pepita walked over and laid her hand on his.

Tildy turned to Bernie. "This man, the one you arrested, is he a pilot?"

Bernie got that intense look again. This time it didn't go away. "A pilot?"

"A helicopter pilot."

"Why do you ask?"

"A helicopter landed near the trailer," Tildy said. "The pilot talked to Dr. Wendy. He sounded mean."

"What did he say?"

"I don't know. Dr. Wendy sent me back over the hill. But I watched from up on top. The pilot had a loud voice. I could hear the sound."

"Did Wendell talk about it after?"

"There was no after," Tildy said. "The next day I was with the goats and the day after that was when he . . . got killed. The day after that I was back here."

Bernie went to the window, parted the curtain, gazed out. "What kind of markings were on the helicopter?"

"I don't know," Tildy said. "It was dark gray."

"And what about the pilot?"

"He had a beard. And he was big. A real big guy, bigger than you."

"Anything else?" Bernie said.

Tildy squeezed her eyes shut. "He had one of those damaged ears — like they get in MMA."

"A cauliflower ear?" Bernie said.

Tildy opened her eyes and nodded. "Does that help?"

"Very much," said Bernie. Good news! I

hadn't been sure where we were going with this. "Can we take the drawing?"

"Sure," said Tildy. "But it's not very good."

We went outside, Bernie motioning Pepita to follow. Out on the street he said, "What's wrong with your husband?"

"They don't know."

Bernie took out his wallet, gave her all the money inside. Pepita's face seemed to be saying no but her hands had other ideas.

TWENTY-NINE

Back in the car, I was thinking along the lines of whether there was a cantina in Los Pozos, and if so would it have an alley in back, where . . . where certain encounters might take place? Bernie looked very thoughtful. Was he also thinking cantina thoughts? I couldn't tell, but very soon we were out of Los Pozos so that was that.

"When Charlie's twelve, I wonder if he'll be . . ." Bernie began. That was followed by a quiet spell and then he laughed and said, "No way."

Meanwhile the moon was sliding down the sky. From time to time, Bernie tapped the brakes, cut the headlights, and peered all around. Why? I had no idea. All I really knew was that our wallet was empty, although on the plus side we had Tildy's piece of cardboard. I sat up nice and tall, like the kind of dude who knows exactly what's going on and why. And all at once I was that dude. Or just about. Was that how it worked? How nice to learn new things!

Bernie got on the phone.

"Hey, Lou. It's me."

"It's the middle of the night," said Captain Stine.

"Tell me something I don't know," Bernie said.

"What's good for you," said Stine.

Then came a long silence. We were bumping along on this bad road but somehow Bernie was sitting very still, his eyes greenish in the glow from the dash. The sight reminded me of Gudrun's eyes, and that led — funny how the mind works — to Bernie and Gudrun and that kiss on her deck, high over the Valley. Gudrun was no friend of mine. Bernie was . . . well, Bernie. So we had a big problem, except the kissing had stopped mid-kiss and pronto for some reason, and the next thing I knew we were out of there. Problem or no problem? I had no answer. Sometimes the mind is no help at all.

"Bernie? Still there? Disturbed my sleep just to give me the silent treatment?"

"There must be a list of licensed helo pilots in the state," Bernie said.

"Are you musing out loud or asking a question?" said Stine.

"I need to know if a man named Mason Venatti is on it. And if he is I want the full CV."

We were back where those cliffs rose on both sides of the road.

"Any point in me asking why?" said Stine.

"First let's see —"

"Not hearing you —"

"First —"

"You've gone all —"

Bernie glanced up at the cliffs. "Lost him," he said. We drove on, came to where the cliffs ended in softly rounded hills, and there, again parked across the road, stood the black roofless pickup with the roll bar.

"A two-way toll?" Bernie stopped the car.

We sat. Were we waiting for the two dudes to come over and collect more money? That wasn't going to be easy, what with Pepita now having all our cash. Would we have to return to Los Pozos and ask for it back? This was turning out to be a complicated night. Plus I was getting hungry. And not just getting — I was all the way there, big time. Was there any food at all in the car? Even a stale biscuit would have been a start. One quick sniff and I had the answer, not a good one.

We waited. The dudes seemed in no hurry. I could see their silhouettes in the moonlight, one sitting up straight in the passenger seat, the driver slumped a bit, possibly napping. Napping? Good grief. I was famished. *Bernie! Do something!*

Then came a surprise, and a welcome one: Bernie opened the car door and said, "Let's move these guys along."

Did this mean I could get Bernie to do things just by thinking them? Could I have been doing it all this time? I hopped out, trotted up beside him. *Bernie? How about scratching between my ears in that spot I can't get to? On the way home, let's swing by Dry Gulch Steakhouse and Saloon for steak tips. After that we can buy a new Frisbee — the old one's getting ratty — and play some fetch. Then we'll probably be hungry again — am I going too fast? — so we could head for —*

I glanced at Bernie. Was he getting all this? I couldn't tell. His eyes were on the pickup and he was on high alert. Bernie has a high-alert smell I don't miss. I was also picking up another smell, also of a kind I don't miss, namely blood. We walked closer, reached the point where Bernie would usually say "Hey" or "Hi" or something else to let folks — especially trigger-happy types — know that we were in the area. But Bernie said nothing. We went right up to the pickup.

Both our dudes had round holes right in

the middle of their foreheads, round holes that had bled a little and stopped. Those bloody holes looked silvery in the moon-light. Then a line of clouds, like a lid, slid over the moon and the holes turned black.

Bernie walked slowly around the pickup. "A cartel thing? I just don't —"

At that moment I picked up one more smell to go with the Bernie-on-high-alert smell and the drying-blood smell. I'd first learned this new smell way back in K-9 school. I'd flunked out on the very last day, in case you've forgotten, but that's not the point. Oh, but if only . . .

Never mind that. The point was this new smell, a very important smell, kind of like a mixture of Legos and wet clay. That smell means business. I ran right up to Bernie, faced him, looked him in the eye and barked a single bark, a bark that also means business.

"What's up, Chet?"

I barked once more, not an especially loud bark, but very sharp. Bernie glanced around. As for what he was seeing, my guess was not much. With the moon gone it was very dark and humans are pretty much blind in the very dark. We do better in the nation within. I could make out the expression in Bernie's eyes, a look he gets when he's thinking real fast. Then, all at once, he said "Let's go," giving me a little push to get me started. Imagine that! And me, a self-starter if there ever was one!

We ran — Bernie at top speed for him, me in what you might call a medium trot — across the road, up the slope that led to the cliff, toward a big boulder. I scrambled in behind it, just knowing that was what Bernie wanted me to do, and he threw himself on top of me. I struggled around, trying to get on top of him.

And then: *KABOOM!*

A tremendous kaboom that shook the air, the earth, and me and Bernie, too. The sky overhead caught fire, orange flames shooting out, some straight up, some sideways, some at us. Hard metal things zinged all around, thwacking into the ground and pinging off the face of our boulder.

Then, just like that, almost a reverse kaboom, if that makes any sense, it was over. The flames died out, the zinging and pinging stopped, the night went still. There were smells, of course, smoke, hot metal, burned plastic, burned, well, meat, I'm sorry to mention, but that was it.

"You okay, Chet?"

Perfectly fine.

"Good job. One of your very best."

I thumped my tail on the ground, maybe thumped it a few more times. I felt tip-top. Mess with us, my friends? Who's next?

Meanwhile there was nothing going on. Back home we'd be having sirens, and people running around, and lots of chatter, but none of that was happening. I peered out from behind the boulder, made out the twisted form of the remains of the pickup and the dark slope rising from the far side of the road.

"Stay," Bernie said, his voice very quiet. He had the .38 Special in his hand.

"Stay" is a biggie in our lives. We stayed, me and Bernie. We don't mess around with the biggies. And if we do, there has to be a real good reason. Slim Jims just out of reach, for example.

But now, behind our boulder on this night that now seemed even quieter than silent, which can happen after a big boom, there were no Slim Jims, no reason at all not to stay. The wind came up. The clouds thinned out and moonlight shone through, although the moon itself remained hidden. Then the clouds thickened and the night darkened again. I'm a lover of the night. I love daytime, too, but isn't there something about the night? You must have noticed.

"If it's the cartels," Bernie said, "there

won't be anyone here till daylight. But if it's . . ."

How nice to hear Bernie's thoughts, even just some of them. Or especially just some of them. All his thoughts would probably have been a little too much. There's only so much brilliance us ordinary brains can handle at once. As for the cartels, we'd once had dealings with a guy called El Primo who offered to pay us big green if we'd —

What was that?

A very soft crunch, coming from somewhere on the slope across the road. I straightened up, sat very still, just at the edge of the boulder. Bernie crouched behind me, his hands on my shoulders, his head over mine.

"Can't see a goddamn thing," he said very softly.

Crunch. And another, and some more. But quiet crunches, the kind made by someone who knows how to move in the dark, even when the footing's tricky. Then a man-shaped shadow — a big man-shaped shadow — separated itself from the greater shadow of the slope and came down onto the road.

A man, for sure. He approached what was left of the pickup, walked slowly around it, went closer. He seemed to make movements with one of his legs. Poking his foot into the wreckage? I thought so. Then he started around the pickup again, this time in a larger circle. He was coming our way when the clouds parted and the moon appeared, brighter than I'd ever seen it. The moonlight turned the shadow-man into a real man, a very big man with a trim beard, kind of handsome except for the cauliflower ear. It was Mason Venatti. He had a short, stubby sort of rifle slung over one shoulder, and was looking down the road.

Bernie stepped away from me, raised the .38 Special. "Mason! Hands up!"

Mason whipped around toward us. He did not put his hands up. Instead — so quick for such a big man — he threw himself on the ground, rolled, twisted, and started firing.

THUNK THUNK THUNK, THUNK THUNK THUNK.

Oh, no. Automatic fire. I knew automatic fire from K-9 school, something you never wanted to deal with. Bernie, too, hit the ground, also twisted around, and seemed to kick at me with his legs, as though to shove me back behind the boulder. What a crazy idea!

THUNK THUNK, THUNK THUNK.

"Ewph." Bernie made a little sound. Was

406

he hit? I got ready to charge across the road and —

"Chet! No!"

THUNK THUNK, THUNK —

And then Bernie, on his knees, got off his first shot. *CRACK!*

Mason cried out, put a hand to his chest, slumped backwards, the machine gun falling onto the road. I heard him breathing — hard breathing, like he'd just run a race — and perhaps a soft gurgle.

Bernie rose and walked slowly toward him, the .38 Special pointed right at Mason's head. I walked with him, side by side. When we reached Mason, Bernie kicked the machine gun away. I sat on it, the only idea I had at that moment.

Bernie gazed down at Mason. Mason gazed up at him. His hands, still clutching his chest, were soaked with blood, like they were getting a coat of molten silver. He opened his mouth. Blood leaked out, but not a lot, not like what was pouring from his chest. He tried to spit it away, couldn't get his lips to work. But he could talk.

"You're fucking doomed," he said. "You don't know what you're dealing with."

"Wrong," said Bernie. "It's chin music. I was slow on the uptake, that's all."

Mason hated that remark. I could see it in

his eyes. A moment later there was nothing. I'd caught last looks in the eyes of a number of men — I'm a pro, don't forget — last looks full of pain, or fear, or even peace, but this one, hatred, was a first.

We examined Bernie's leg in the moonlight. There seemed to be a chunk missing from the side of the thigh.

"Just a scratch," Bernie said.

Whew! Was I glad to hear that or what? Bernie got out the first-aid kit, patched himself up, a patch that bled through so he did it again, way better this time. He found a fresh pair of jeans under my seat and we hit the road.

The first milky light was poking into the sky when the phone buzzed.

"Hey, Bernie, Lou. Lost you back there. Everything okay?"

"Yup."

"Got some info on that name, Mason Venatti. Bottom line — watch your step around him."

"Yeah?"

"Former marine helo pilot, decorated many times, but ended up with a dishonorable discharge, involved in some sort of atrocity, although that's not the word in the file. Killed a man in a barroom brawl outside of San Antonio two years ago, self-defense, according to the jury. Now doing some sort of contract work for Lobb and Edmonds. That's a fancy pants law firm downtown, in case you don't know."

"Uh-huh," Bernie said.

"Any idea why they'd want a type like that?"

"I'll ask around."

"You don't want to mix it up with this guy," Stine said.

"I hear you," said Bernie.

THIRTY

"Now," said Bernie, "I'm going to do something stupid." He glanced at me. "You're thinking what's new, huh?"

Me? Not really. In fact, I hadn't been thinking at all, was instead just letting my mind have a nice quiet rest while I watched the sky turn brighter and brighter. But if Bernie wanted me to think what's new, then that was that. I immediately thought to myself, "What's new, Chetster?" Nothing came right away.

Meanwhile Bernie got on the phone.

"Hello?" said Suzie.

Humans all sound pretty much the same when the phone wakes them from a sound sleep: confused and not too happy about it.

"Uh, it's me, Bernie."

"I know."

"Hope I didn't wake you."

"No. I was up." In the background a sleepy-sounding man said something I didn't catch. I began to wonder whether this call was . . . not a stupid idea, no way Bernie could ever have a stupid idea, but perhaps not his best.

"I'd like to see you," Bernie said.

There was a long pause. "What about?"

"Just briefly."

Was *just briefly* a good answer to *what about*? I would have guessed not, but I was wrong. "We're at Rancho Grande," Suzie said, "in one of the casitas. Number seven, behind the peacock garden."

Humans are not always easy to understand. I'd learned that over and over in my career and was now learning it again. Good things just keep happening to me.

I'm fine with peacocks up to the moment when they spread those huge fans or tails or whatever they were. And as we walked by a nice little garden behind Rancho Grande, wouldn't you know it? The biggest peacock I'd ever seen strolled out from behind a flowering bush, turned his eyes on me — nasty and mean, no doubt about it — and did exactly what he shouldn't have done. I'm the well-behaved type, but there's only so much anyone can —

"Ch-et? Chet!"

We kept going, no problem whatsoever,

411

with Bernie trailing closely behind me for some reason, and soon stood before a pretty pink casita. Bernie took a deep breath and knocked on the door. After some time when nothing happened, I smelled Suzie. At the same moment, Bernie raised his hand to knock. Suzie opened the door while his fist was still up in the air. Bernie jammed it in his pocket.

"Hi, Bernie," said Suzie. She gave me a quick pat. Suzie looked great, her face kind of rosy even though she has the kind of skin that doesn't really get rosy.

"Uh," Bernie said, his gaze on her like . . . like it was beyond his control, locked on Suzie forever. "Sorry," he said.

"For what?"

"Disturbing you." Bernie looked down. "So early."

"You're not disturbing me," Suzie said. "What's up?"

Jacques appeared behind Suzie, carrying a bicycle, the speedy-looking kind. "Morning everybody! Hi, Bernie. Hey, Chet!" He came outside, hopped on the bike and zoomed off. We all watched him till he was out of sight.

"Come on in," Suzie said.

"That's all right," said Bernie. "I need to ask you something."

412

"Shoot."

"Do you know a lawyer named Gudrun Burr?"

"At Lobb and Edmonds? We've met."

"Did she mention me?"

"She did, in fact. It turns out she's representing the suspect you brought in on some murder case. I hadn't known that."

"So you were meeting about something else?"

"Correct. She just happened to know about . . . you and me." Suzie's eyes narrowed. "Why would we be meeting about you?"

Bernie smiled a small smile. "Good point," he said. "Can I ask what the subject was?"

"Sure," said Suzie. "The story I mentioned — the one Jacques and I are working on, the one we're hoping to use to launch the platform."

"The endowment fund thing?"

"More or less," Suzie said.

"What's Gudrun Burr's role?" Bernie said.

"She's a troubleshooter — a very formidable troubleshooter according to a few people who've come in contact with her."

"She's troubleshooting for the endowment fund?" Bernie said.

"That's not clear. But I really can't get into the details."

Bernie got an idea. I could see it on his face. "Or maybe she's working for a Swiss company?"

Suzie gave Bernie a close look. "There are a number of Swiss — putatively Swiss — companies involved. Do you know something, Bernie? Where are you going with this?"

"I'm not sure," Bernie said. "I could give a better answer if I knew who Gudrun's working for. Can't you trust me to keep a secret?"

Suzie reached out, as though to touch Bernie's chest, but didn't quite do it. Then she sighed. "Goes without saying," she said. She thought for a moment or two and went on. "It's not just Gudrun Burr — it's Lobb and Edmonds in general, and a couple of other big firms, one in LA, one in Chicago. They represent the Veritan endowment fund."

"One hundred billion dollars?"

"And rising all the time," Suzie said. "But time is what they've got, even more than money. They think far into the future and their goals are colossal."

"For example?" Bernie said.

"For example, there's our story. Veritan is buying up lots of land in the state — and in New Mexico and parts of California as well — rural, urban, productive, non-productive, doesn't matter. The only point of commonality is the price, always over market, often way over market. At least that's what we have so far. The data isn't easy to come by. There's a screen of offshore entities that's hard to penetrate, but the whole thing is very strange."

"Is this what you were meeting about at the Veritan Club?"

"Exactly. Loudon DeBrusk is the CEO of the endowment fund. He doesn't acknowledge the overseas companies — at the same time saying there's nothing illegal about them, which is probably true. As for the rationale behind this sort of drunken-sailor spending spree, he says Veritan is simply buying into the future of America."

"It's patriotic?"

"He used that very word," Suzie said. "But why pay more than the land is worth? He denied that was the case, despite the numbers — at least the ones Jacques and I have found — being clear. We just don't get it."

"Thank you," Bernie said.

"For what?"

"This is a huge help."

"How?"

"I'll tell you later," Bernie said. "But there is one more thing." Bernie opened his mouth, closed it, opened it again.

"Speak," said Suzie.

Bernie looked down. He took a deep breath. "Did you . . . tell Gudrun . . ."

"Tell her what?"

"That — that the reason you and I . . . or the reason you no longer wanted to . . ." His head came up. "Oh, Christ, was because I loved —"

He gestured at me with his chin. What I was suddenly doing in this incomprehensible conversation was a complete mystery.

"— more than you," Bernie went on.

Suzie put her hand to her chest. "What a foul thing to do!" she said. "Never!"

"Whew," said Bernie. "That's so good to know!" He turned to me. "Come on, Chet."

"What?" said Suzie. "You're leaving?"

I was surprised myself, although hitting the road is part of our business plan.

"Where are you going?" Suzie called after us.

"To get your wedding present," Bernie called back.

We parked in front of a small adobe building I recognized. Bernie grabbed our piece of cardboard — very important evidence for reasons I hoped would someday be clear to me — and went to the front door, a glass door of the dark-tinted kind. Bernie tried the handle. Locked. He pressed a buzzer. A voice spoke from a little speaker, a man's voice I recognized.

"Who's there?"

"Chet and Bernie."

"Excuse me?"

"You know who we are," Bernie said. "Open up."

"No can do. I'm rather busy right now."

"Curse of the modern age."

"Agreed. You're welcome to call and schedule an appoint—"

SMASHEROO! Bernie kicked in the door. Not the glass part — that didn't even break. His foot went right for the lock, which was proper technique for kicking in doors. We strolled inside.

And there was Hoskin Phipps, his smooth pinkish face turning red, his tortoiseshell glasses crooked on top of his head. He backed away, hands raised. "This is outrageous," he said. "I'm calling the police."

"In a few minutes," Bernie said. He walked right up to Hoskin, raised his hand. Hoskin flinched, like Bernie was about to smack him one, but all Bernie did was take careful hold of the tortoiseshell glasses and place them on Hoskin's nose. "First we've got something for you to look at." Bernie turned to the nearest desk, swept everything

417

off in a lovely crashing way, and set down our piece of cardboard. Then he made a little finger gesture for Hoskin to come closer. Hoskin came closer.

"Tell me what you see here," Bernie said.

Hoskin glanced at Tildy's drawing. "No idea."

"Here's a clue," Bernie said. "This line represents ground level at Dollhouse Canyon."

Hoskin took a more careful look this time. His eyes shifted, then shifted again.

"We're waiting," Bernie said.

Hoskin licked his lips, dry-looking lips, and his tongue looked dry as well. My own tongue felt nice and moist. I considered licking my muzzle, decided to put it off till later. It's nice to have something to look forward to in this life.

"Where did you get this?" Hoskin said.

"Hoskin? Are you listening?"

Hoskin nodded.

"You're not asking the questions. Got it?"

"You have no right to bully me," Hoskin said.

Bernie hardly ever gets angry, but when he does it's always a treat to see. He grabbed Hoskin by the front of his button-down shirt, lifted him right off the ground, and plunked him into a chair — not gently —

and shoved the chair up to the desk, giving Hoskin a close-up view of Tildy's drawing.

"I have a weak heart," Hoskin said.

"I'll say," said Bernie. "Now let's have it."

Hoskin straightened out his shirt and pointed to the drawing. "This is the perched aquifer I told you about. But I don't understand all this fuss."

"Liar," Bernie said, not raising his voice at all but at the same time sounding pretty scary. I was getting very good feelings about the case. Bernie rested his fingertip on the cardboard, down toward the bottom. "What's this?"

Hoskin shrugged. "Perhaps some sort of speculative —"

Bernie smacked the back of Hoskin's head, not very hard, although his glasses flew off and landed on the floor. I snapped them up and gnawed a bit on a tortoiseshell arm. It didn't smell at all of tortoise, which was kind of disappointing. I let go of the glasses.

"It . . . it resembles an upwardly extruding formation," said Hoskin.

"Meaning an aquifer?" Bernie said.

Hoskin nodded.

"A big one?"

"These terms are relative."

"Compared to the other one."

419

"Yes, bigger."

"How much bigger?"

"I haven't determined that yet. All I —" Hoskin stopped himself.

Bernie looked down at him. Hoskin wouldn't meet his gaze. "You got paid to produce an accurate hydrology report," Bernie said. "You withheld crucial information. Why?"

"I don't agree with your characterization," Hoskin said.

"It's all over," Bernie said. "You may end up in jail. The time to eliminate your personal worst-case scenario is now."

"I wouldn't be so sure about things if I were you," Hoskin said.

"Because it's Veritan on the other side?"

Hoskin didn't answer.

"Why are they buying up so much land?" Bernie said. "And why are they paying so much for it?"

"You're really not very bright, are you?" Hoskin said. "The goddamn land isn't worth anything. Only the water has value."

"They're buying up all the water in the West?"

"Of course not. Just our fair share. The motive is totally altruistic. We're on the side of conservation. This . . . this ownership will give us more power to do good. Sometimes the people need a little nudge."

"Who elected you — who elected Veritan — to be the nudger?" Bernie said.

"That's a rather naïve position to take," said Hoskin. "If you don't mind my saying so."

"I do mind." Bernie picked the tortoise-shell glasses off the floor and very slowly and carefully put them back on Hoskin's face, getting them nice and straight, just right. It seemed to take forever. "Wendell Nero got nudged to death," he said.

Hoskin went a bit teary. "Oh my god — I had nothing to do with that."

"Who did?"

"It was her. Her and that thuggish side-kick."

"You're talking about Gudrun Burr and Mason Venatti?"

"They were only supposed to persuade Wendell, bribe him, perhaps, with threatening as the last option."

"But he wasn't the bribable type?"

Hoskin shook his head.

"And also not the kind who's easily scared," Bernie said.

"So it appears."

I felt an enormous surge of strength in Bernie, got ready for something very bad to happen to Hoskin. But then Bernie got a grip. The effort made him shiver the tiniest bit. "Which one cut Wendell's throat — Gudrun or Mason?"

"I don't know firsthand," Hoskin said.

"Who's your source?"

"I . . . I can't recall. I was very upset at the time. Wendell and I weren't friends, but there was a mutual —"

"Shut up," Bernie said.

Hoskin shut up.

Then came a strange quiet time, where Bernie just gazed at Tildy's drawing. Soon Hoskin was gazing at it, too. Finally he raised his head. "It was her. Evidently Wendell told them he was going to call the police. She . . . she lost her temper. She's said to have a temper." He touched the cardboard. "There's a kind of ruthlessness in the land these days."

"I don't disagree," Bernie said. "Why didn't she take Wendell's cell phone and laptop?"

"A stupid mistake on her part," said Hoskin. "As will happen when temper gets the best of one. The potential import hadn't even crossed her mind until I —" Hoskin went silent. Bernie gazed at him. Hoskin looked down.

"Here," Bernie said, picking up a bottle of water.

"I'm not thirsty," Hoskin said.

"Drink," said Bernie.

Hoskin took a sip.

"More," Bernie said.

Hoskin drank more. We found some duct tape, got him comfortably settled in a chair, and hit the road.

"More," Bernie said.

THIRTY-ONE

We drove along Upper Camino Royale, as high above the Valley as you can get, and came to the tall metal gate. Last time a bird had been perched on one of the gateposts. Now there was a bird on each, both of them watching us with their unfriendly little eyes.

"This could be tricky," Bernie said.

But just as before, a man's voice spoke. "Welcome, Mr. Little. Drive on through."

So it wasn't tricky at all! Today was off to a great start. We'd already duct-taped a perp — assuming Hoskin was a perp, since we hardly ever duct-taped non-perps — and we hadn't even had breakfast yet. That, by the way, was a small problem, but of the kind that can blow up into something very big, as I'd learned way too many times.

We followed the long curving driveway of polished pavers toward Gudrun's house, that strange arrangement of boxes that by night had seemed so easily toppleable off the cliff edge, and now by day seemed even more so. We parked in front of the door but while we were still in the car, Gudrun's voice came from somewhere above.

"Hey, there," she said, sounding very friendly. "I've been expecting you. Come around to the back."

Bernie took the .38 Special from the glove box. We got out of the car. Bernie didn't tuck the gun in his waistband or stick it in his pocket, instead held it by his side. When had that ever happened? All at once, I remembered the one and only time: very late — too late, as it turned out — on the night of the broom closet case. The little girl's name was Gail, a name I can't forget.

We followed a path lined with flower beds. It led almost to the edge of a cliff, where it ended in a sort of walkway that I didn't want to walk on at all. The floor part of the walkway was some sort of thick glass, and so were the walls, which were much too low, in my opinion. This walkway followed the cliff edge, but out in midair, and led to another one of those boxes, this one also in midair, although it maybe was being held up by a sort of metal arm rising from below — kind of how a waiter carries a tray. Whoa! What a strange thought! Not me at all. The truth was my mind was sort of spinning out here in midair, and —

"Chet? We're all right, big guy."

Oh. Good to hear. I'd almost been slightly worried there for a second, which I'm pretty sure is a very short time.

Meanwhile we were almost at the end of the walkway. There stood this outdoor glass box, similar to those that made up the whole house, except for having no roof. I could tell that from how a fountain in the box was spraying a feathery jet of water into the sky. The fountain itself — and the entire inside of the box — couldn't be seen at all, on account of those glass walls being the darkened kind.

"Come on in," said Gudrun from inside.

A glass door that had seemed like part of the wall slowly opened. We stepped through. Usually — actually always — I'm the first one through any doorway, but now Bernie blocked me. Yes, blocked me. There was no other way to put it. He went through first, with me behind him, as close as I could get.

There are big surprises and small surprises in our line of work. A small surprise would have been Gudrun waiting for us with a gun in her hand, even though her voice had been sounding so friendly today. I wouldn't have been very surprised by that small surprise, on account of the way Bernie was carrying the .38 Special by his side. He could raise it and make it talk its .38 Special talk real quick from that position, take it from me.

But he did not. Far from it. When Gudrun said, "Please let go of the gun, Bernie," he did as he was told.

"And kick it away, if you don't mind."

Bernie kicked it away.

What we had here was a big surprise. We were on a sort of patio, the glass walls somehow not as high as they'd looked from outside, no higher than my head if I'd been standing on my hind legs. There was a green-glass fountain, its shape not an animal or anything else that made sense to me, and a lawn chair. Gudrun stood behind the lawn chair and held no gun.

None of that was the big surprise. The big surprise was the person sitting in the chair, namely Tildy. And what Gudrun did have in her hand, namely a knife, a red-handled knife with a very thin blade, but long. She held it by her side, the same way Bernie had held the .38 Special.

Oh, poor Tildy! Would I ever forget the look on her face? It was the face of a kid who had a great big scream inside her but wouldn't let it out. Her eyes, wet but not overflowing, were fixed on us, me and Bernie, and sending us desperate messages.

There were desperate human smells in the air as well, Tildy's, and other human smells I'd hardly ever encountered, at least not together, crazed and murderous. Those were Gudrun's.

Crazed and murderous for sure — smells don't lie, one of the reasons I'm so good at this business, as Bernie has explained to more than one perp — but on the outside Gudrun looked relaxed.

"I could use someone like you, Bernie," she said. "Especially now that Mason's gone. Call it a classic Darwinian demonstration." She laughed. "Not that you and I will be breeding — you made that very clear. But I'd never let that stand in the way of building a productive professional relationship."

"You're out of your mind," Bernie said, his voice quiet. Also his hand was on my head, just touching. Were we in command? That was my takeaway.

Gudrun smiled. She almost kept looking relaxed, but one eyelid came down the slightest bit over one of those green eyes, and started to twitch, not a lot, just enough for me to notice.

"Any chance you'd want to take that comment back?" she said.

Bernie shook his head.

"What if you knew Wendell Nero slurred me in those exact words?" Gudrun said.

"Is that why you killed him?" said Bernie.

Gudrun reached out with her free hand, touched Tildy's hair. Tildy made a tiny sound deep in her throat, tiny but terrible.

"Wendell's . . . end result was his own doing," Gudrun said. "We weren't asking a lot."

"You were asking him to betray his life's work," said Bernie.

"My my," said Gudrun. "You have a feminine way of thinking. I'd never have guessed."

"Fine with me," Bernie said. "But what we need to talk about now is how to stop all this before anyone else gets hurt."

"Please," said Gudrun. "You must be more of a realist than that." She glanced down at Tildy. "You're a smart girl, Tildy, it turns out. Explain to Bernie here what a realist is."

"I . . . I . . . I can't," Tildy said.

Gudrun touched her hair again. "Go on," she said. "This isn't a judgmental crowd."

"That's enough," Bernie said.

"Ah," said Gudrun. "The almost-but-not-quite apple of my eye doesn't seem to understand the pecking order here." She raised the knife, the handle held delicately between finger and thumb. "First comes me." She lowered the knife. "I'm a reasonable person, Bernie. It's my defining characteristic. Reasonable people know how to make deals. Following me so far?"

"Go on," Bernie said.

"I'll go on when I'm good and ready. You don't define me. Is that clear?"

Bernie nodded.

"Say it's clear."

Bernie's voice got very thick. "It's clear," he said.

"You know what we mean by an NDA, Bernie?" said Gudrun.

"A non-disclosure agreement."

"Bingo." Gudrun had a wicker basket at her feet. She reached down, took out a folder. "Sign these papers and you walk out of here with Tildy."

"What's to stop me from breaking the agreement?" Bernie said.

"Good question," said Gudrun, "although a little strange that you'd be the one to raise it. The answer is that Chet will be in my care for a temporary but undefined period, the end date of which will depend on the finalization of certain business arrangements and your continuing good behavior."

"Out of the question," said Bernie.

"That's just your emotional reaction,"

Gudrun said. "I'm confident that the rational part of you soon takes command in situations like this." She reached into the wicker basket again, took out a strange jumble of things, tossed the jumble to Bernie, his hands sort of catching it on their own. "Let's get started," Gudrun said.

Bernie gazed at the jumble. So did I. At first I didn't make sense of what I was seeing. And then I did. What Bernie had in his hands were a leash and a muzzle. He dropped them on the floor.

"You're delusional," he said.

Gudrun took a firmer grip on the knife, held it close to Tildy's throat, although not touching. Tildy made a tiny little squeak, a bit like a baby having a bad dream. "Why are you not getting this?" Gudrun said.

"Hurt her and I'll kill you," Bernie said.

"But it would be too late," Gudrun said. "And even then I like my chances. Now muzzle your dog."

Bernie shook his head.

Gudrun moved the knife. The point touched the side of Tildy's neck. And now, finally, Tildy let out the scream that had been building inside her. Had I ever heard a sound so terrible? And meanwhile there was the sight of her neck, such a child-like, innocent neck, if that makes any sense.

Gudrun raised her voice. "Zip it."

A tiny drop of blood appeared on Tildy's neck. She went silent, although tears now streamed down her face.

"Bend down," Gudrun said. "Pick up the muzzle. Do the right thing."

Bernie looked at me. For a moment I thought tears were going to start streaming down his face, too. But why? And in the end, they did not. Instead he bent down and picked up the muzzle.

"Easy, big guy."

Sure thing. If Bernie said easy then I was at ease. He opened the wide end of the muzzle and slipped it over my face. No one had ever muzzled me before except for two perps, real bad guys who'd gotten what they deserved. Bernie was not a bad guy. He was the very best. And besides he was Bernie. I let him muzzle me, no problem. Bernie had to have his reasons. Wasn't he always the smartest human in the room? Snap snap — and I was all buckled in.

"The leash," Gudrun said.

Bernie hooked on the leash.

"Now send him over."

Bernie took my head in his hands, gazed deep in my eyes. Oh, no! He looked so unhappy, the unhappiest I'd ever seen him. What was going on?

432

"Go, Chet," he said, and pointed toward Gudrun.

Did I want to go over to Gudrun? Certainly not. But Bernie always knows what he's doing. That's why he's in charge of the thinking at the Little Detective Agency. I bring other things to the table.

I walked over to Gudrun, not fast, but I did it. She grabbed the leash with one hand, stepping slightly away from Tildy. And now — whoa! — the knife was at my throat. I felt its sharpness through my fur.

"Get the folder out of the basket, Tildy," Gudrun said.

Tildy, still sitting in the chair, took the folder from the basket.

"Take it to Bernie. There's a pen inside. He's going to sign the agreement. Bring it back. And then you're free to go, no harm done."

Tildy rose, very slowly, like her legs weren't giving her much help. Gudrun glanced at me, then turned her gaze to Bernie. If she wasn't scared by the look on his face, she was scared of nothing. The knife was still at my throat. Tildy took a first hesitant step, one of her hands still on the arm of the chair. Both of Gudrun's hands were busy, one holding the leash, the other holding the knife. One more point:

Gudrun's eyes were still on Bernie.

Right then was when Tildy did an amazing thing. She dropped the folder, grabbed the arm of the chair so she now had both hands on it, whipped around, the muscles in her arms sticking out like cords, and heaved it at Gudrun.

Gudrun hadn't seen this coming! The chair hit her in the chest. She reeled back, almost fell, let go of the leash and — and dropped the knife! It clattered across the floor. I charged after it, completely forgetting about the muzzle. How was I ever going to pick up the knife while wearing a muzzle? That thought didn't even occur to me. I charged my hardest charge.

Meanwhile Gudrun was charging, too, charging for the same thing as me, the red-handled knife. We dove for it at the exact same moment and crashed together. Gudrun went flying. Don't forget I'm a hundred-plus pounder.

Gudrun flew. She hit the rail of the low glass wall, clutched at it, missed, did a whole sort of somersault, and suddenly spun over to the other side of the rail, all of that meaning she was turned toward us but in midair, high over the Valley. The expression on her face was all about not believing. And then she was gone.

Bernie ripped the muzzle off my face. He knelt and brought me and Tildy in close.

Loudon DeBrusk, who had something to do with the Veritan Endowment Fund, whatever that was, exactly, wanted to meet us at the Veritan Club. Bernie laughed in his face — not really, since it was a phone call, but close enough — and told him the venue — his exact word — would be the 7-Eleven parking lot under the Rio Vista Bridge approach.

DeBrusk's driver opened the back door of the long black car and DeBrusk came over to us, Bernie leaning against the Porsche and me leaning against Bernie. He held out his hand for shaking. Bernie ignored it.

"I just wanted to thank you for all your work on this," DeBrusk said.

"Oh?" said Bernie.

"We at the fund are simply not constituted to cope with a rogue employee — in this case not even an employee, but a contract worker."

"So that's how it's going to be?" Bernie said.

"Absolutely," said DeBrusk. "We couldn't be sorrier about allowing someone like her to slip through our screening process."

"She slipped through a number of times,"

Bernie said.

"Excuse me?"

"She was a Veritan graduate, and a graduate of Veritan Law — in fact came first in her class. Also taught there a few semesters, I believe. That's three slip-ups for starters."

DeBrusk smiled the kind of smile that's only a slight upturn of the lips, no more. "Do I detect the whiff of class resentment?" he said.

A whiff of what? I'd sniffed in more whiffs in a morning than a dude like this would deal with in a lifetime, and I'd never come across anything of the kind, and certainly not now. Wasn't I supposed to be grabbing DeBrusk by the pant leg? *Bernie! Ándale!*

But Bernie just said, "Nope."

"Glad to hear that," said DeBrusk. "And you yourself might be interested to hear that the endowment is undertaking a top-to-bottom reassessment of our investment plan, with special reference to land use, pricing, and transparency."

"Are you quitting or waiting till they fire you?" Bernie said.

DeBrusk's snowy eyebrows rose. "Neither." He laughed. "As far as I know."

"So the fall guy will come from the higher-ups?" said Bernie.

DeBrusk stopped laughing.

"I've seen Suzie Sanchez's story," Bernie said. "You've got a supporting role, but not insignificant."

DeBrusk glanced around like he heard somebody coming, but the 7-Eleven parking lot was empty except for us.

"Netflix bought the rights yesterday," Bernie said. "But you know how they streamline these things. You may end up on the cutting room floor."

That didn't sound good, but DeBrusk's mood seemed to brighten. "We happen to own a sizable chunk of Netflix. Don't I have a cousin on the board?" He reached into his pocket, took out an envelope. "One last thing. Please accept this as a token of gratitude from the Veritan community."

Bernie turned and hopped in the car. Hopped right in! Bernie! Even with his wounded leg. I hopped in right after him.

"Don't you even want to see the amount?" DeBrusk said.

Va-voom!

Well, maybe what with our finances being the way they were, it might have been . . . but too late. Rubber burned. That was us.

Felicia, together with Wendell's two other wives, or perhaps girlfriends — some cases remaining complicated right to the end —

took us out to lunch. They had very small salads and several bottles of white wine, later switching to rosé. Bernie had a burger and a beer. I had the remains — generous remains — of a bone-in ribeye, thanks to a friendly gentleman at the next table.

"What do we owe you?" Felicia said.

Bernie named a figure. Too high? Way too high? I could tell from the looks on the faces of the ladies — all those faces now kind of pinkish — that we had a problem.

"Tell you what," Felicia said.

"We'll each of us," began the youngest one.

"Pony up that amount," said the one in the middle.

"Oh, there's no need for —" Bernie began.

"Shut up, Bernie," Felicia said, and I'm afraid I was with her on that. "Wendell was —"

"Worth it," they all said together. Out came their checkbooks, slap, slap, slap on the table.

What a great lunch! And no pony ever appeared! We were on a roll.

There were two fine parties, the first down in Mexico when we took Tildy home. Pepita made enough food to last the whole town for two days, and don't forget the drinking part, although Bernie wanted to for about a week after that. Before the drinking really got going, we had a quiet little talk with Diego.

"I've decided to sell anyway," Diego said.

"Not to a Swiss company?" said Bernie.

"Oh, no. It's a group of investors from the Valley. One of them says he's a friend of yours."

"Malcolm?"

"That's right. Is it true? He's a friend?"

Bernie thought about that, then nodded.

"Glad to hear that," Diego said. "He's actually been a little . . . off-putting during the meetings, but if he's a friend of yours I won't worry."

"Um," said Bernie.

"I'm selling for two reasons," Diego said. "First, these people want to continue making wine on the land and they're keeping the name. Second, Jim's heart is no longer in it, if it ever was. You can't fake the passion, Bernie, and the wine is always the proof."

They clinked glasses.

The second party was Suzie's wedding, which happened after the monsoons, when things had cooled down and the air was clear. So many flowers, including a nice creamy one in Jacques's lapel. Lots of folks made a big fuss over me and Bernie, which he seemed to tire of pretty fast, although I did not. Waiters came around with little trays. Suzie had arranged a special one just for me. Bacon wrapped in bacon! Can you believe it? But that was Suzie, really the best of the best. She and Jacques slipped gold rings on each other's fingers, the gold glittering brightly even from where we were sitting, toward the back. Actually by ourselves in the very last row. Then Suzie raised her face, so beautifully, and she and Jacques kissed, not a long kiss but it sent out a wave I could feel.

We left shortly after, me and Bernie. When we got home, old man Heydrich was outside watering his lawn. He saw us coming and shut down his sprinklers. That was new.

"Hmph," said Bernie.

We parked in our driveway. Bernie went inside for the tools. We got to work on our blue boat, *Sea of Love,* but had hardly begun before Florian Machado came walking up.

"Out on bail?" Bernie said.

"Yes, sir," said Florian. "Just wanted to thank you, first thing. For, like, everything."

"No problem," Bernie said. "Any idea what Butchie did with Wendell's phone and laptop?"

"Um," said Florian. "He never had them. I woulda sold to him, but the window kind of closed on that plan, if you know what I'm sayin'."

"I don't," Bernie said. "Did you take the damn things or not?"

"Oh, I took them, all right. No slip-ups there. But that's as far as I got, on account of you."

"On account of me?"

"Showing up how you did, a bit early in the day. I'm one of them night owls, by nature."

Bernie gave Florian a long long look, maybe the longest look I'd ever seen him give anyone. Then he said, "Are you telling us Wendell's phone and laptop are on the boat?"

"Far as I know," said Florian.

"Get up here," Bernie told him.

Florian climbed the ladder, went toward what we in boating circles call the bow. He stopped at the coiled, rusty anchor chain lying on top of a hatch cover, the hatch cover where I'd smelled fishiness on our first visit. Now the fishy smell was just about gone. Florian shoved the chain aside with his foot, raised the hatch cover, reached inside, and took out a paper bag.

"Fish sandwich I never got to eat."

Florian dropped it on the deck, reached in again, this time hauling out a cell phone and a laptop. He held them up for us to take a real good look. He had a big smile on his face, like he'd just won a prize.

Bernie was not smiling at all. "Why did you tell us you'd sold them to Butchie?"

Florian shrugged his big, soft shoulders. "By then it was the story, you know. Kind of true, since it's what I woulda done, namely unload the stuff to Butchie. So I stuck to it, in spite of all the browbeating."

"Browbeating?" Bernie said.

"From my lawyer, Ms. Burr. A real piece of work. Like how she got herself bein' my lawyer? Wheels within wheels, my man. Anyways, she wouldn't believe me, kept browbeating, calling me a liar."

"She told you she needed the phone and laptop for bargaining chips?" Bernie said.

"Same as you did," said Florian.

Bernie didn't answer.

"Hope all that had nothin' to do with how Butchie ended up," Florian said.

Bernie reached for a screwdriver, started unscrewing screws in a very rough sort of way, as though he didn't like them. Florian watched him. Did he catch the hot look in Bernie's eyes, almost on fire for a moment?

Maybe not. "Boat's coming along pretty

good," he said.

"Uh-huh."

"Tell you what — it's yours."

"Thanks," said Bernie.

"That name — *Sea of Love* — was already on it," Florian said. "Boat belonged to some hippie lady who took her around the world. I was gonna change it to *Get Wasted* but I guess you can call her whatever you want."

"We're keeping the name," Bernie said.

"Beautiful," said Florian. "Nice talkin'."

He stepped over the side, started down the ladder, somehow forgetting that he still had the phone and the laptop. I reminded him in no uncertain terms.

ACKNOWLEDGMENTS

Many thanks to Kristin Sevick for her wise and sensitive editing of this book, and to Linda Quinton for her support of Chet and Bernie.

ABOUT THE AUTHOR

Spencer Quinn is the bestselling author of the Chet and Bernie mystery series, as well as the #1 *New York Times* bestselling Bowser and Birdie series for middle-grade readers. He lives on Cape Cod with his wife Diana — and dogs Audrey and Pearl.

The employees of Thorndike Press hope you have enjoyed this Large Print book. All our Thorndike, Wheeler, and Kennebec Large Print titles are designed for easy reading, and all our books are made to last. Other Thorndike Press Large Print books are available at your library, through selected bookstores, or directly from us.

For information about titles, please call:
  (800) 223-1244

or visit our website at:
  gale.com/thorndike

To share your comments, please write:
  Publisher
  Thorndike Press
  10 Water St., Suite 310
  Waterville, ME 04901